Whispering Vines

Also Available by Amy Schisler

Novels
A Place to Call Home
Picture Me
Whispering Vines
Summer's Squall
The Devil's Fortune

Chincoteague Island Trilogy
Island of Miracles
Island of Promise
Island of Hope

Children's Books
Crabbing With Granddad
The Greatest Gift

Collaborations
Stations of the Cross Meditations for Moms (with Anne Kennedy, Susan Anthony, Chandi Owen, and Wendy Clark)

Whispering Vines

By Amy Schisler

ISBN-13: 978-1-7346907-6-7

Published by:
Chesapeake Sunrise Publishing
Amy Schisler
Bozman, MD
2020

Acknowledgements

Whispering Vines called for not only imagination but also much research. It also required the help of many to aid in accuracy and contributions. The owners of La Dama Vineyard in Verona answered my many questions about wine making. Learning the intricacies of wine tasting was truly the best part of my research! Antonella Fantoni, the most superb tour guide in all of Europe, shared her vast amount of knowledge and answering my many inquiries about Florence, Italian history, art, and Robbia and his work. Thank you!

Vince Graziani, of Plan-It Italy, planned spectacular trips for us, especially for, insisting we visit Verona. Thank you for introducing me to Antonella and for reading my manuscript and helping me with my use of the Italian language, the history of Italy, and the accuracy of the recipes within the story. Your expertise in all things Italian was invaluable to me throughout my writing and research.

Thank you Bianca, Maryann and Nonna Nina for the recipes. Alex couldn't have mastered the art of Italian cooking without you! Knowing you is one of the most wonderful parts in my life, and I'm grateful for your friendship.

Thank you, Aunt Debbie, for being a wonderful critic. Every book I write is better with your suggestions. Thank you, Judy Reveal, my fabulous editor. Your edits improved not only the story but my overall writing. Thank you Alexa Jacobs for your support, advice, and friendship. You rock!

Thank you, Scott and Evelyn, of Henderson Design for your cover design, ads, and promos. Your creative elements greatly enhanced my work and helped to bring my vision to life through the cover, video promos, and the Belle Uve logo.

Thank you, Mom and Dad, for being critics, assistants, promoters, and fans. Thank you, Ken, Rebecca, Katie Ann, and Morgan for your unending support. I love you all.

To the unknown heroes and heroines of
World War II
and all of those who aid in the fight for righteousness.

Dear Readers,

The history of Italy is a long and fascinating one. Italy has existed since the 1st Century BC but was confined to the region now known as the 'toe' of the boot. The rest of modern-day Italy went through a series of conquests and wars under many flags, including Germany, Austria, Hungary, the Vatican (known at the time as the Papal States), and Napoleonic France, to name just a few. Italy, as we know it, didn't exist until 1870, thus making it an even younger republic than the United States.

What makes Italy special is that each region has maintained its individuality despite unification. Each has its own distinct history, cuisine, fashion, and colloquialisms. While all sharer the Italian language, certain words and phrases are inherently Venetian, Tuscan, etc. Every major city feels like a different world in comparison to neighbors to the North or South. I fell in love with Italy when I first visited there in 2012 and have felt compelled to return over and over. In 2015, while visiting a vineyard in the Valpolicella district of Veneto (formerly part of Venice), I felt a story coming to life—that of a struggling vineyard and the young woman hand-chosen by its dying owner to save the vineyard and the man running it. I wanted the reader to see Italy through the eyes of a foreigner visiting the wonderful and romantic world for the first time and falling in love with both the country and the man she meets there. I hope I've done justice to the centuries-old families, businesses, and magnificent art and architecture.

I hope you, too, will fall in love with Italy through my words and descriptions. Come with me to this world of intoxicating beauty where wine and art are held to a higher standard and where romance and intrigue can be found among the *Whispering Vines*.

Amy Schisler

Italy's Valpolicella District

November 4, 1943

It is done, and I am more afraid than ever. Roberto and I will take tonight's train from my beloved home. It is safest that way. Nobody else knows what happened last night... We will take the secret to our graves. Whether that be sooner or later, it is in God's hands.

May He bless this land and my mother. May she forgive me for running and never discover what we have done. And may God forgive us for the sin we have committed.

Standing on the little bench, Isa carefully put the worn, leather-bound journal back in its hiding place high in the rafters of the barn's loft and climbed down the ladder. With her satchel in hand, she walked to their meeting place, the olive tree near the west field. When Roberto arrived in silence, she turned back to take one more look at the house, the barn, and the fields of grapevines. She knelt by the fresh pile of dirt and wept for her loss. She knew that once she left, she would never return. She prayed that her mother would forgive her for leaving and that she and Roberto would depart from Italy alive.

Chapter One
Baltimore's Little Italy, 2015

Alex wiped the tear from her cheek and wished that her memories could be wiped away as easily. The grey sky and the scent of the coming rain perfectly matched her mood as she hopped on her bike and headed to work. 'Work' was anything but; at least as far as Alex was concerned, but even so, she was not looking forward to it today.

Alex rode her bike to the small house just outside of Little Italy in the heart of Baltimore. In spite of the impending showers, the sound of baby birds, chirping for food, filled the air. It had been a cold and wet spring, and Alex hoped that the weather would begin to warm soon, especially since she had no car and relied on her bicycle to get her to work and class. The smart thing would have been to take a taxi this morning, with the forecast as it was, but Alex didn't care if she got wet. She was in a foul mood and intended to stay that way, though it would be hard once she was in the presence of Signora Isabella Fonticelli. Though Signora had lived in America since just before the end of the war, never World War II or the War in Europe, but just 'The War,' Signora had never been called Mrs. Fonticelli. She was always Signora.

At eighty-seven years old, Signora had a sharp mind and humorous wit, and Alex loved her dearly. From the moment Alex saw the scrawled writing on the formal stationery pinned to the bulletin board in the campus student center, she had the unmistakable feeling that she was meant to take the job. Not that Alex had any experience with elderly people or as a caregiver. She just felt compelled to call the number, as if the writing was a musical composition meant only for Alex to play. It called to her, a melodious tune that entranced her and had her taking the paper down and putting it in her pocket without even realizing she had done it.

Almost a year later, Alex was Signora's most trusted companion, and Alex had the grandmother she always longed for. Aside from making sure Signora ate and took her medicine, Alex learned to play bridge and read aloud every book she could find from the classic, *Rebecca*, Alex's favorite, to *Dante's Inferno*, at Signora's insistence. What she did most, however, was practice her music on Signora's piano. It wasn't a baby grand or a Steinway, but it was in tune, and Signora loved to be carried away by Alex's playing.

Alex parked her bike inside the gated alley next to the house and used her key to enter the kitchen door on the side of the little abode. The faint aroma of last night's dinner still hung in the air, a pesto sauce over shrimp and pasta, the strong scent of garlic clinging to the room. She took off her coat and shivered. The house was much too cold for the elderly woman, and Alex worried that the faint, musty smell indicated the possibility of mold hiding within the walls or carpeting of the old house.

"Signora," Alex called as she wandered through the kitchen to the thermostat in the tiny hallway and adjusted the temperature by a couple degrees. "I'm here. Are you awake?" Hearing no answer, Alex walked upstairs.

When Alex walked into the bedroom, Signora was sitting on the side of the perfectly made-up bed, already dressed and wearing her finest jewelry. A stranger might have thought she had somewhere to go, but Alex knew that this was just the way Signora always looked.

"I keep telling you that I will make the bed and help you get dressed. You never listen to me," Alex scolded, bending over to give Signora a peck on each cheek.

"You're late," Signora said, faking an air of superiority.

"I am not, and you know it." Alex smiled. "I got here the same time I arrive every morning."

"You're late every morning," Signora replied, but her smile and twinkling eyes gave her away. She was just an old tease, and Alex loved her for it. "An old woman could die waiting for breakfast with you looking after her."

"I might be worried if there was an old woman here." Alex put her arm around Signora and smiled, her bad mood already giving way to the lightheartedness that only Signora could bring out in her on this rotten day. "Ready?" Alex asked before helping the older woman up and out into the hallway.

"I don't know why you won't let someone put in a stair lift or help move your bed and personal items downstairs," Alex said, not for the first time, as they descended slowly to the first floor.

"Because I can still get up and down the steps just fine," Signora told her. "And when I can't, I might as well be dead." Alex didn't reply. It was an argument she was used to losing.

They made their way to the cozy little kitchen, and Alex helped Signora sit down at the table, the same one her dear husband had made for her as a wedding present seventy years ago when Signora was just seventeen and trying to make a new home in the New World.

"Now make me breakfast," Signora prodded, "and then tell me why you were up half the night crying."

Standing at the counter with her back to the older woman, Alex closed her eyes and braced herself on the Formica. "Is it really that obvious?"

"Patrick?" Signora asked. Alex nodded, trying to hold back the tears. "I told you not to trust an Irish boy."

Alex smiled. Had anyone else said that, she would have been offended. After all, she was an O'Donnell herself. But she knew that Signora only had her best interest at heart. Alex busied herself with putting on a cup of coffee and making breakfast. Following a recipe Signora had taught her early on, Alex made a hole in the middle of two pieces of fresh, Italian bread. She poured a little olive oil in a pan and browned one side of the slices. After flipping them, she cracked an egg into each hole and let them cook, flipping the toast and eggs once more to cook the eggs all the way through. While they cooked, she sliced a red pepper to go with the eggs and poured two glasses of orange juice and two cups of coffee. Signora patiently sipped her coffee and waited for Alex to finish cooking as the scent of eggs, toast, and coffee filled the tiny kitchen.

Once they were both seated and Alex had taken a sip of her coffee, she took a deep breath.

"We broke up," she began. "I suspected he might be cheating on me, but I never imagined it was with my own roommate." She shook her head, but no tears came to the surface.

"Sandra?"

Alex nodded. "I caught them. That's all I'm going to say. I won't rehash it because it was horrible, but now it's over. I should have let him go a long time ago."

Signora shook her head. "The little hussy."

Alex laughed. "I hate the thought of going back to that townhouse, but graduation will be here soon enough."

"At least you discovered the real person he is before it was too late. And I'm sure you will find somewhere else to live." Signora placed her hand over Alex's and squeezed it.

Alex smiled at the older woman. "What would I do without you?"

"Have a real social life, go out and enjoy yourself on a Friday night, meet a nice man."

Alex laughed at the thought of a social life. Growing up, she had always had a boyfriend, but nothing ever seemed to last. She preferred being alone—reading, playing piano, painting, or going outside to take pictures.

"That wasn't my life before I met you, and it wouldn't be my life if I didn't have you. I don't need a social life or a man."

"Oh, my dear Alexandra, life is so much more wonderful when you have someone to share it with." Signora looked across the room to the framed photo of her and Roberto on their wedding day. There was no white dress, no veil, not even any guests, but Roberto was a handsome man with a beard and slight smile, and Signora was beautiful with long, black hair and dark eyes. Alex often wondered what that day was like, but it was one of many things Signora refused to talk about. All she ever said was that she and Roberto were deeply in love and fleeing the War, and that it was one of the most frightening days of her life. Alex could see the fear in their eyes, and she guessed that the War made everyone afraid, even on their wedding day. Still, Alex was always curious about the day, the couple, and their lives during and after the War, but Signora was quiet about it all.

"Love is all that matters," Signora said, turning back to the younger woman. "Life brings hardship, and pain, and more loss than you think you can survive, but in the end, love will carry you through the agony and restore the breath you need to keep living. You must have love, or you have nothing."

"Maybe someday," Alex told her, "but for now, I have you, and you're all I need."

Alex stood and cleared the table. *Maybe there is someone out there for me, but I sure as heck haven't found him yet.*

Signora watched Alex and thought about her life at that age. By twenty-two, she had seen things that no human being should have to witness. She had already lived two lives, suffered unimaginable losses, escaped the War, overcome the stigma of being a refugee, gotten married, and learned that most things in life never turn out the way you imagine them when you're young and in love. But she was stronger and wiser for what she had seen and learned, and she knew that Alex would be, too. Their lives were so much more alike than Alex knew, and Signora firmly believed that the right person and the right life were out there waiting for the young woman. Alex just needed to find the confidence in herself to follow her dreams. The time was almost at hand; Signora could feel it. She hoped that Alex was ready for what was to lie ahead.

That night, Alex arrived at the welcoming little house just after nine. She let herself in and hurried to the living room where she usually found Signora reading or already asleep in her cushioned armchair. Alex stopped abruptly at the door when she saw Signora, her eyes closed, the book open on her lap. *She looks so peaceful*, Alex thought before her heart skipped a beat. There was something about her, something about the look on her face, the way her body rested in the chair.

"No," Alex cried as she rushed to Signora's side. She felt for a pulse as she reached for the phone in her pocket. "Please, no," Alex pleaded through tears while she waited for the dispatcher to answer. "You're all I have. What will I do without you?"

"911. What is the nature of your emergency?"

Alex was barely able to answer. The lump in her throat grew as she tried to gather her thoughts and speak the words she had been dreading for the past year. Closing her eyes and taking a deep breath through her nose, she calmly relayed the emergency and then waited for the ambulance while her world fell apart.

Monday morning came much too fast. The sun shone bright, and the birds were singing as Alex opened the door. She supposed that it made sense—that it would rain on the day Signora died and be sunny on the day Alex would officially tell her goodbye. Signora would have liked the poetry in that. She would have said that the angels were crying at her death but rejoicing in having her home.

As Signora had requested, a funeral Mass was celebrated at the small church that Signora had attended since coming to America in 1944. Alex sat in the front pew, the only 'family' member present. The home healthcare nurse who visited Signora every afternoon was also there, as were a few of the families from the parish who wished to pay their respects. Alex noticed an older man, perhaps in his sixties, whom she did not recognize. After the burial in the small cemetery behind the church, the man approached Alex.

"Ms. O'Donnell?" he asked once Alex had a chance to say a tearful goodbye to Signora at the gravesite. She looked at the man and tried to place him.

"Yes?" She answered him in a questioning voice. The man reached out his hand.

"My name is Peter Owen. I've heard a lot about you." His grip was firm, and his eyes were both kind and sad. He was tall with a solid build and a shiny, bald head that gave him quite a distinguished air. His aftershave smelled expensive but not offensive. Alex raised an eyebrow in question.

"I'm with the law firm of Kennedy, Owen, and Warren. Signora Fonticelli was a client of mine for many years, and she was very fond of you."

With her hand still in his, Alex smiled faintly. "And I of her," she said quietly.

Peter smiled back and let go of her hand. "I have some business to discuss with you. It's not urgent, but I would like to get it taken care of at your earliest convenience. We could go to lunch, or you could tell me when a better time would be to meet."

"Lunch would be nice." She smiled. Peter's smile grew as he suggested a place and led Alex to his car.

Lunch at Da Mimmo, a favorite of the Baltimore business crowd, was very nice, and Alex enjoyed sharing stories about Signora with Peter. He was fit and trim and looked darn good for his age, not that Alex knew what that was. She was never good at guessing ages. He was charming and kind, and Alex couldn't help but wonder why all men couldn't be like him. Their coffee had just arrived when Peter opened his briefcase and took out a manila folder.

"I would like to go over the contents of Signora Fonticelli's will," Peter said as he opened the folder.

Alex wasn't sure how to react. She picked up her napkin from her lap and wiped her mouth. "Okay," she said hesitantly. "I'm not sure how that affects me."

Peter put on a pair of reading glasses, glanced at the file, and then looked over the lenses at Alex. "I assume Signora Fonticelli never mentioned anything to you about her will."

Alex shook her head. "Nothing."

Peter took off his glasses and closed the folder. "This may come as a shock to you." He put down the file and folded his hands on the table.

Alex held her breath as he leveled his gaze on her. Everyone else in the restaurant seemed to fade away as she waited for him to go on.

"Alex, do you know anything about Signora Fonticelli's estate and holdings?"

Alex shook her head, unable to speak.

"Of course, there is the house in Baltimore." Peter paused, and Alex nodded. It would be just like Signora to leave Alex her home, knowing that Alex was weeks away from graduation and would need to be thinking about her future. Peter went on, "In addition, there is the vineyard and villa—"

"Excuse me?" Alex stopped him. "Vineyard? Villa?" Her head began to spin. She had no idea where this was heading.

"Yes, just outside of Verona in the Valpolicella district." He paused for a second and smiled at Alex. "My Italian is not that good, but Signora insisted I learn to at least pronounce that correctly." Alex smiled and motioned for him to go on though her mind was yelling for him to stop. Alex didn't know what was coming, but she had a growing feeling that it was going to be earth shattering, at least for her.

Peter picked up the folder again, opened it, removed a document, and replaced his reading glasses. He cleared his throat. "I, Isabella Abelli Fonticelli, being of sound mind and body, do hereby bequeath the following:

To Alexandra O'Donnell, my dearest companion and caregiver, my house at 117 Trinity Street and all of its contents, to be done with as she wishes (though I recommend selling it all and taking the money—you'll need to pay off your college loans)." Peter looked at Alex and smiled.

"She always did like to give me advice on how to run my life," Alex said quietly as tears formed in her eyes. As she suspected, the house. That wasn't such a big deal after all. "That was very sweet of her."

"There's more," Peter said, and Alex gasped in surprise as Peter looked back down at the document. "I also leave Alexandra one half of my family's vineyard, Belle Uve, to be shared with my great-nephew, Nicola Giordano."

Alex placed her hands on the table to steady herself as the earth shattering commenced. She wished she had not had that glass of wine with her lunch. It suddenly left a sour taste in her mouth, and the Italian cuisine that had smelled so wonderful just a few minutes before, now seemed strong and overpowering. "Bell... what?"

"Belle Uve, which until last week, Signora Fonticelli shared with her great-nephew who inherited his grandfather's half of the estate. The name means 'beautiful grapes.' Signora Fonticelli stipulates that you and her great-nephew, Nicola, are to share the estate and run the winery together. I have papers and pictures for you with all the details about the estate. I'm afraid that it's not as glamorous as it sounds. The winery doesn't seem to be as profitable as it once was." Peter began to pull more documents and photographs out of the folder, but his words seemed to be coming from the other end of a distant tunnel. Alex felt dizzy. "Signora Fonticelli and her great-nephew already had a contract that dealt with how they maintained their shares and profits. Those conditions will remain unchanged. You will simply inherit her shares and assume her profits."

"No, please, stop." Alex shook her head in confusion. "I don't understand. I don't live in Italy. I know nothing about wine or vineyards or estates. I know that Signora grew up on a vineyard, but I've never heard of Nicola Geor—whatever his name was. Talk about shares and profits is something I've never tried to understand. This must be a mistake."

Peter took off his glasses and looked at Alex with sincere compassion. "I'm afraid I didn't do a very good job preparing you for this. I did say it would be a shock."

"To say the least," Alex said as she buried her face in her hands. She looked up and shook her head. "I don't know what to say. What do I do?"

"I'm afraid I can't answer that. If you wish, I can continue to handle the affairs of the vineyard, putting the profits, if there ever are any, into a portfolio for you. You wouldn't have to do anything except, perhaps, hire an accountant to look over my shoulder, which is the smart thing to do these days. Would you like to take the papers and photographs with you and go through them?"

Alex nodded, her mouth agape, as she reached a shaky hand for her cup. "Yes, I guess so…" she whispered before she gulped down the lukewarm, now bitter-tasting coffee she had ordered after finishing her wine and tried to figure out what just happened.

"Do you have a passport?"

Alex looked at Peter and blinked. "Uh, no. I never needed one."

"If you decide to go to Italy, even just to see the estate, you will need a passport. I can tell you how to expedite the process if you want to go any time soon. In addition, if you decide to stay..."

Peter continued talking, and the phrases 'work visa' and 'dual citizenship' floated between them like the scent of the coffee, but Alex became lost in her own thoughts. She spent her entire life dreaming of going to Italy, seeing the famed Uffizi Gallery in Florence, riding in a gondola on the Gran Canal of Venice, visiting the Vatican. But never in her wildest dreams had she ever imagined that something like this would be the catalyst to take her there. She had a lot to think about, but one thought ran through her mind over and over as she stared unseeing at Peter putting together the stack of papers. With no family to speak of, no boyfriend, and no job tying her down, what did she have to lose?

Nicola ripped up the letter from the Office of Peter Owen in Baltimore, Maryland.

"Che cosa?" Maria asked.

Nicola let out a string of expletives in Italian and threw the pieces of paper at Maria. "Prozia Isa's share of the vineyard. She left it to some American."

Maria was stunned. "I do not understand. An American? Perhaps he will sell it to you?"

"Non lo so," Nicola said, shaking his head. "But it is not a 'he.' The American is a woman."

"What will you do?" Maria asked.

Nicola paced the floor in the winery. His face was red, and he felt like he could punch someone. He had been working at the vineyard almost his entire life and had been running it since he graduated from college. This was his business, his home, and he was not going to share it with anyone.

Chapter Two

Graduation day was bright and sunny, but Alex couldn't see past the fog of sadness that had settled into her being. She watched the crowds as they lined up to go inside as soon as the doors opened. Friends called and waved as they went through the 'Graduate Entrance,' but Alex couldn't bring herself to go in quite yet. So many emotions and thoughts rippled through her. The smell of lilacs somewhere nearby reminded Alex of her childhood home and all that she was leaving behind. This was indeed the end of life as she knew it, and she couldn't decide how she felt about it. Commencement was a good word for it—a beginning and not an end.

Watching the parents, grandparents, siblings, fiancés, and even spouses hug her fellow classmates as they parted ways for the ceremony, Alex felt that familiar tug at her heart. A solitary tear rolled down her cheek as she thought about her father, her brother, and now Signora, all watching from above. Sandra and Patrick would have been her only family here today, yet even they were lost to her. They both reached out to her after Signora's passing, but Alex rejected their attempts to comfort her. As much as she hated being alone, Alex was taking her life into her own hands and making her own decisions. She would find the strength and the courage to make a new life for herself, and maybe, just maybe, someday her mother would come around and be a part of it.

Though she didn't want to admit it to anyone, including herself, Alex stood alone outside not because she wasn't ready to go in, but because she was an optimist at heart. She hoped, against all odds, that her mother would walk around the corner, camera in one hand and a gift in the other, smiling broadly, proud of all that her daughter had overcome to get to this day. Realizing the absurdity of that happening, Alex brushed away her tear and took a deep breath. She was graduating today, moving on, making a break with the past, and embarking on the adventure of a lifetime. With cap in hand, she entered the arena and closed the door on the life she knew. From this day forward, life was an open door, and Alex was ready to walk through it.

Alex had always wondered what it would be like to fly on an airplane, but she never imagined how miserable it actually would be. Perhaps her first flight should have been something short rather than the grueling overnight flight from JFK to Frankfurt and then on to Verona. The seats were tiny, the food was awful, and she barely slept thanks to the screaming baby behind her and the snoring man next to her. He was actually sound asleep before the wheels even retracted into the plane at takeoff. Alex assumed he was a seasoned traveler, which she most certainly was not.

Opening her carry-on, Alex pulled out the worn notebook from Signora's kitchen. She lightly fingered the leather book as memories came flooding back to her. Though Signora knew every recipe by heart, she always referred to the cookbook and had Alex follow it like a Bible. Alex would always remember when Signora first told her that the recipe book was the only real connection she had to her family and her beloved homeland. Alex opened the book and read the note from Signora's grandmother. Though she knew no Italian, she had memorized the words that Signora read to her each time they whipped up one of the delicious recipes, and she could now interpret the few sentences on her own.

Dearest Isa,

I pray that you are well and will return to us soon. Nothing is the same without you here. I am sending all of your favorite recipes so that I know you are eating well in America. Paolo helped me with American measurements, so I hope they are correct. Take care of yourself, and know that I love you and pray for you. Nonno also sends his love.

God bless you always,
Nonna Nina

Alex hoped that the little book, so loved by Signora, would give her a feeling of security on this journey and that it would help her find her place in this new world. Cooking always brought comfort to her, much like playing the piano. She supposed that it was another way to let her creative juices flow, and she prayed for the opportunity to show Mr. Giordano that she could pull her own weight in both the vineyard and the villa. Alex leafed through the book for a few minutes before tucking it away and settling down to try to get some sleep on the long, overseas flight.

It was eleven in the morning when Alex, stiff and still sleepy, disembarked from the plane at Verona Villafranca Airport. Once the plane landed, Alex carried her travel bag and laptop case, one on each shoulder, and made the trek to baggage claim. Her whole body ached by the time she saw her suitcases tumble onto the conveyor. At that moment, she hated herself for bringing practically her entire wardrobe with her. They had clothing stores in Italy. Why had she brought so much? She desperately looked around for a solution to carrying all of the bags herself and spied a rack of luggage carts. She rushed over and was thankful that the machine took credit cards since she hadn't had time to get Euros before leaving the U.S.

Ten minutes later, Alex stood in the taxi line with her laptop case, carry-on bag, and three large suitcases. She probably could have bought an entire new wardrobe for the cost of the baggage fees she paid to haul her stuff with her. Live and learn, she thought. It's all here now. She gave the attendant the piece of paper with the hotel address on it and waited as he spoke to the driver in Italian.

"Grazie," she said to the driver with a smile as he managed to fit all of her things into the car. She hoped her pronunciation was correct since the only phrases she had learned so far were from her $5.00 airport guidebook.

"Prego," he answered. Alex conjured up an image of a jar of spaghetti sauce. She began to doubt that her four years of Spanish and a cheap guidebook would help her understand Italian.

With her nose pressed to the window, Alex watched the modern façade of the airport give way to rolling fields of what she thought might be olive trees interrupted by the occasional warehouse or train yard. She delighted in the scenery, but her euphoria faded as they entered the city of Verona, and Alex saw that the suburbs weren't unlike those in the Chicago or Baltimore area—houses on top of each other, lots of cars, schools, stores, and the like. Continuing on, though, she realized that many of the buildings downtown were the same ones that had stood there for hundreds of years. She suddenly felt very small and very young as the taxi came to a stop outside of the Hotel Bologna in the oldest part of Verona. The sight of the 15th Century buildings gave her a thrill but also made her realize just how young her own country was and how little she had experienced in the world.

Feeling a sudden surge of energy, Alex checked into the hotel and graciously thanked the hotel staff for agreeing to store her massive amount of luggage until her room was ready. She used the lobby bathroom and splashed water on her face. This was her lifelong dream—she was in Italy. The country where artists and musicians from all over the world came to see the works of the masters. Before the death of her father and the virtual loss of her mother, Alex, like most Fine Arts Majors, dreamed of spending her junior year in Florence, learning art and music history from the experts and traveling around Europe to see masterpieces such as the *David*, the *Pieta*, the *Mona Lisa*, *Sunflowers*, and more. Once on her own, she never imagined she would have the opportunity to leave Baltimore, let alone travel abroad.

Out on the sidewalk, Alex closed her eyes and inhaled the smells of the city. She was sure she could identify the very aromas of pizza, pasta, wine, and a host of delicacies that she couldn't wait to taste. She let all of her senses soak up the city, the warm sun beating down on her upturned face, the smells of garlic and seafood from the restaurants, the sounds of the vespers as they raced alongside the cars, and the sights of ancient and modern melded together in a beautiful architectural collage. She took a deep breath and smiled, ready to explore. Turning right, she went just a short distance to the end of the block and stood in awe as she gawked at the giant structure before her. Having done her homework, she knew that Verona was home to the ancient Arena, even older than the famed Coliseum in Rome that it resembled, but she was nevertheless shocked at the enormity of the round, stone arena before her. The entire area around the arena was a plaza with restaurants, ancient columns, and buildings older than anything she had ever seen. As she walked, Alex took it all in: the ancient ruins of the Arena, the scents of strong espresso and the freshly baked goodness of flaky and buttery cornetti amidst the chatter of a multitude of languages.

The aroma of a nearby restaurant pulled her gaze from the Arena to the menu displayed on the sideboard, and Alex realized how famished she was. After taking her seat, she quickly found a dish that sounded intriguing, thanks to the English translations alongside the Italian descriptions, and reached for the wine list. She scanned the list until she found just what she wanted. She ordered *Tagliatelle con Funghi Porcini e Timo*— tagliatelle pasta with Porcini mushrooms and thyme— from the menu and a glass of wine from Belle Uve. Alex was anxious to taste the product which was now fifty percent hers.

Alex pointed to a white wine, but the waiter shook his head.

"No, this is white. You will want red."

Alex looked at the waiter, surprised that he would tell a customer no. "I would like the white," she firmly told him with more conviction than she felt.

The waiter gave Alex a look of disapproval, but he did not argue further. Alex knew that she was going to need to develop a more mature attitude toward wine, but she had never quite developed a taste for reds. She simply felt more comfortable starting with the whites and working her way up to the heartier wines.

As Alex waited for her wine, she noticed a very good-looking man walk in with a case bearing the distinctive logo of Belle Uve. She immediately perked up, paying attention to the exchange between the man bearing the case and another man behind the bar. She wondered how many employees the vineyard had. This man was young, not much older than she, with dark brown hair and a body that could make people swoon. He must get a pretty good workout on the vineyard.

Alex watched as the man shook hands with the man at the bar and then turned to speak to another restaurant employee. He was friendly and obviously well-liked. He didn't seem to be in a hurry, or if he was, he was too polite to let it show. Everyone seemed to know him, and he gave each person his undivided attention.

When the wine arrived, Alex took a hesitant sip and was pleasantly surprised that it was good, in fact, very good. However, Alex acknowledged to herself that she knew nothing about wines and couldn't really say whether it was just very good, remarkable, or wouldn't even be palatable to a real wine taster.

As she sipped the drink, the man from the vineyard, her vineyard, she reminded herself, said his final goodbyes and headed toward the door.

"Ciao, Nicola," her waiter called and waved as the man left. Alex almost choked on the piece of bread she had just popped into her mouth. She watched Nicola Giordano walk out into the Verona sunlight and signaled for her waiter.

"Another glass, please," she managed to say, motioning to the wine. When her food arrived, she smiled and thanked the waiter but hardly tasted her first authentic Italian meal.

By the time she finished her lunch, her eyes were droopy, and she realized her second wind had come and gone. Making her way back to her hotel, she happily discovered that her room was ready and her bags safely tucked inside. She almost cried with relief. She stretched out on the bed and was soon fast asleep.

When Alex awoke, it was late evening, and the sun was beginning to set. Was this what she had heard referred to as the 'Tuscan Sun,' she wondered as she watched the orange ball disappear into the glowing horizon outside of her window. Remembering something Peter had said about the region, Alex pulled out her travel guide of Italy and looked at the regional map. No, Tuscany was further south. Oh well, she thought as she flipped through the pages. The Veneto region obviously has beautiful sunsets as well. Alex turned to a dog-eared page and scanned the lines she had highlighted. Realizing how long it had been since she left Baltimore, Alex suddenly felt the uncleanliness of almost forty-eight hours without a shower and headed to the bathroom. Once showered and dressed, she pulled back her auburn hair, brushed her teeth, slipped her feet into her sandals, and grabbed her purse before heading out the door.

After stopping to ask for directions at the front desk, Alex headed toward the shopping district in the opposite direction of the Arena. Here, the storefronts were all glass and housed the same businesses found in every modern shopping mall—H&M, Benetton, and scads of others—but the buildings themselves were unlike any Alex had seen before. While utilizing modern industry standards for boutiques and chain stores, the designers had managed to retain the structure and charm of the Fourteenth and Fifteenth Century buildings. Alex was amazed at the modern pedestrian-only street lined with store after store nestled into a world that was over two-thousand years old.

She browsed some of the shops and took note of the fashion trends. She tried to think of ways she could update her own meager wardrobe at little cost. Scarves were everywhere, so she would most certainly need to purchase a few more to add to her paltry collection. Alex stopped at one corner to marvel at the glass sidewalk that allowed a look underground where ancient ruins could be seen beneath the modern pavement. Glancing to the right, she saw the remains of a stone structure, a building or an arch perhaps, that had been preserved when the present city had been built. She caressed the soft marble and shook her head in disbelief at the thought that this piece of architecture was thousands of years old.

Alex wandered down Via Mazzini. Around every corner, she looked for Nicola. Did he live here in Verona or on the vineyard? Perhaps he lived in one of the newer homes she passed on her way from the airport. Maybe he was married and had a beautiful, exotic wife and large Italian family. Would they accept her? He seemed so friendly, so popular when she saw him earlier. Would he embrace her like a long-lost relative?

Alex checked her map and then searched for Via Scudo di Francia. Once on the right street, she stopped at the Bottega del Vino for dinner. Though it was almost nine o'clock, the restaurants were just beginning to receive their evening diners. Alex did not have a reservation, but she hoped that obtaining a table for one would not be a problem, and it was not. She was seated at one of the small, outside tables and, scanning the menu, chose antipasti, a first course, and a second course. *When in Rome, or Verona,* she mused. She found herself looking around, half expecting to see Nicola walk in again.

Alex was anxious to peruse the wine list but even after knowing what was in store, she was still blown away at the over 10,000 choices of wine that were before her. Bottega del Vino was a wine lover's dream restaurant, and it took several minutes before Alex found what she was searching for. Spotting an Amarone, the dark, red signature wine of the region, from Belle Uve, Alex pointed to the wine she wanted, and the waiter smiled in approval.

"Very good choice, Signorina. You have exquisite taste."

Alex was pleased that she had chosen wisely and that Belle Uve had a wine that was considered a top-notch wine.

She waited in anticipation for the server to bring her glass and pretended to know what she was doing when he presented the bottle and the cork for her approval. The wine did not disappoint. Even for someone who knew nothing about wines, Alex knew that this was indeed 'exquisite.' Not a red wine drinker herself, she was surprised at the delight she felt as she swallowed the warm liquid. She could taste the wine throughout her entire mouth, and even in the back of her nose. It went down so smoothly that she felt an almost soothing sensation in her throat. She had no idea how to describe anything she tasted or felt, and she suddenly realized she had a lot more to learn than she already imagined. Tomorrow was going to be quite an interesting day.

Waking up to the morning sun streaming through the hotel window, Alex stretched and smiled. She couldn't remember the last time she had such a good night's sleep. She was afraid that thoughts and misgivings about today, not to mention her late afternoon nap, would keep her up most of the night, but the food, wine, travel, and relaxed atmosphere lulled her to sleep. There were no dreams about Patrick or more of the recurring nightmares about the car accident. There was just sleep.

After a quick shower and a bite to eat in the hotel restaurant, Alex headed outside and looked for a taxi. There was no use stalling. She had a task to perform, and she might as well get it done. Every decision she made from this point on was dependent upon the outcome of today's journey.

"Sì, allora," the driver said to Alex as he returned to her the paper containing the address. Alex assumed that meant he could take her there since he exited the taxi and opened the back door, motioning for her to climb in.

"American?" The driver asked once they were underway.

"Sì," Alex answered, and she wondered what made it so obvious.

"I visited my cousin in Orlando once. It was very nice there."

"Sì," Alex agreed. "But there are many other places much more beautiful. You should go back and visit New England or the Rockies. They are both very different from Orlando." Alex had made a trip to New England with her family once but had never been to the Rockies. She had seen pictures, though, and could only imagine their beauty.

"Sì, sì, someday," the driver said.

Alex settled back and enjoyed the scenery. Once again, the city gave way to a countryside dotted with trees and trellised vines.

"Are those olive trees?"

"Sì, many olive trees here."

"And those plants that are tied to the wooden stakes? Grapevines?"

"Sì, sì, they grow on, how you say in English, arbors?"

"Yes, I think that's the word." Alex's quick study on vineyards was beginning to come back to her, at least she hoped.

She watched as the many fields of olive trees and grapevines rushed past. Some stretched high up on rolling hills and seemed to go on forever. She noticed several tiny shacks here and there amongst the grape arbors and thought it odd that there would be outhouses scattered through the field.

"What are those tiny buildings?"

"Ah, they are for the tenders, the keepers of the grapes. Um…" He seemed to search for the right English words and phrases. "Sometimes, the workers stay there to watch the grapes. In bad weather."

"Oh, I see," said Alex, though she wasn't entirely sure she understood.

She read the signs outside of the vineyards that they passed, but they were all unfamiliar to her. And then she spotted the logo of Belle Uve on a sign ahead. Though the sign looked old and weather beaten, the logo was clever. A glass of red wine splashed over the words Belle Uve. Obviously some thought had gone into creating the eye-catching design that now adorned each bottle of wine that was sold by the vineyard, and Alex liked it instantly. She wondered how it could be creatively marketed.

Turning into the drive, the taxi slowed at what must have been the main building. It didn't look like much—a green-roofed, aluminum barn-like structure. Alex began to wonder exactly what Signora had dragged her into. Not far from the barn stood a traditional looking Italian house that Alex could only describe as a villa. It was a two-story white building with a red terra-cotta roof and a welcoming front porch. It looked old, well taken care of, and just perfect. Surrounding the two buildings as far as she could see, were rows and rows of green, leafy arbors. Opening the door of the taxi, she noticed that the air smelled fresh and sweet, and the gentle breeze that caressed her skin caused the grape leaves to sway ever so slightly as Alex gazed out at a world so different from Baltimore or Chicago.

On shaky legs, she got out of the door and barely paid attention to what the driver was saying as he told her a price. She didn't even register what she was paying when she handed him some of the Euros she had gotten from the ATM in the shopping district the night before. She held her breath as she watched him get back into the car, close the door, and drive away, leaving her feeling more alone than she had on graduation day.

Alex pushed open the door and looked around the building. There was a counter in front of a wall of shelves that were lined with bottles of wine, all bearing the Belle Uve label. The smell of wine hung in the air, an inviting aroma rather than the stale smell of alcohol in a college bar or fraternity house, not that she had been to many of either one. The room looked nice, freshly painted, judging by the faint smell that was mixed in the air with the wine, and decorated with framed photographs of the grapes, the vineyard, and the sun setting over the field. Alex stared, mesmerized by the photographs and wondered who had taken them. They weren't just pictures. They were art. Obviously someone with a keen eye had composed these beautiful shots.

"Posso aiutarla?" Alex jumped at the sound of the voice behind her. She turned and came face-to-face with the man she now believed was Nicola Giordano, just as handsome as she remembered him from the day before and with the most compelling dark eyes and an inquisitive expression. She caught herself staring at him and hoped he wouldn't recognize her.

"I'm sorry?"

"Ah, non parli italiano?"

"No. English?" The man did not answer Alex's question. Instead, his inquisitive expression vanished, and a storm seemed to cross his face.

"What do you want?" He asked angrily. *No wonder the vineyard isn't doing well financially. What a way to treat a guest and potential customer.*

"Um, a tour?" Alex blurted out the first thing that came to her mind and regretted it instantly. She found herself unable to tell him the truth.

The man looked Alex over, seemingly assessing her, or the situation, or both. Several seconds ticked by, and Alex waited patiently and quite nervously for an answer.

"No, no tour. Goodbye." The man promptly turned and began walking toward a door marked 'uffizi.'

"But wait." Alex began to follow him and almost ran right into him when he abruptly stopped as the door opened and a pretty, young woman walked out.

"Nicola?" She looked at the man with her eyebrow raised in question. Nicola began speaking in Italian, and a disagreement ensued between the two. The only word Alex could pick up on was "American." Finally, the young woman made her way around Nicola and walked toward Alex with her hand outstretched. As Alex reached to shake her hand, Nicola stormed into the other room and slammed the door behind him. Alex was shocked that the friendly man from the restaurant could instantly become so rude.

"Prego," the woman said, and Alex wondered again about the use of the familiar, yet at the same time, unfamiliar word. "I'm afraid my boss is in a, um, how do you say? Foul? Si, foul mood today. How may I help you?"

Alex liked the woman immediately and wondered if she and Nicola had more than a business relationship. Alex hoped not, not for her own sake but for this woman's. Who would want to be in any type of romantic relationship with him?

Remembering that the woman was waiting for an answer, Alex smiled and asked again for a tour of the vineyard. She figured it was too late to turn back now.

"I've been told that many of the vineyards give tours. Is that correct?"

"Sì," the woman answered as she walked behind the counter. "Many vineyards do give tours, but we do not." Alex noted the change in her tone and wondered about it.

"Oh." Alex acted surprised even though she had not seen any mention of tours anywhere on the vineyard's paltry web site. "I thought… Could you give me one anyway? I will pay for it. I've come all this way, and my taxi has already left and won't return for a couple of hours."

Alex gave her a pitiful smile and hoped that the woman would be sympathetic.

"Well, I don't know…" She hesitated and looked away.

"Please," Alex begged. She went to the counter and leaned across it. This was not going at all how she planned, and she continued to dig her hole deeper. "I won't take up much of your time. I just, I um…" Alex was beginning to panic. She tried to think of something to say, a way to explain. Suddenly, she blurted out the words, "I'm writing an article, you see, on Italian wines and vineyards. My boss asked me to write it, and he paid for me to come all the way over here from New York, and I didn't have the guts to tell him that I know nothing about wine or grapes, or any of this." She threw open her arms to indicate her surroundings and couldn't believe she had just said that. Alex felt as if a stranger had taken over her body, and she wished a hole would appear and swallow her up.

The woman's hesitation instantly disappeared. "An article? Oh, perhaps then…" She rushed toward the closed door. "Please, wait."

After a few minutes, which Alex needed to calm herself down and say a prayer, the door opened, and Nicola came out. He went straight to Alex and took her hand. Bowing before her, he kissed her hand, and looked up at her apologetically. She blushed, not in embarrassment but from guilt. Was she really going to continue this charade?

"Mi dispiace, I am sorry," he said with a small smile. "I misunderstood. Please." He let go of her hand and waved his hand in front of them to usher her toward the front door. "I am Nicola, owner of Belle Uve, and I would be happy to show you around." The suave Italian man from the restaurant had returned.

"Thank you," Alex said, and in her mind she uttered apologies over and over as the guilt continued to plague her.

Alex and Nicola exited the building and walked around back to the fields. Nicola opened his arms and gestured at the many tidy rows of plants that clung to the stakes as far as the eye could see.

"These are the white grapes," Nicola began, and Alex pulled out her notebook to take notes. She hadn't planned on telling the lie about writing an article, but she had planned on taking notes for her own benefit. There was so much to learn. She tried to concentrate on what Nicola was saying. "They are much more difficult to grow and don't produce as strong a bouquet or heady taste as the red grapes."

Alex nodded and listened as Nicola explained the process of growing and harvesting the grapes. Every single grape is harvested by hand, he told her, and she was amazed. "This protects the grapes and ensures quality." Alex looked around and imagined the time and manpower it must take to harvest them properly.

"Who picks the grapes?" She asked.

"We do," Nicola told her. "Myself, Maria, and Giovanni and Luigi, Maria's brothers."

"That's all?" She asked in amazement. "How long does it take?"

"Many hours over several days, but we are good and fast. It is something we have done for many years, since childhood. But we do hire workers to help at the peak of the harvest."

Alex listened to Nicola talk about the green grapes versus the red grapes in the neighboring field and tried to take as many notes and ask as many questions as she could. After about 20 minutes, Nicola told her to walk with him to the other side of the building.

"You speak very good English," Alex commented as they walked.

"I spent many years learning both English and French. I've traveled to vineyards in France, New Zealand, and America. It is very expensive, but I want to learn everything I can to improve our, uh, operation. There are many new methods in other places, and I want to use the very best here."

Alex was impressed. "Did you go to school to learn about running a business?"

Nicola nodded. "Sì, I went to university in Bologna. I have a degree in Business and a Master's in Food and Wine."

Wow! He has more education than I have, Alex thought. *How snobbish of me to think that I would be the smarter one just because he was raised on a vineyard in the country.*

Nicola explained the process of loading the grapes into the enormous vats where fermentation takes place. Alex was surprised to learn that, for red wine, the grapes, skins, leaves, and stems were all loaded together and would be separated after fermentation. The temperature is closely regulated as the process takes place. After going through the crusher, which is the first step for the white wine, the juice is fermented again.

Alex followed Nicola inside, her head spinning with information. How would she ever learn this trade? Was coming here a colossal mistake? She should be applying for teaching or museum curator positions or other jobs suited to her degree instead of fooling herself that she could live this amazing European fantasy.

"Is everything okay?" Nicola asked when they stopped in a room filled with barrels of every imaginable size, including floor to ceiling, at least ten feet above their heads. "You do not look well. Do you need to sit down? Perhaps the heat was too much for you."

Now, standing in the cool cellar, Alex could feel the sweat that was running down her back and sticking to her armpits. She was so preoccupied outside that she hadn't even noticed. But she knew that it wasn't the heat or the strong aroma of the previous fermentation that was bothering her. The deceit, the enormity of her hasty trip to Italy, the unknown future looming in front of her, and the vast amount of information she would be expected to learn were all crushing her as if she were balancing one of those barrels on her shoulders.

"Perhaps I should sit," Alex said meekly. Nicola ran into another room and returned with two folding chairs. Opening them up, he gestured for her to sit and then sat next to her in the dimly lit room. "I'm so sorry," Alex said, though Nicola certainly didn't understand the extent of her apology.

"No, it is fine," he said. "Some water perhaps?"

Alex nodded, placed her purse and notebook on the floor, and watched as he quickly left the room again. When he returned, he handed her a glass of water and sat back down. As she drank, Alex noticed the concern in his eyes, deep brown eyes the color of dark chocolate. He seemed so different from the man who had walked out on her when she first arrived. She looked away, fearing that if he looked deeply into her own eyes, her sin would reveal itself.

Taking another sip, Alex smiled. "I think I'm okay now. Thank you." She looked around the room. "Shall we continue?"

Nicola raised an eyebrow and leaned back in his chair, assessing her for a moment. "Are you sure?"

"Yes," Alex said emphatically as she bent down to pick up her things. "I know you're a busy man. I don't want to take up any more of your time than necessary."

He continued to look at her skeptically for another minute and then rose, closing the chair, and reached for her hand to help her up. "If you are sure."

"I'm sure," Alex said with a smile. Nicola closed her chair as well but leaned them both against a nearby barrel rather than putting them away.

He went on to explain the difference between the barrels, the types of wood, which ones were used for the best reserve wines and which ones contained old and new vintages. Alex asked about the term 'vintage,' how one knows when a wine is 'fine,' and how long they are aged. Nicola answered all of her questions and offered questions of his own to ensure that she understood, at least rudimentarily, what he was teaching her.

They continued through another two rooms with Nicola explaining to Alex which wines were further processed, which ones were still being aged, and how they were all bottled and labeled. When they were through, Nicola led her into a room with a long table and several chairs. On one wall, were a small refrigerator and a shelf housing several bottles of red wines. Alex assumed, based on her small bit of research, the white wines were being kept cold while the reds remained at room temperature. Hanging beneath the shelves were several rows of wine glasses. On the longer wall in front of the table were a series of sketches that ended with the Belle Uve logo which Alex now easily recognized.

"Would you like to taste?"

"Sì, sì." Alex found herself saying, and she blushed at her obvious enthusiasm. Nicola laughed.

"Then you are feeling better," he said with a smile, and Alex noticed the way his cheeks dipped into deep dimples at the corners of his mouth when his smile was genuine. She blushed even more and hoped Nicola didn't notice.

She watched as he carefully removed a wine glass from the rack and placed it in front of her. "Just one?" she asked. "Won't you join me?"

Nicola shook his head. "No, I still have much work to do today, but thank you." He reached into the refrigerator and pulled out a bottle of white wine. Unscrewing the cap, he poured some of the golden liquid into her glass.

"No cork," she commented.

"No, this is new. Many scoff at the idea of using a screw top, but some of the top vineyards around the world are now using them. They cost less, and contrary to the old teachings, they do not change the taste of the wine. A cork, however, can rot and can indeed change the taste if the wine is not stored properly or is stored for too long."

"Too long? But I thought wine was supposed to be stored for a long time before drinking."

"Ah, you have already forgotten what I have told you." Nicola smiled as he replaced the top and sat the bottle on the table. "Only some wines are meant to be aged. Most wine is best when fresh."

Alex nodded and reached for the glass, but Nicola stopped her by placing his hand on her arm. Alex froze at his touch. "Not so fast," he said and smiled. "You must first smell the wine."

Alex did as she was told and found herself closing her eyes in order to fully enjoy the scent. She tried to identify the essence of the grapes, or something like that, but truthfully, she wasn't really sure what she should be noting.

"Smelling is part of tasting," Nicola said quietly as she sat and slowly inhaled through her nose, her eyes closed, her lips parted. "Now," he gently added, "look at the wine, the color, the way the light hits it."

Alex opened her eyes and looked at the beautiful liquid in her glass.

"Swirl it gently and watch how it reacts. I will show you in a few minutes how different wines have different legs, the height and slide of the wine on the glass." Alex did as she was told, unsure whether or not she was swirling it correctly.

"Very good," Nicola said. "Notice how the wine clings to the glass just slightly before sliding back down.

In a moment, you will see longer legs, a more robust wine."

Alex nodded and waited for the next instruction. Nicola motioned for her to drink, and she put the glass to her lips as their eyes met over the rim. Alex thought she saw his Adam's Apple move as she took a sip, and she found it hard to look away. She remembered why she was here and tried to concentrate on the taste, but she found herself lost in his gaze. Lowering the glass, she gave him a small smile.

"It is very good," she said.

Nicola was staring at Alex and then seemed to reawaken when she spoke. He quickly turned to the shelf behind her and took down another bottle. "Good, yes, but not great," he admitted.

Alex finished the wine in her glass and tilted it toward Nicola so that he could pour some of the red wine for her, but he took the glass away and replaced it with a clean one. She repeated the steps he had told her and noticed that this wine had a stronger scent. Nicola pointed out the longer legs, though Alex still wasn't sure what she was supposed to notice as the wine sloshed around the glass. She nodded and took a sip. This wine filled her mouth and nose with a heady scent and taste. She smiled and nodded as she swished it in her mouth and finally swallowed it.

"You're right, the first wine was good, but this wine is great." She finished the rest of the wine in her glass and sighed.

Nicola laughed. "You are easy to please," he said, and Alex felt momentarily stung by his comment. She frowned. "Just wait," he said as he opened a third bottle.

Alex watched as he poured the wine into a new glass. Taking it from him, she put it to her nose and didn't even have to inhale in order for the bouquet to fill her nostrils. She swirled it around and watched the liquid cling a little more heavily to the sides of the glass. Then she sipped the deep purple taste of Heaven. She opened her eyes wide as her whole mouth and nose filled with the robust flavor. Her taste buds felt alive, and her throat tingled as she swallowed the thick potable. It was even better than it had been at the restaurant now that she knew the proper way to taste it.

"Ah," was all she could manage, and again Nicola laughed his rich laugh that filled the room around her. Was she drunk? Her head began to spin with the flavor of the wine and the sound of his laughter.

"Great?"

"Sì," she replied. "Great." Then she turned toward him. "No, like a taste of Heaven." She voiced the thought that had come to her when she tasted the wine.

"Bravo," Nicola said and clapped his hands together. "That is our best wine, an award winner, I believe. Alas, no prizes have come to us for it yet."

"Why not?" Alex asked. She could scarcely believe that a better wine existed, even with her limited knowledge.

Nicola shrugged. "There are many Amarone grapes in this region that produce such good wine. It is a hard competition."

Alex thought about that. How could this be improved, she wondered. What more are the judges looking for?

The afternoon sun reached through the window as if it, too, felt the need to caress the auburn tresses that rested on her shoulder. Nicola was entranced, perhaps even bewitched, by her hair, her smile, the light that danced in her eyes like the stars danced on a lake on a moonlit summer night. He watched her and wondered what she was thinking. He also wondered what brought her here, to his vineyard, into his life? Surely God was playing a trick on him, sending this American into his life for a day, a few hours, and then whisking her away. He sensed something in her, something mysterious, and suddenly, he didn't want the tour to end. And it wasn't sexual. She just seemed… different, and Nicola had spent enough time in the States to know that not all women fit the stereotypes that Italians believed about the fast and loose American girls. This one seemed genuine, kind, and even innocent. It was as if he could see the goodness in her soul.

Nicola pulled out the chair beside this enchanting woman and sat down. At the moment, it dawned on him that he did not know her name.

"So, Signorina…" Nicola looked at her questioningly.

"Oh, I'm so sorry," she said as she reached out her hand. "I am, uh, I'm Annie." She smiled as he took her hand.

"It is very nice to meet you, Annie. What else can I tell you for your article?"

She appeared slightly confused and then looked down at her notepad and blushed. "Oh! I was enjoying myself so much that I forgot I'm supposed to be working." She smiled and picked up the pad and paper. "Can you tell me about the history of the vineyard?"

"I would be honored," and Nicola proceeded to tell her about the vineyard that had been started by his great-great grandfather at the turn of the 20th Century. The vineyard passed down through the generations, and he inherited half of the vineyard from his grandfather who passed away.

"The other half belonged to my prozia who just recently died as well." He tried not to think about what would happen to that half of the business now. When he turned back to her, he saw the pain in her eyes and wondered if she, too, had experienced a recent loss. A moment of uncertainty nagged at him, but he brushed it aside.

"I'm so sorry," she said as she reached over and took a hold of his hand. "Were you close?"

Nicola shook his head. "We never met," he told her. "She begged me to come when I was in the States, but she was in the East, and I was in the West, and I was young and selfish and enjoying my freedom. I should have gone," he said wistfully and looked down at his hand in hers. Suddenly feeling quite warm, and remembering the woman in his life, he pulled his hand away and stood up. He opened a window and paced for a minute to clear his head before sitting back down.

"So," he continued. "I came back to Italy and began to put my knowledge to work. I want to make Belle Uve a prize-winning vineyard that will honor my family."

"I believe you will do that." Annie smiled. He held her gaze and resisted the temptation to fix a stray hair that curled beside her face; its deep auburn mixed with brown was a stark contrast to her ivory skin.

"I'm feeling very hungry," he said suddenly. "Would you care to go for lunch and continue learning about great Italian wines?" He wasn't sure where that had come from. He never intended to say such a thing, and his girlfriend would not be pleased if she found out, to say the least.

Nicola thought that Annie looked uncomfortable, and he wished he could take back the offer. "Oh thank you so much. I do appreciate it." She began to stand. "But I have to get back. I need to write this while it's fresh in my mind."

Nicola nodded, "Of course." He stood back so that she could pass in front of him, and the scent of her shampoo wafted to his nose, strawberry and something else, vanilla? "Will you come back?" he asked and then felt foolish. "I mean, for more information?" What was wrong with him? He would be a dead man if word got out that he asked another woman to lunch and then inquired about when he would see her again.

She hesitated. "I don't know. Maybe," she said, but she failed to look at him. Her face was bright red, and she hurried through the door. He admonished himself for acting so impetuously. What kind of man did she think he was?

When he walked to the door and looked into the main room, Annie was talking to Maria. He watched as Maria took a bottle from the shelf and handed it to her. Annie nodded and pointed to another one. In the end, she bought one white, and two each of the reds. When she finished paying for her purchases, Nicola went into the room and held out a bottle of Amarone. From the corner of his eye, he saw a taxi pull up out front.

"It was a pleasure, Signorina. Please accept this gift as a token of my appreciation for visiting us and writing about our vineyard." Alex hesitated as she took the bottle and reached for his hand.

"Thank you," she said, and Nicola noticed a quiver in her voice. Instead of shaking her outstretched hand, he took it gently in his own hand and lifted it to his lips. He lightly kissed the back of her hand and felt a torrent of emotions race through his body. "Until we meet again," he said and held onto her a moment longer while their eyes met and held each other's gaze.

Blushing and seeming quite nervous, she smiled
weakly and thanked him again before hurrying from the
building.

"Wow," Maria said as Nicola stood, watching her
leave. She practically knocked over the driver in her
haste to get into the backseat. He watched the car drive
away and turned to Maria.

"Wow, what?" he asked in Italian.

"I never thought I'd see you act that way toward
her," Maria said in astonishment.

"What are you talking about?" Nicola went to the
counter as Maria pointed to the computer screen.

There on the screen, the credit card information
stood out like a flashing emergency light—Alexandra
O'Donnell.

So much for his intuition about the 'nice, American
girl.'

Without saying a word, Nicola turned on his heel
and went into the office, slamming the door so hard that
the bottles on the wall shook. He cursed, not at her but
at himself, for making such poor observations about her
character. She was indeed a witch who had cast a spell
over him, and now that the spell was broken, he would
not be made a fool of again.

Alex tilted her head back onto the seat of the taxi
and closed her eyes. She couldn't believe what she had

just done. She liked Nicola, she truly did. He was…well, he was darn good looking for a start; but, in spite of that temper, she could tell that he was also a gentleman. He was so concerned when he thought she was having a heat stroke, and all the while she was having a good, old fashioned guilt trip. When he told her the history of the vineyard and how he never even met Signora, she wanted to cry. But when he asked her to have lunch with him, all of the wine in her stomach began to turn sour, and she knew she had to leave. Immediately.

How could she face him now? How could she tell him the truth? She saw how he reacted when she arrived, and he didn't have time for a stupid American. That's how he would react when she went back, only worse. She looked at the bottle of fine wine and began to cry. He was so kind to her, and she did nothing but lie to him. She should just turn around right now and head back there and try to make amends. That would be the best thing to do. Yes, she would tell the driver to turn back now. It was decided.

But Alex remained silent in the back of the taxi as it passed by the olive groves and vineyards on its way back to Verona. She let the tears trail down her cheek and prayed that when she did arrive at the vineyard to claim her share, Nicola would understand. More than likely, he would not.

Two days later, Alex stepped out of a taxi wearing her best suit and finest jewelry, rather, Signora's finest jewelry that came with the house in Baltimore. It had taken her that long to get up the nerve to go back. The taxi driver took all of the luggage out of the car, and Alex handed him the fare along with a nice tip. She was just summoning her strength when she heard the door open behind her. She took a deep breath and turned to face Nicola, but he was not there.

"You are a brave woman," Maria said. "I like that." Her smile was wide and welcoming. "Come, I have been waiting for you."

"How…?" Alex began.

"You used your credit card," Maria said. "Perhaps a, how do you say, Freudian mistake?"

"Slip," Alex said quietly.

"Prego?"

"It's a Freudian slip." She sighed. "I guess I'm not as good at acting as I thought I was." She managed a weak smile.

"Oh, you were good all right. Nicola suspected, from the second you walked in, who you were, but you convinced him otherwise. It is not easy to trick him, so you should give yourself more credit."

"Thank you, I guess." Alex followed Maria into the villa that stood across the parking lot from the winery building. She marveled at the photos and old furniture. It was just as she imagined it would be, and not unlike Signora's house except for the obviously Italian exterior with its white stucco and red roof. The floors were made of polished red stone and were covered with beautiful throw rugs, and light, airy curtains swayed in the breeze. The long, wooden kitchen table was old and rustic, and Alex imagined Signora sitting on one of its benches as a child.

They went up the narrow staircase, and Maria opened the door to the room at the end of the hall.

"This is yours," she said. "I prepared it for you when we first learned of you. I had a feeling you would come."

The room was small but not uncomfortably so. It had a four-poster bed and a lace coverlet with matching window curtains. The dresser was old and large, and the wardrobe was magnificent. On the nightstand, sat an old lamp on top of a doily, and Alex wondered, as she ran her hand along the bedding, if all of the linens in the room were handmade by someone in Signora's family.

"It's perfect," Alex said. "Thank you."

"Il piacere e' mio. It is my pleasure," Maria said with a smile. "You picked a good time to come. Nicola is in town on business. He will return in a couple hours, so you have time to get settled."

"He's very angry?"

"Sì, sì, he is very angry." Maria leaned against the wall and thought for a moment. "You see, he thought that someday this would be his. He has run it by himself for many years. His grandfather was ill for a long time, so even when Nicola was away studying, he was still making all of the decisions here. He has been running Belle Uve since he was quindici, ah, ten and five?"

"Fifteen," Alex said.

"Sì, fifteen. So you see, he did not expect to share it. Finding out about you was a, ah, what is the word?"

"A shock?"

"Sì, sì, a shock. He felt tricked."

"Yes, I can see that." Alex sat on the bed and thought about what she had done. "And then I tricked him again."

"Sì," Maria nodded. "Now he does not trust you. He thinks you are going to try to take over his home and business."

Alex laughed out loud. "I hardly think so! He already knows that I know nothing about the business. I proved that the other day."

"Ah, but he does not know how much was trick."

Alex thought about that. She wasn't *that* good an actress. Sure, a couple of high school plays and several supporting roles in dramatic productions in college, but honestly, did he think she *really* knew about the wine business?

"Well, I can tell you right now, everything that I know about wine making I learned from a guidebook, the Internet, and from Nicola two days ago."

Maria nodded, seemingly satisfied. "You can unpack. I will have Luigi bring up your bags."

Alex watched her leave and wondered again what her relationship with Nicola was. They were obviously close and had worked together for a long time. Were they involved? And if so, why would Nicola have asked her to lunch? Alex had heard rumors about Italian men.

Perhaps they were true, she thought, as she opened the bag she had carried up with her.

Maria was showing Alex how to work the computer and how to translate the notations and products when Nicola walked into the building. He came to a dead stop when he saw the two women behind the counter.

"Prego," Maria said as she slipped out and went into the office. She had explained to Alex that 'prego' had many meanings, one of them being 'pardon.'

After releasing what Alex assumed was a string of profanities under his breath, Nicola turned toward her.

"What are you doing here?"

"I believe I live here now," Alex said defiantly, but her legs felt like jelly underneath her, and she was sure they would give out at any minute.

"You *live* here? No, no," Nicola said as his face turned blood red. "You do not *live* here. *I* live here. This is *my* house, my *family's* house. This is not *your* house." His voice rose in both volume and intensity with each sentence. "You can get your things and leave." He shouted at her, his hands now splayed on the counter, their faces almost touching.

"Nicola..." She tried to remain calm, "we should speak about this calmly and ration—"

"Speak about this? No, we will not 'speak about this.' You will leave." He turned and pointed to the front door.

"I will not." Alex felt her own ire rise as he tried to bully her out of what was rightfully hers. And it was rightfully hers. Signora had been the only family she had for the past year, and she wanted Alex to be a part of this.

"Then I will call the polizia and have them get you out." He continued to shout.

"Go right ahead," she shouted back, standing on her tiptoes so that she matched his height. "I'm. Not. Leaving." She folded her arms across her chest and stood looking at him defiantly.

"Oh yes you are," and with that, he went around the counter and picked her up, tossing her over his shoulder in a fireman's carry, and walked out the door. Alex kicked and screamed and beat her fists on his back until he dropped her into the dirt, her blouse and the skirt of her best suit now covered with the dry, June dust. When he turned to go back inside, Alex jumped up and grabbed the back of his shirt.

"You will not manhandle me like that, do you understand?" She yelled as he struggled to get away. They both heard laughing and turned their heads to see Luigi and Giovanni pointing and holding their stomachs. They laughed so hard, Alex thought they might begin crying. She let go of Nicola's shirt, and he stomped inside as she tried to regain some dignity by dusting off her clothes and pulling her skirt back down to a decent length. Maria walked out with a smirk on her face and fussed at the men in Italian. Alex assumed that she told them to go back to work. They sauntered off but continued to laugh.

"He will calm down," Maria assured her. "Someday," she added with a smile as she went back inside.

Alex stood in the dirt parking lot with her hands on her hips and tried to decide what to do. She had no desire to go back inside while Nicola was there, so she walked to the villa. Sitting at the wooden table in the cheery kitchen, she put her head down and closed her eyes. This wasn't going to be easy. Not by a mile.

Nicola fumed. He stood in the office and looked out the window at the rows of neatly kept grapevines. How was he supposed to share this with a complete stranger, especially one he didn't trust?

"She is nice, you know," Maria said from the doorway. "She wants to learn."

"She wants to take over my business," Nicola said without turning around.

"I do not think so," Maria said as she took a seat in the chair by her desk. "I have the feeling that she has nowhere else to go. She brought so many clothes but only two photographs. I saw them when I took her some fresh towels. There is one of her with her family, parents and a brother perhaps. It did not look recent. And then there was one of her and a woman I believe is your aunt."

Nicola turned to face her, and Maria saw the pain on his face. "Why?" he asked. "Why did she do this to me? Why after all of these years did she have to interfere? And from the grave, no less? She could have come over when my grandfather died, and the business and home went fully to her. Instead, she gave me half of the estate and let me take over the running of it. She never wanted anything to do with the vineyard. Why now?"

Maria shook her head. "I do not know, Nicola, but she must have had a reason."

"Well I wish to hell I knew what it was." He turned back to the window.

"Then ask her," Maria said.

"I cannot very well do that, now, can I?"

"No, but you can ask Alexandra, I mean Alex. Maybe she knows."

"Ha," he scoffed. "I bet she knows all right. She talked my aunt into giving her the most valuable thing she owned."

"I do not think so, Nicola." He didn't move, but Maria saw his shoulders tense and knew he was listening. "She told me that she had no idea any of this existed. She was as surprised as you were."

Nicola shook his head and turned back to her. "I do not believe it," he said adamantly, though he had a fleeting memory of their first meeting and how he had believed that she was kind and innocent. Obviously he was wrong. "I do not believe a word she says, and I think she knew exactly what she was getting and how much it was worth."

"Then the joke is on her, is it not? Because it is not worth the ground it sits on." Maria stood and left the room while Nicola clenched his jaw at her biting words. He closed his eyes and took a deep breath. Somehow, he was going to turn things around. Belle Uve was going to be the most profitable vineyard in Valpolicella with or without the meddling Alexandra.

Chapter Three

After a restless night, Alex stayed in her room until she knew that Nicola had left the house. She ate breakfast in the cozy kitchen and tried to decide what to do with her day. She needed some time to gather her thoughts but was curious about the estate, so she decided to explore the property. Careful not to run into Nicola, she walked down a path between the vines to the barn she spied from her window. Sitting in the middle of the fields, she assumed that the barn was part of the estate. When she came close, Alex realized that the structure was rather old and worn, and she wondered if it was even safe to poke around inside.

Carefully opening the door, Alex peeked inside. She saw several pieces of farm equipment that looked fairly new, so she presumed that the barn was still in use and proceeded inside. The smell of oil, gasoline, and dirt filled the air, and dust clung to the sun rays as Alex pushed open the doors. A sudden movement to her left made Alex jump, but it was just a barn cat racing through the building, perhaps chasing a mouse. The thought didn't bother Alex. She had never been one of those girly girls who stood on a chair and screamed at the sight of a rodent.

Alex noticed stalls and wondered if, at one time, the barn housed animals. The stalls were now filled with extra barrels, tubing, boxes of bottles, and other wine making supplies. There was a ladder to a loft that looked like it was still in pretty good condition, and she walked to it for a closer inspection. Deciding that the ladder seemed sturdy enough, Alex gripped the rungs and climbed to the top, her curiosity getting the better of her. The loft was empty except for a bench by the window, and she wondered what the loft was used for and why a bench would be there. Taking a look out the window, Alex could see the villa and the winery. The leaves on the grapevines waved gently in the breeze, and the smell of grapes wafted through the window. She saw Nicola walking among the vines and gasped, ducking out of sight when she thought he looked up toward the window. Peering out once again, she saw him inspecting the plants while Luigi and Giovanni worked on an irrigation pipe in a neighboring field.

The light breeze drifted through the window, but the loft was still hot and stuffy with the early June heat. Alex headed back toward the ladder, but her sneaker hit something under the straw. She bent down and brushed away the hay to find an old, leather-bound book. It was loosely tied with a ribbon that had mostly deteriorated over time. When Alex picked up the book, the ribbon disintegrated and fell away, and the soft leather flaked off a bit in the bottom corner. Alex delicately paged through the book and found that the sheets were yellow with age, but the ink, for the most part, was still dark and legible. She opened the book to the first page.

The journal was written in Italian, but Alex could make out just enough of the words to cause her heartbeat to quicken and her throat to tighten. Among the words she knew were *December 10, 1942* and *Isabella Abelli*, whom Alex knew better as Signora Fonticelli.

After leaving the barn, she stealthily walked to the office and asked Maria about Internet access. She was pleased to find that both the house and the business had wifi and a fast connection. She hastily retreated to her room, hiding the journal in her waistband. Alex sat on her bed and powered on her laptop. She waited anxiously for it to finish starting up. As soon as the computer was up and running, Alex opened the sophisticated translation software she bought before leaving home and typed into the box the first paragraph in the journal.

December 20, 1942

I, Isabella Abelli, have a confession to make. While the world goes to pieces all around me, I have found a reason to be happy. I may not know many things. I do not know what will happen to our country. I do not know why Hitler does the things he does, why he is trusted by our leader. I do not know why they have plunged the entire world into this darkness we call war. I do not know what will happen to me, my family, our little world here at Belle Uve, but I do know one thing. Today I met the man I will marry.

Alex read the translation again and wondered about this girl. How old was Signora when she wrote this? She certainly didn't sound like the Signora whom Alex knew—the one who seemed to know everything and never faltered in her advice. This Isabella Abelli was a girl, probably a teenager, just finding her way in the world. She was an enigma to Alex, and Alex longed to know more. However, she felt that old pang of guilt once again. Shouldn't she tell Nicola about her discovery? Wouldn't he want to see it? Or perhaps he had seen it years ago and had left it lying up in the loft, uninterested in its contents, the musings of a young girl whom he had never met.

Alex ran her fingers across the writing and pondered what she should do. She closed her eyes and asked for help.

Signora, please give me some guidance here. Please help me know what to do.

No answer came.

Nicola watched the taxi pull up in front of the vineyard early the following morning. He followed it with his gaze as it pulled away with Alex inside of it. Maria walked to the window and stood beside him.

"She is leaving?" he asked.

"No. She said she needed to empty her head and asked if she could make dinner for us. She is going to the store. I told her to ask Luigi to take her, but she said no." Maria shook her head. "She needs a car." She looked at Nicola and saw that he was trying to hold back a grin. She nudged him. "What?"

"Clear her head, not empty it. Though I like that thought." He laughed as he went outside, leaving Maria to ponder the American idiom.

Nicola wandered in and out of the rows of the vineyard, sampling a grape here and there to be sure that they were ripening well. His mind was elsewhere, though, and he was annoyed with himself for not concentrating on the vineyard. He was more annoyed with Alex, however, and the way that she had been inserted into his life. He actually liked Annie and would have enjoyed taking her to lunch, getting to know her. But Alex was a different story. He wanted no parts of her. She was nothing more than a pest hovering over his crop, savoring the fruit, and leaving him the spoils. That's how he saw her, as someone who just wanted to reap the benefits of the business he was trying so hard to save.

Vineyards were everywhere now. They were becoming more and more popular the world over, with modern technologies that allowed almost any climate to produce a grape cultivated just for that region. It was hard enough to compete with other Italian wines, but in this global economy, Nicola had to figure out how to compete not just in Europe but in every country on the map. For now, he concentrated just on Italy, hoping to win a prize, to become known in his own country for an outstanding vintage. Then he could slowly begin exporting to wineries and stores around the globe. The last thing he needed was this legal mess that he was going to have to deal with in regard to Alex.

Exactly what did she want from him? She couldn't possibly believe that she could just walk in here and be his partner. She knew nothing about grapes, wine, or even Italy. She spoke no Italian. How would she be able to communicate with customers or interact with business associates? What did she think she could possibly offer him?

Nicola shook his head and tried to ignore the hurt and anger that he felt toward his great-aunt. From what little he knew about her, she was well-regarded by the rest of his family, most of them gone now. There were some whisperings about something in the past that had prevented her from ever returning to Italy, but nobody ever spoke about it. Nicola had no idea what it could have been, and he wasn't sure that it wasn't made up, no more than a family legend. As far as he knew, she and her young betrothed fled Italy during the war, marrying in haste before catching a train that took them from Italy and then a boat that took them to America. He didn't know how they managed to escape the war-torn country or why they left, but they were held in high esteem by everyone who remembered them, so it couldn't have been a mere, cowardly escape from the War.

What reason could Prozia Isabella have had to leave half of his vineyard to this stranger? Didn't she trust him to keep it going? Nicola did not understand and could not fathom why this was happening.

"She is beautiful, no?"

Nicola's thoughts were shattered by Luigi who seemed to appear from nowhere.

"Prego?"

"Signorina Alex è molto bella," Luigi said with a smile. "Maybe I should ask her on a date." He winked at Nicola.

"Go right ahead," Nicola said before turning and walking away. His words conveyed disgust, but his stomach clenched at the thought of his cousin taking Alex out for a night on the town. What if they hit it off? What if they married? Then Alex would truly be part of the family. Nicola shook his head and tried to put the image out of his mind. He couldn't care less what Alex did, but he didn't want anyone to encourage her to become any more a part of the family than she already assumed she was by virtue of the will.

Nicola went back inside and headed straight to the tasting room. He reached for a bottle of wine and poured himself a glass. *Now she has me drinking on the job, something I have never done.* Tossing the wine down his throat as if it were a cheap whiskey, he glared out the window at Luigi's back. The smooth liquid did nothing to ease the knot that sat like a rock in the pit of his stomach.

Alex needed some time to think and some space to breathe. Nicola did not want her at the villa, but she was determined to show him that she belonged there. In just the short time since she had sat her suitcases down in Signora's old bedroom, Alex knew that she was home. Now she just had to convince Nicola. She decided to cook dinner for him and the others at the vineyard, but first, she needed to spend a few hours to herself.

Deciding that she should expose herself to some more Italian culture and history, she asked the taxi driver to take her back to the heart of Verona. She felt that a visit to *Juliet's House* was in order. According to her guidebook, the Montagues and Capulets truly did exist during Shakespeare's time, although there never was any account of an actual Romeo or Juliet. The Capulet family home, however, still lured in millions of tourists each year, all wanting to stand on the famous balcony overlooking the courtyard where Romeo allegedly pledged his love to Juliet. Alex had been Juliet's understudy in the university's production of *Romeo and Juliet* her sophomore year; and like Juliet, Alex's life had been no picnic, so she felt an odd affinity to the tragic heroine.

The house wasn't hard to find. Even at the early hour, tourists were flocking to the courtyard that was lined with walls covered with graffiti—messages to Juliet asking for help finding or keeping true love. A bronze statue of Juliet stood in the middle, and dozens of people gathered around to take pictures with the tragic heroine. Alex opted not to rub the breasts of the statue even though she could use all the luck they were said to give to those so bold. She paid the small fee and followed the narrow stairs to the top floor. Along the way, she read the framed quotes from the play and took notice of the costumes and furniture from movie sets that now adorned the house.

It all seemed so familiar to her, like she was back on the stage preparing for opening night. Alex stood in line for her turn to go out on the balcony. Feeling slightly embarrassed, she took a selfie on her phone and wished, not for the first time, that she had someone to send it to. Then she thought of her childhood friend, Cindy, the only person, other than the quick email to her mother, she contacted before heading to Italy. She would send it to Cindy later.

After killing a good couple of hours in the city, Alex hailed a taxi to take her to the market. With her shopping list in hand, she prayed for Signora's help to make a dinner that would knock Nicola, Maria, and the guys off their feet.

The taxi driver dropped off Alex and her packages a few hours later. At this rate, she was going to spend all the money she inherited from Signora on taxi fare. She really needed to think about buying a small, inexpensive car. Perhaps Giovanni or Luigi would go with her and help her find one. She had no experience purchasing a car in the States. How could she possibly know where and how to find one in Italy?

She trudged into the villa with her groceries and began unloading them onto the large, stone countertop.

It wasn't long before the kitchen smelled like a five-star restaurant in the heart of any Italian city. Of the many things Alex had to thank Signora for, learning to cook authentic Italian food was one of them. Rather than buying the pre-packaged pasta, Alex made her own, some soft and smooth tortellini that she twisted around a ball of fresh cheeses seasoned with spices. While the pasta cooked, she made a tomato and cream sauce that was Signora's favorite and warmed the freshly baked bread she found in a pastry shop. She was just cleaning up her work area and preparing to call everyone in when Nicola stepped into the room.

He eyed her with interest and walked over to the stove to see what she had cooked. He lifted the wooden spoon and gave Alex a questioning look. She nodded and watched as he dipped the spoon into the sauce. Alex swallowed hard with trepidation as he blew gently on the steaming sauce, with his lips puckered and his eyes closed to avoid the steam. When he tasted it, she saw the surprise on his face. He turned toward her.

"It is…" He hesitated. "It is like my grandmother's sauce. I…" his words faltered. "I have not tasted anything close to this in years."

Alex smiled. "Then I guess I finally did something right." She breathed with relief as Maria, Luigi, and Giovanni breezed into the kitchen. Alex could practically see them salivating.

"Please." She nervously gestured to the table, already set with the china she found in the kitchen cabinets. "Sit down, and I will put the food on the table."

They did as they were told after washing up, and Alex used the beautiful, handmade pasta dishes to serve the meal. They said grace with their heads bowed, and then they all dug in like they were ravenous.

Over dinner, Maria, Luigi, and Giovanni told tales about growing up on the vineyard. They were, it turned out, the children of Nicola's aunt on his father's side, cousins to Nicola but not related to Signora. Alex marveled at their tales and found herself feeling giddy from the stories, laughter, food, and no doubt, the wine. She almost felt at home, except for the weight of Nicola's silence and his heavy stare, a constant reminder that he would never accept her as one of them, no matter how good a cook she was.

When the meal was over, Luigi and Nicola went to the living room to watch soccer—which Alex learned was calcio in Italian—while Alex and Maria cleared the table and washed and dried the dishes. Maria tried to insist that Alex let her do the work since Alex had cooked, but Alex resisted giving up this chance to be a part of the family, even if only in her own mind. Giovanni made a hasty exit, taking home a helping of the pasta and sauce to his wife and baby. He gave Alex the customary two-cheek kisses before leaving and told her how much his wife would love to meet her. Alex's heart melted, and she insisted that she and the baby come over the next time they all shared a meal. That was when Alex learned that they all ate together every Sunday afternoon after Mass, an old-world custom that their family had kept up through the years. Alex looked forward to meeting Adriana and baby Marco that weekend, that is, if Nicola didn't put his foot down and forbid her from going. *Just let him try.*

After Luigi and Maria said their goodbyes, Alex and Nicola stood in the awkward silence.

"I'm going to go to bed and read for a bit," Alex finally said. She turned toward the steps, but Nicola reached for her arm and stopped her.

"Thank you," he said quietly, "for dinner. It was buonissimo."

Alex blushed and gently pulled her arm from his loose grip. "You're welcome, Nicola." She took a step and then stopped and turned back to him. "I'm sorry," she began. "I never wanted this." At that moment, Alex wasn't sure if she meant the inheritance or the lingering animosity between them. "I just, I just wanted a family, and Signora gave that to me for the short time I took care of her. It was enough for me. I never knew about…" She stopped as the tears began to flow. "I'm sorry," she said again before fleeing up the stairs to her room, leaving Nicola behind to ponder her words.

That night, as she lay in bed, the journal that was hidden in the nightstand drawer seemed to whisper to her, as if Isabella's voice was carried in on the breeze that wafted through the open window. Alex didn't want to keep any secrets from Nicola. Perhaps the journal could be the thing to bring them together, a mutual curiosity that could convince him to allow her to be a part of this world into which she had been plunged like Alice into the rabbit hole. She drifted off to sleep with Signora's ghost whispering in her ear,

While the world goes to pieces all around me, I have found a reason to be happy....

Tomato and Cream Sauce

See if you can find real, Italian tomatoes
in cans for this recipe.
¼ pound butter
3 tablespoons finely chopped yellow onion
3 tablespoons finely chopped carrot
3 tablespoons finely chopped celery
2 ½ cups canned Italian tomatoes with juice
2 teaspoons salt
¼ teaspoon granulated sugar
½ cup heavy cream

Put all ingredients except cream into s
aucepan and cook at lowest
simmer for 1 hour, uncovered.
Stir occasionally.
Puree and bring to simmer. Add cream
and cook for one minute
while stirring.
Serve immediately over tortellini.

Chapter Four

Alex woke up early the next morning and took a shower, dressed, and quietly made her way to the kitchen. Strong coffee and the faint smell of some kind of cheese hung in the air along with the scent of a meat, perhaps sausage. She grabbed a container of fresh yogurt out of the refrigerator and scooped it into one of the beautiful dessert bowls along with some fresh berries that she had purchased on her grocery trip the day before. She sliced off a piece of fresh bread and made a cup of coffee from what was left in the coffee maker.

After eating, she wandered across the driveway to see what was going on at the vineyard. She could hear the brothers speaking to each other in Italian from the fields, but Nicola did not appear to be with them. She entered the building and found Maria working on the computer behind the counter. Maria's face brightened, and she smiled at Alex, a warm, welcoming smile.

"Buongiorno," she said cheerfully. "Would you like another lesson?" She motioned toward the computer.

"Sì," Alex said with a smile. "I'd like to learn the computer as well as some Italian. If I'm going to live in Italy, I should know how to speak the language, right?"

Maria nodded. "Sì, sì, you will learn it in time. It will come naturally if we all try to work with you in every day talking."

Alex wasn't so sure about that, but she guessed that diving in headfirst was one way to learn.

For the next hour, the two women went over the information on the screen. Alex learned the words she needed to know to work the sales and inventory software, and Maria helped her learn how to say, "May I help you" and other phrases and sentences that she would use most frequently.

"Do not worry, I will never leave you alone," Maria assured her. "At least not until you are ready."

Alex believed that could be years.

They heard a car pull into the driveway and both looked up when the door opened, and a woman, around Alex's age, dressed at the height of Italian fashion walked in, her entire demeanor commanding attention and respect. She looked and even smelled like an aristocrat, not that Alex had been around any aristocrats. This woman gave off an air of importance, and Alex was intrigued by her while at the same time feeling completely inadequate in her capri pants and cute, matching t-shirt.

Maria smiled, but Alex had already gotten to know her well enough to know that the smile was not genuine. "Buongiorno, Evangelina," Maria said without the warmth that Alex had come to know and recognize.

The woman did not reply to the greeting but proceeded to ask a question with an air of superiority.

Maria answered, and the woman went to the office door, opened it, and went in without knocking. She closed the door behind her, and Alex could feel Maria tense. Alex raised an eyebrow in question.

"Evangelina Lombardi," Maria said with a shake of her head. "She has been after Nicola for years. I'm not sure if it's him or the vineyard that interests her more." Maria wrinkled her nose in disgust. "She does not, how do you say, have his best interests in her heart?"

"Hmm." Alex leaned toward the door to see if she could hear any of the conversation going on behind it. She turned back to Maria. "And how does Nicola feel about her?"

Maria shrugged. "I do not know. He does not ever talk about her to me or tell me anything, but they do spend a lot of time together. Everyone says they are a couple, and he does not deny it. It puzzles me. Her family and Nicola's family go back very far, to the War or before, I think. Her madre's family were butchers, but her padre has a large fortune."

"Funny," Alex said. "I didn't get the impression that he was seeing anyone. Other than you perhaps, before I knew you were his cousin, of course!"

Maria spit out a loud laugh. "Boy, were you on the wrong road!"

"Wrong track," Alex corrected her. "But yeah, I guess I was. Entirely on the wrong track." She thought about the way Nicola had touched her arm the night before. She had dismissed it as nothing more than a small truce, which it obviously was.

After a few minutes, Evangelina and Nicola emerged from the office. Alex noticed how stiff Nicola seemed to be while Evangelina couldn't stop touching his arm, his shoulder, his back, as they walked toward the counter. Nicola and Maria had a brief exchange of words, and Alex pretended not to notice the way Evangelina sized her up. Finally, she turned toward the woman and reached out her hand.

"Alexandra O'Donnell," she said. "I'm Nicola' business partner."

Evangelina stared at the outstretched hand for a moment and then raised her eyes to glare at Alex. "Non capisco," she said coldly before placing her hand on Nicola's back and practically pushing him out the door.

"Humph," Maria scoffed. "She understood you perfectly. She is just a, what word would you say?"

"And I understand you perfectly, Maria. My thoughts exactly." The two women watched through the window as the fancy, metallic blue, Alfa Romeo Princess glided out of the driveway. Alex hoped she didn't have to win over the snotty Evangelina in order to win over Nicola. She had enough on her hands already.

Nicola hardly heard anything that Evangelina said on the ride to Verona. She was hosting a cocktail party for a visiting celebrity making a movie in the city, and she wanted Nicola's opinion on the placement of the bar on the terrazzo in her backyard. Nicola had no idea why she needed him to tell her to put the bar in the same location she always put it, but he wasn't in the mood to argue with her, and it gave him an excuse to leave the vineyard for a while. He stared out the window at the fields of grapevines and olive trees and found himself wondering what Alex's home was like back in America. Did she live in the countryside like he did, or did she live in a city? He knew that she was a recent graduate from a college in Baltimore, but had she always lived there, or was there another place she called home? And why couldn't he get her off of his mind? Perhaps a Google search later would satisfy his curiosity and make thoughts of her go away.

"Niki, did you hear a word I just said?"

Nicola brought his attention back to Evangelina. "I am sorry, my mind must have wandered off. What were you saying?"

Evangelina pouted and stared at the road ahead. "No, I will not repeat," she said after a moment. "You are not paying me any attention today." She puckered her lip out farther.

Nicola reached over and patted her leg. "I am sorry," he said. "Please, I have a lot on my mind these days."

"The woman living in your house? Your 'business partner'?" she said the phrase like one would have said "Your rotten fish," or "Your ex-wife."

"Yes, Alex is the root of it," Nicola admitted. "I have to rethink how I do everything, how I can give her some authority without giving up control. It has been very confusing and frustrating for me."

"I see nothing confusing. Just get rid of her. Send her back to America."

"I would if I could, believe me, but I have gone over every document and looked at every possible loophole, and I am afraid I am stuck with her." Nicola sighed and shrugged his shoulders. He looked at Evangelina with a pitiful gaze.

"It is okay, my love, I know how to make you forget about your new 'partner.'" She reached across the car and put her hand on his thigh. She looked at him out of the corner of her eye with a sultry smile and moved her hand upward.

Nicola reached down, picked up her hand, and placed it back on the steering wheel. "Now, now, Eva, you do not want to wreck the new car Papà just bought you."

The pout reappeared, and Evangelina sneered at him as she pressed down the accelerator and sped up the car. "Niki, you do know how to ruin a girl's fun."

Nicola turned back toward the window and wondered what was wrong with him. Every hot-blooded male for at least thirty kilometers would give his right arm to go to bed with Eva. They'd been together off and on for years now, and he knew that Eva was ready to make a commitment. He thought he was, too, but suddenly, her touch didn't excite him like it normally did. Maybe he was coming down with something.

Maria and Alex sat behind the counter and ate the caprese salad that Maria fixed for them. Alex was nervous the entire time that Maria was in the villa, but nobody called or came into the winery, and Alex appreciated Maria's trust in her. Still, she was happy that Maria returned quickly.

"So, Maria," Alex began tentatively, "yesterday, I was exploring a little."

The phone rang, and Alex was relieved to have the interruption. Maria took an order from a restaurant in Bologna, and Alex watched the transaction, trying to learn the steps as well as the words. When she hung up, Maria turned and looked at Alex expectantly.

Alex continued, "I was up in the barn, and I found something…" she hesitated.

Maria's expression changed. "Something bad?"

Alex shook her head. "No, nothing like that."

"Then just tell."

Taking a deep breath, Alex began, "I found a journal. I think it's Signora's, Prozia Isabella. I can't read it, but I typed the first paragraph into my laptop, and I'm sure she wrote it when she was quite young, a teenager perhaps."

Maria sat in silence as she thought about the information. After a few minutes, she spoke. "And you want to read it?"

Alex nodded. "I do, but only if you, and Nicola of course, think it's okay. I should ask him right? I should see if it's okay with him or if he wants to read it himself, shouldn't I?"

"I think, yes, you should ask. It is not my say, but his. I think if you do not ask him, he will say you kept information from him again. I do not know if he will care what it says, but he will want to know you are reading it."

"I thought so, too. You know him so much better than I do, and I trust you. What should I say? Will he be angry that I didn't go to him right away?"

Maria rolled her lips together and thought about it. "I do not think so. Not if you go to him today and say that you forgot about it yesterday, and then he was gone today when you remembered. I think he might like to know what you find, but then again, he may say it was written so long ago that it does not matter anymore."

Alex nodded and thought about what his reaction might be. After a few minutes, Maria inquired, "What did it say? The paragraph that you read?"

"That she had met the man she was going to marry." Alex smiled as she remembered the feeling she had when she read the words.

Maria smiled, too. "How romantic," she said. "Did it say anything else?"

"Not much," Alex told her. "It was written during the War, and she said that the world was falling to pieces around her."

"Si, then she was a teenager, for she left toward the end of the War when she was just seventeen or eighteen." Maria's eyes lit up. "In fact, she left with a boy. I wonder if he is the one."

"A boy, or a man?"

"Well, they were both young, as I said, not more than seventeen, at least Isabella. I don't know much about the man, or boy. I suppose everyone seemed older than they were during those years. Nicola could tell you more. She was his family, not mine."

Alex thought about how horrible it must have been to live in Europe during that time. She closed her eyes and remembered the Signora she knew. She tried to imagine her as the teenaged girl in the journal. They just seemed so different. She needed to know more, to know how this naïve young Isabella became the elegant and wise Signora.

"I will show it to Nicola tonight," she said. "Maybe together, we can learn about the woman who threw us into this mess."

"If Evangelina lets him out of her grasp," Maria said, shaking her head. "Maybe you can talk some sense into him."

"Oh, I don't know about that. I don't think I have any influence over Nicola at all."

"Not yet, perhaps, but I think that will change." Maria stood and took Alex's plate. Alex watched her go outside to take the dishes back to the villa and thought about the two different sides of Nicola she had seen, particularly his angry side.

I don't know about that, Maria. I'm not sure I could ever have the influence over Nicola that Evangelina has, or if I even want to.

It was late afternoon when Nicola barged into the winery looking like he was returning from the trenches of war. He seemed out of breath, his expression hard, his jaw clenched, and his hands curled into fists. He practically snarled at Maria and Alex as he slammed the door behind him.

Maria asked Nicola a question, and he shook his head and exhaled as he answered. His words were fast and filled with irritation. Maria shook her head, tsked her tongue, and made another comment. Nicola spat back an answer and retreated to the office, not sparing that door either. The bottles on the wall shook as they had the day Alex first arrived at the vineyard.

Eyes wide, Alex turned to Maria and released the breath she hadn't realized she was holding. "What was that?"

"You will get used to it. It is the effect *Eva* has on him." Maria tried to suppress a smile.

"You really don't like her," Alex stated.

Maria shook her head and laughed. "I cannot stand her!"

"Nicola doesn't seem overly fond of her either. Why does he put up with her?"

"As I said, the families are old friends, and Eva always gets what she wants. And there is the sex, of course." Maria laughed at Alex's shocked expression. "No, really, he says he loves her, and everyone says that someday he will marry her, but so far, that has not happened. He is very, I don't know how to say, strange when it comes to Eva. He does not act like a man in love. I think it is just what he thinks the family expects him to do, but he is taking a long time to do it. Like I told you, he does not talk about her or their relationship to me. And he probably does not talk to his mother either. She would want him happy and not worrying about what is expected."

"We have an expression in America, why buy the cow when you can get the milk for free? Maybe Nicola doesn't think they need to get married if he's getting everything he wants already, if you know what I mean."

"I do not know," Maria said. "Nicola is a good man. I know you have not seen that yet, but he has been very good to me, and I know that he has a good heart. He would not use Evangelina or anyone for sex or anything else. I truly think he would rather not be with her. He has tried to tell her that maybe they are not right for each other, but she becomes more painful, and he goes back to her." Alex smiled at Maria's attempt to speak English and realized just how little effort she was making at learning Italian. At least that would get her mind off of Nicola and Eva, though she wasn't sure why she even cared, other than the fact that she did not want to spend the rest of her life sharing a business with that woman.

Suddenly, she thought again of the journal and how she wished she could understand it. "I'm guessing this is not a good time to talk to Nicola about the journal."

Maria pressed her lips together and shook her head. "No, I would wait. It is best you leave him alone for now."

Later that afternoon, Luigi and Giovanni came in to tell the ladies goodbye. Maria shut down the computer and gathered her things before bidding Alex a good night and heading home. Alex realized that Nicola must have snuck out the back door from the office. There hadn't been any sounds coming from behind the door in quite a while, and a heavy silence fell over the building. Alex turned off the lights and locked the front door before slipping out and walking to the villa.

She ate a quiet dinner alone and wondered where Nicola was and what he was doing. It wasn't until she was in bed reading, holding off the temptation to translate more of the journal, that she heard him come upstairs and go to bed. Unable to fall asleep, once she turned out the light, Alex tossed and turned as many thoughts drifted through her mind. How would she ever fit in here? Would Nicola ever accept her as a partner and friend? Mostly, what secrets might Signora's journal hold, and did she really want to know them?

Chapter Five

On Saturday, Luigi took Alex car shopping. He was a hopeless flirt, and she couldn't help but flirt back. It seemed that they both understood that nothing would come of it, but it was fun to let go and enjoy herself with a man, and the attention was flattering and something she needed these days. She didn't see Nicola before they left, and she wondered if he was truly that busy or if he was avoiding her. Returning late that afternoon, the new owner of a used, blue Fiat, Alex found Nicola in the kitchen.

"Oh my gosh, that smells heavenly," Alex said as she hung her purse on a chair.

"I cooked for two," Nicola said without looking at her.

"Oh," Alex said, peering into the next room. "I'm sorry. I will just make myself something quick and get out of your way."

Nicola turned toward her and gave her a small smile. "I cooked for us. For you and me," he clarified when he saw the question in her gaze.

"For us," Alex repeated. "Why, thank you. I didn't expect that." She hesitated a moment, trying to hide her nervousness, and then went to the cabinet and took out two glasses. "Wine?"

"Sì, grazie." Nicola turned back to the stove, and Alex poured them each a glass of wine. She took a sip of hers as she set his on the counter near the stove. She watched as he tossed spinach, mushrooms, and something she couldn't identify in a pan of olive oil and spices.

"What's that?" She motioned toward the black paste in the pan.

"Truffles," Nicola answered and turned down the heat as he uncovered a hot pot of pasta—linguine, Alex guessed—and reached for a plate.

"What are truffles?" Alex asked.

Nicola raised his eyebrows. "You have never tasted truffles? They are a bit like mushrooms but stronger in taste. You might not like them."

Alex smiled widely. "There isn't much I don't like, so bring it on." She took a plate and helped herself to a small piece of steak. She then handed it to Nicola for him to add a healthy serving of the sautéed mixture.

"Maria said that you don't cook. In fact, she said that I would probably be expected to cook for both of us every night."

Nicola laughed. "My cousin knows me better than that. Sì, many Italian men let the women do the chores, but I have lived alone for many years. I cook, or I starve."

"Good point," Alex said and raised her glass to him before taking a sip. She thought about Evangelina and remembered that Maria said she and Nicola had been together for years. "What about Evangelina?"

Nicola looked at her with a quizzical expression. "What about Eva?"

"Doesn't she ever cook for you?"

Nicola exploded with laughter. "Eva, cook?" He continued to laugh and shake his head. "Eva is very good at choosing the best restaurant, but cooking? No, that is not something Eva is good at."

Oh, I bet I can guess what she's good at, Alex thought as she looked away to hide her rolling eyes.

"No talk about Eva tonight. Let us eat," Nicola said, and Alex couldn't have agreed more.

They took their time with the dinner—tender and juicy steak, garlic potatoes, and the spinach mixture. Alex raved about the meal and practically fell in love with the truffle paste, though it truly was strong in taste, as Nicola had warned her. It was unlike anything she had ever tasted. They made small talk as they ate.

Toward the end of their meal, Alex couldn't contain her curiosity any longer.

"Why are you doing this?" she asked abruptly.

Nicola looked confused. "What am I doing?"

Alex swept her hands over the table. "This, the dinner, the conversation, you being nice to me. What are you up to?"

Nicola raised an eyebrow and stared at Alex for a moment before answering. "I decided that this feud is useless. I can either hate you and try to drive you away, perhaps fight you legally. Or I can accept that we might work together." He sat back and shrugged. "I will admit that I am not happy with it, but I can try to make it work."

Alex thought about what he said and appreciated his honesty, but she was now the one who was confused. Pushing the images of Nicola with Eva out of her mind, she looked at him with curiosity. "What does Eva have to say about this?"

"It is not her concern."

"But won't she own part of it someday?" Alex asked.

Nicola stopped his glass in mid-air and just stared at Alex. He paused before setting the glass back down on the table.

"What do you mean?"

"Well, Maria says that you and Eva will probably get married eventually. Will she be okay with working with me?"

Nicola's laugh was deep and hearty. "Eva does not work."

"Whatever," Alex said as she stood and began to clear the dishes. She was mystified as to what he saw in that woman but didn't feel like wasting any more time on the spoiled Evangelina. "I'm just glad you won't be dropping me in the dirt or slamming doors in my face anymore."

"We will see, bella, we will see." Nicola laughed again as he stood to help. Alex would have thought that Nicola was actually calling her beautiful if she hadn't heard him use the same word and tone with Maria several times. And she also knew that Luigi wasn't the only flirt in Italy. It seemed to come naturally to the men here.

As they washed and dried the dishes, Alex thought it might be a good time to bring up the journal. Nicola was in a good mood, and the ice had been broken between them.

"Nicola," she began tentatively. "I have something to tell you…" She stopped speaking and took a deep breath. The easy atmosphere they had enjoyed for the past hour became tense as Nicola stopped drying a plate and eyed her suspiciously. Alex swallowed and turned off the water, laying her dishrag on the side of the sink. She turned to Nicola.

"I found something a couple days ago. I wasn't trying to hide it." She quickly tried to reassure him. "I just haven't had a chance to talk to you. There was business to be attended to and then Evangelina and then car shopping." She took a breath and tried to slow down her rapidly beating heart. "Please, know that I wasn't trying to snoop or keep secrets."

"Just say what you found," Nicola said impatiently, throwing the towel on the counter and putting the plate down on top of the other one. There was no flirtatiousness there now.

"It may not be anything, really. It's just a journal. A journal that I believe belonged to your Great-Aunt." She watched him and tried to read his expression. After a moment, he shrugged, picked up the plates, and put them away.

"It sounds like nothing," he said. "I thought you were going to tell me it was something important."

"Oh, but it is important," she said pleadingly, and she grabbed his arm to force him to turn back to her. "It is very important to me. You see, you have Eva, and Maria, and Luigi, and Giovanni, and their families, and your friends. But I have no one. Finding the journal…" She searched for the words without noticing that her grasp had tightened around his arm. "Finding it was like finding a long-lost friend."

She stopped talking, and Nicola remained quiet, waiting for her to go on. She looked out the window above the sink. The last light of the setting sun shone behind the fields, turning the tops of the grapevines a pinkish-purple color, which reminded her of the sunsets back in the mountains of Western Maryland where she and kids from school went hiking in the fall. She bit her lip and tried to think of how to best explain what she was feeling. Finally, she looked back at Nicola who was gazing at her with the most beautiful look of concern. Alex gave him a small smile.

"She was all I had left in the world, and now she is gone. You did not know her, the woman she was, how deeply she loved. Loved everything: her husband, her country, both of them—the U.S. and Italy—the family she left behind, and little things. Things like a piano concerto played with mistakes but played with love, a classic book that she had read before but enjoyed again when she closed her eyes and listened to the melody of the prose, the roses that bloomed in her small back yard." She closed her eyes and pictured the gardens, so lovingly attended to by Signor Fonticelli and then by his wife in his memory. She could almost hear the soft music of the old, but in-tune, piano. When she opened her eyes, her breath caught in her throat at the way that Nicola was looking at her. She realized that she was still holding his arm and let go.

"I'm sorry," she said quickly, pink blush covering her cheeks and spreading across her face. Nicola reached his hand toward her cheek and then stopped himself, taking a step back.

"It is okay," he said quietly. "I do not mind if you read her journal."

Hastily, Alex shook her head. "No, you see, that's the problem. I cannot read it. Not without your help." She had no idea why those words had spilled from her mouth. She could use her app and read the journal just fine, but she now realized that she would lose something in the translation, the human connection.

She looked at him with pleading in her eyes, but he turned back to the counter and picked up the wine glasses.

Putting them away, he answered, "You do not need me. I did not know her. I would not be able to tell you anything."

"You don't understand," she said with frustration. "I can't read it. It's in Italian."

Nicola turned back to her and smiled. Then he began to laugh. "Then you have a problem, no?" he asked, teasingly.

Exasperated, she followed him as he left the room and called out to him. "Nicola! Don't do that to me!"

He stopped at the foot of the stairs and looked back at her, smiling. She couldn't tell if he was teasing her or if reading the journal together was more intimate than he wanted their relationship to be.

Realizing that she truly needed this, the chance to have someone to share this gift with, she resisted allowing her translation software to be her aid and companion. She swallowed her pride and begged, with as much maturity and dignity as she could muster.

"Please, I need your help. I know you don't really like me and don't want me here, even if you are willing to let me stay. I understand that this is a business relationship and that you have some sort of thing going with Evangelina, but could you be a gentleman, please, for just a short time each night, and help a lady in need?" She could see the smirk playing at his lips and hated herself for being so desperate, but she firmly felt that she did not want to read the journal alone and that, for some reason, it was Nicola with whom she was supposed to read it.

"Okay," he gave in. "Where is this journal? I can see that you will not leave me alone until you show it to me."

Alex let out her breath and raced up the stairs. She called back when she reached the top, "I'll be right back."

Why did she intrigue him so? One minute he resented her, and the next, he was amused. Before Nicola could ponder his feelings, Alex was back with an old, worn, leather book in her hand. She handed the journal to him, and he inspected it. Though it was old, he could see that the ink was still legible. He flipped through some pages and noticed how fragile the cover and binding were.

"Where did you find this?" he asked as he turned it over in his hand.

"In the barn," she answered. "It was up in the loft. I hit it with my foot and found it covered with straw."

"What a strange place for it to be," he remarked.

"I thought so, too, unless that's where she hid it."

"But to be there for so many years and not be found? How can that be?"

"I don't know, but it was almost like, well… you'll think I'm silly." She looked away.

"No, I will not," he insisted.

Alex sighed and looked at the book in his hands. "It was almost like she led me to it. Like I was meant to find it."

Nicola smiled at her words and at the way the blush once again spread across her cheeks.

"See, you think I'm a nut," she said.

"No," he assured her. "I do not. I think you are hoping to hold onto someone you lost." He took her hand and led her to the couch, trying to ignore the way his own hand tingled at the touch.

"Let us see," he said as he opened the book. Alex listened as he translated the first page. "Ah, a young woman in love. Are you making me read a romance book?" Nicola teased, the flirting thus resumed.

"Shut up and keep reading," she said with annoyance.

"I do not think I can do both," he teased again, enjoying the way it made sparks go off in her eyes. "Is that an American thing? To be able to speak and remain quiet at the same time?"

She shot him a nasty look, and he gave in. "Okay, I will keep reading."

He read the next page out loud in Italian and then handed it to Alex. "You look at the words, and I will tell you what is said."

She moved closer to him and held the book open for them both to see. He relayed Signora's thoughts to her.

December 23, 1942

I saw him again today, the handsome young man who was helping at the winter market. We got a light dusting of snow last night, which is not usual this time of year, and I was hurrying in the cold to get some meat for mother. School is out for the holiday, and the Christmas dance at Our Lady of the Roses is tonight. Will he be there? I cannot help wondering. I think he smiled at me when he saw me. I like to think he did.

Alex smiled. "She's so cute. A young girl infatuated with a handsome young boy. Do you think he went to the dance?" She looked at Nicola with joy and innocence, and his heart missed a beat. She didn't seem to even notice how close they were on the couch or how fast his heart was beating. Nicola reminded himself that, in spite of the intimacy of the moment, she was his business partner and nothing else.

"I know the answer, but maybe I do not tell," he teased.

Alex nudged him with her shoulder. "That's not fair. You can read ahead and see what it says, but I can't. You also know who she married in real life. It's just mean if you don't tell me."

Nicola laughed and continued.

December 24, 1942

It is midnight, the first moments of Christmas Eve. Mamma and Papà let me stay at the dance until it ended at 11:00. It was a magical evening. I wore the red dress that Mamma made for me. It is a beautiful dress. When he walked into the church hall, our eyes met, and I knew my life had changed forever. He didn't wait a respectable amount of time to seek me out. He came right to me at that very second and took my hand. He didn't even ask me to dance. The band began to play a waltz, and he swept me across the floor without moving his eyes from mine. We danced all night, his beautiful brown eyes gazing into mine. Isa, he called me. Not Isabella, but a name just for us, like I was a different person, born anew in his arms. His name is Roberto, and he finished school last year and wishes to go to university in the fall if this war ever ends. We are very lucky to live here where we are not bothered so much by the war. Papà says that will end soon. He does not like

Mussolini or Hitler. He says that this war will not end well for us. But tonight, there is no war here, and I will go to sleep happy.

Alex was quiet when Nicola closed the book. She looked sleepy but content. "Well, what do you think?" he asked her.

"I think that I'm making you read a romance book," she said with a smile. Nicola couldn't resist smiling back.

"I think this was a trick. You wanted to read an Italian romance and needed me to do it for you. Why me? Why not Maria?"

"I know you think I'm just a silly girl wanting to read a romantic story, but remember, we both know how this ends. The idyllic life that Isa was living at that moment won't last forever. It rarely does," she added wistfully, and Nicola wondered about her past.

"Sometimes it does," he said quietly and then abruptly stood. Telling Alex good night, he headed off to bed. In spite of himself, he was looking forward to tomorrow, which confused him. In only a matter of days, he had accepted this stranger into his home and into his business. Though they enjoyed the evening together, and he did admit to finding her charming, Nicola was at war with himself about the whole situation. Was he letting her fall too easily into his life? He truly did not know the answer.

Chapter Six

Sunday was a whirlwind of non-stop commotion, and Alex loved every minute of it. The day began with Mass at Our Lady of the Roses Church. Though Alex had been saying the prayers all her life, she found herself stumbling over them as she tried to whisper them in English along with the Italian voices. The Homily, though said by a lively and invigorating young priest, was completely lost on her, and she found herself daydreaming about Isa. Where had she sat? Was there an inscription on a window dedicated to her family like in so many of the American churches? Had she sung in the choir? Knelt along that same Communion rail for her First Eucharist? Looking around the church, the thoughts swirling in her mind, Alex felt almost dizzy. Standing beside Nicola didn't help, especially when she caught Evangelina's dagger-like stare and turned to see the woman giving her a look that had no place in the holy building.

After Mass, Nicola introduced Alex to Father Rulli who welcomed her to the parish. He even offered to give her a copy of his Homily, translated into English. Alex blushed and wondered if he knew that her mind was elsewhere while he was at the pulpit. Their conversation was interrupted by Giovanni, Adrianna, and baby

Marco, followed by Luigi, Maria, and a man introduced to Alex as Pietro. After many air kisses, the group headed toward their cars to leave for Giovanni and Adrianna's house for dinner.

Alex, who was riding with Nicola, waited patiently by the car while he said goodbye to Eva. She watched the exchange with interest, noting the sparks that flew, and wished she could hear and understand what they were saying. After a few minutes, Eva turned to look at Alex and shot her a smile that could freeze water. Alex returned a half-hearted smile as Nicola attempted to give Eva a hug and kiss that were rebuffed when Eva simply turned her back on him and walked away. Alex averted her gaze and tried to hide her surprise.

"Is Eva joining us for dinner?" she asked casually as Nicola opened the car door for her.

"No, she is busy," was his curt reply. Alex bit her lip as she tried not to smile. The woman obviously didn't like her, and Alex was so looking forward to the family meal. She was more than relieved that Eva's stare and rudeness would not put a damper on the event.

"Why did you never even mention Pietro to me?" Alex asked Maria as they put together the antipasti, a nice mixture of cheese and sausages wrapped in pancetta and called bocconcini fritti. Adrianna's seafood sauté filled the kitchen with a heavenly aroma as they worked.

Maria blushed. "It is new. I was still deciding if I liked him." They both laughed, and Adrianna teased them about keeping on task.

Though baby Marco was the only child at the table, the room was filled with noise as they ate—conversation, laughter, teasing, and ridicule filled the room. They tried to speak in English or translate for Alex, but she felt guilty that they had to do so and tried to keep up with the stories they told in their rushed voices. She reminded herself that she had only been in Italy just over a week, even though it already seemed as if she had been there for years. The language would come in time, but she was impatient to feel like a part of this wonderful family she had suddenly inherited. And that's when it hit her. Signora hadn't left her a vineyard. She had left her a family. Alex beamed as she watched her new family interact and silently thanked Signora for giving her just what she needed the most.

That evening, Alex floated down the stairs in her comfy shorts and t-shirt and settled onto the couch. She had never felt so content in her life. Nicola had also changed into shorts and a t-shirt and waited for her in the living room, the soggiorno. He looked at her curiously as she entered the room.

"What?" she asked.

"You look, different," he said after a moment.

"I don't know why," she said casually. "Maybe I'm just worn out after a whole day with the Giordano/Minnelli family."

"No," he said as he joined her on the couch and reached for the journal on the table in front of them. "You do not look tired. You look happy, very happy. I do not think I have seen you look truly happy since you arrived here."

"I haven't been truly happy for a very long time," she confessed, and realized for the first time the truth in her statement. "I thought I was happy in college when I was with…my friends." She shook her head. "But that was not happiness. I think it was complacency." It occurred to Alex that Nicola might not quite understand, not knowing any of her background. "I think that I was telling myself that I was happy, but I wasn't, not really."

"And being with my family makes you happy?" Nicola asked. He wasn't teasing, nor was he flirting or anything like it. Alex felt that he was genuinely curious about her feelings.

"Yes, it does. I can't quite describe what it is, why it's different from what I've felt before, but it feels good." She turned to face him. "Thank you, Nicola. Thank you for allowing me to stay and to be a part of this vineyard and your family."

Nicola smiled but did not say anything. He opened the journal and turned to the next entry.

December 26, 1942

The war rages on. There has been heavy bombing in Southern Italy by the United States, but we continue to be spared. Father has been very quiet since Christmas Day. He stayed late after Mass and came home just before dinner, looking worried and, dare I say, old. He knows something that he is not saying. I do hope that he won't have to go fight. So far, the older doctors have not had to go. They are necessary at home. I pray this is not going to change.

I have not seen Roberto since the dance, but I dream of him, and for now that is enough.

"Did her father go to war?" Alex asked.

"I do not know," Nicola answered thoughtfully, his expression one of puzzlement. "He is already very old in my memories. My family never talked very much about the War when I was growing up. I think they wanted to forget it. The men who did fight, like my grandfather, Isa's brother, did not talk about what they saw."

"I can understand why. My great-grandfather fought in the War. He was in France. He never spoke about it until the last few years of his life, and never around us children, just to our parents. From the bits I overheard, it was, as you said, something he wanted to forget." She sighed and thought about her family, her real family. They had been happy once, a long time ago.

"Shall I go on?" Nicola asked, breaking into her thoughts, and Alex nodded.

December 31, 1942

A note appeared today. I say appeared because I do not know how it got here. When I went to check on the animals, it was tacked to the barn door with my name on it. I do not know how he knew that I would be the first one out of the house and that I would go to the barn to begin my chores. I knew as soon as I saw it, even before I opened it, that it was from Roberto.

Under the writing, a faded and worn note was stuck to the page. What appeared to be Scotch tape was barely holding it into the book. Nicola read it.

"Dear Isa, I must see you tonight. I must begin the new year with you. Please come to the barn at midnight. Yours, Roberto"

I can barely breathe. Do I dare sneak out? If Papà catches us, we will both be sent to our graves. I have never done anything so secretive, so bold. God in Heaven, forgive me. I know that I will go.

January 1, 1943
Just before midnight, I tiptoed out of my room and down the hall. I was sure that Mamma and Papá could hear my heart beating in the silent night. He was waiting for me in the barn, and I rushed into his arms. Before I could speak, he held his finger to my lips, and I felt dizzy at the feel of his skin on such an intimate place. Shh, he told me, and he led me up the ladder and into the loft. A blanket was laid out, and my heart began to race. This was not what I wanted, not what I planned. I barely knew him. But he took my hand and turned my palm up and kissed it. My

stomach flipped, and my mind went blank. I didn't even know I had closed my eyes until he said quietly, "Isa, look at me." I opened my eyes and looked deeply into his. I drowned in them like they were a pool of warm chocolate. "I want to give you something," he said as he led me to the blanket. I followed, though I knew I should not. I tried not to look into his eyes for I knew I would be lost. I expected him to do something, I didn't know what, something I had only read about in the books my father forbade me from reading. "Happy new year," Roberto said, and I turned to see him holding a small box. I took it with hesitation and opened it. Inside was a key. "It is the key to my heart," Roberto said. "Keep it until I return."

I was so confused. "Where are you going?" I asked. "To war," he told me, and I shook my head. I knew I heard wrong. "To war?" I whispered. "Yes, my love, but I will be back," he promised. And then he leaned in and kissed me. The kiss was chaste, pure, and beautiful. It was a kiss that will haunt my dreams, and tease me with its perfection, and leave me longing for more, like the last glimpse of the perfect sunset. When he leaned back, and I opened my eyes, I could still feel his lips on mine. "Wait for me," he said. I nodded and watched as he stood and went down the ladder. I crawled to the edge and looked over. He stood on the floor of the barn and smiled up at me, and I tried to smile back.

A tear rolled down Alex's cheek. Her heart was heavy with sadness and with dread. "She must have thought their love was over before it really began," she said.

Nicola did not answer. He reached over and wiped away the tear. "He promised to come back," he said quietly, looking into her eyes.

"Pools of chocolate," she said, almost to her herself.

"Scuse?"

"Your eyes," Alex said and then blushed. She looked away and pretended to yawn. "I'm dying to know what happened next, but I'm so tired. I think I will go to bed and dream about Roberto's return." She stood and gave Nicola a sad smile. "Good night, Nicola. Thank you for today."

Nicola watched Alex walk up the stairs and then looked back down at the journal in his lap. Nicola was an educated man. He had read all of the ancient philosophers, Shakespeare, Dante, and contemporary Italian and American authors, but he had never read anything that moved him the way Isa's writing had. He didn't know if it was the words she used, the emotions they conveyed, or the sensual way she described her feelings. He couldn't help but wonder if it was the fact that he was reading them to and with Alex that made him feel the way he did. He realized that sharing this intimate tale with Alex was going to be much harder than he had bargained.

During the next few days, Alex spent a lot of time learning about the wine business from both Nicola and Maria. She was beginning to use more Italian words and phrases and had the computer system down pat. She was sure that growing up in a house with her brother, a computer genius, was a big help because she knew her way around the machine, and technology came easily to her. It was a trait that left most of her Fine Arts classmates envious.

The days were filled with learning, and the nights were filled with a restless longing that Alex couldn't explain other than loneliness. Nicola was quite willing to work with her in and around the vineyard, but he seemed to be avoiding her at night. He often came into the house after dinner but then retreated back to his office in the winery to do 'work,' or he left the house, presumably to see Eva. Alex tried to figure out what she might have said or done to create this situation, when they seemed to be getting along so well, but she couldn't find the root of the problem. Perhaps Nicola had told Eva about the journal, and she didn't like them reading it together. The journal lay on the table where they left it several days before, and Alex felt it calling out to her.

Over the course of the week, Alex confided in Maria about her family. Alex lost her mother on the day their family learned of her brother, Chad's death. That was likely what compelled her to devote so much time and energy to Signora—that and the fact that she truly loved the older woman.

"It was a relationship that neither Sandra nor Patrick ever understood, but I can't blame them," she told Maria. "They had their own families, somewhere to go for holidays, someone with whom to reminisce about the past. They didn't understand how it felt to have no one."

"No one?" Maria asked. "You do not have family?"

"Not really," Alex said with tears in her eyes. "My freshman year of college…" She hesitated and swallowed down the lump in her throat. "My brother was murdered."

Maria gasped. "Murdered?"

"Yes," Alex said. "He was the victim of a hit man who was chasing after Chad's friend, Melissa. It's a long story, but I'm sure all the details are still all over the Internet if you really want to read about it."

Alex wiped away a tear, and Maria gently laid her hand on Alex's shoulder.

"When my father finally came out of mourning, I lost him in a car accident on our first family vacation since Chad's death."

Again, Maria gasped. "Oh, Alex, I am so sorry."

Alex nodded as she struggled to maintain control over her emotions. "For some reason that I will never be able to explain, my mother blamed me. The vacation was my father's attempt to put things back together again, but it only made things worse. Not that I'm blaming him," Alex was quick to add. "My mother certainly didn't. She blamed me." Alex looked away and blinked. Her tone turned bitter as she shook her head and continued, "We were hit by a drunk driver just before we made it back to Chicago. I'll never understand why my mother crawled into her own cave after Chad's death rather than embracing the child she still had, but I suppose that everyone grieves in their own way." Alex shrugged and reached for a tissue to blow her nose.

"Chad's friend, Melissa, reached out to me after the guy was caught who was chasing her, but I had no desire to become friends with her. Melissa has a new life of her own now, a fiancé, a Godmother she never knew existed, and a whole new life, according to the many articles and television interviews that I read online once I felt up to it. I guess that's what happens. Life goes on." Alex tried to smile.

"Si, life goes on. And now you have a new life, here with us."

Maria leaned over and hugged Alex, and for the first time in a long time, Alex knew that she finally had a friend she could trust.

On Friday, the vineyard was a wave of energy as several cases of wine were distributed to restaurants and stores throughout the region. The tourist season was well underway, as were Evangelina's plans for her celebrity welcome party. Nicola was out the previous night and again that morning making sure that the party was well stocked with the best wines. He also took several fancy brochures about the vineyard that Alex insisted they print and casually place around the house and patio. Both Nicola and Maria were impressed with her combination of computer skills and eye for design and thus gave her the task of updating all of their marketing materials.

It was close to noon when the door opened and a woman, perhaps in her sixties, entered. The woman was a stranger, but Alex caught her breath at the familiarity of her voice and the way she moved. Her face was so familiar that Alex was taken aback and wondered where she had seen her. The woman went directly to Alex with a wide, genuine smile and outstretched arms.

"Alex, mia bella, you must be Alex." Before Alex could respond, she found herself wrapped in the woman's arms.

"Yes, I am," Alex said tentatively. "And you are?"

"No, please do not say he did not tell you I was coming." She looked hurt, and Alex felt guilty for not knowing what was going on. At that moment, Maria walked into the room and squealed with delight. She ran to the woman and threw her arms around her.

"Zia Marta," Maria exclaimed and gushed words of Italian that were too fast for Alex to follow.

"Oh, Alex, meet my Zia Marta, Nicola's mother," Maria said as the woman beamed at them both as if they were all lifelong friends reunited after a long hiatus.

"Oh, I'm so sorry. I should have known. You look so much…" Alex couldn't say the words.

"Like my Zia Isabella," Marta said, shaking her head. "Sì, I have been told my entire life how much I looked like her. My father often called me Isabella by mistake. I am sorry if seeing me has shocked you."

Alex steadied herself and reached for the woman's hand. "Just a bit, but I am so happy to meet you. Nicola didn't tell me that you were coming."

"I do not know what he is thinking these days. He seems to be lost in thought each time I try to speak to him on the phone. I thought it would be best if I came up to check on him."

"Zia Marta, you and Alex should take your bags to the house and visit for a while," Maria suggested. "The men are all out making deliveries, and I can handle things here."

"I would love that," Marta said warmly as she laced her arm around Alex's. "We have so much to talk about."

As they made their way to the villa, Marta asked Alex about her trip from America and if she was finding the house and the climate comfortable. Alex found herself opening up to Marta for reasons she couldn't explain, and before long, the entire story of her deception and the first few rough days in the house were tumbling out of her. Rather than judging, Marta laughed and absorbed every little detail as if it were a pastry crumb. Alex felt terrible that she had never even asked Nicola about his own parents. She was so used to not having any of her own to speak of that she didn't find it at all unusual that he seemed to not have any either. He spoke of his grandfather often, and somehow, Alex made the mental leap that, perhaps, he was estranged from his parents as she was from hers. Alex was thrilled to learn that he was not, and she welcomed Marta into her life as warmly as Marta welcomed Alex into hers.

"You did bring your best reserve, Nicola, sì?" Eva asked as Nicola placed several bottles of red and white wine on the counter behind the bar.

"Of course, Eva." He tried to hide his frustration. Eva had plenty of things to do to get ready for her cocktail party, but she had been following him around all afternoon like a shadow.

"What are these?" Eva picked up one of the pamphlets that Alex made and scrutinized it.

"Information about the vineyard." Nicola glanced up and then returned to arranging the bottles behind the bar.

"You have never done this before. Why are you doing it now? Do you not think it is distasteful to advertise your business to my guests?"

"No." Nicola stopped what he was doing and turned to face Eva. "It is customary for businesses who sponsor events to advertise. Unless you want to pay full price…"

Eva's jaw twitched, and her eyes turned into daggers. "What do you mean 'pay full price?' I have never paid full price, and you have never brought these…" She held one of the pamphlets up over the bar and waved it in front of his face. "these advertisements to one of my parties."

"Eva." Nicola reached across and took her hand, trying to appease her while holding firm. "You know that I am trying to expand our base, and I need to let potential clients know about the vineyard and how to purchase from us. Your guests are very connected, both here and in Los Angeles. If they like my wine, perhaps they will want to serve it at future parties or use it on their sets. Imagine, my wine on an American movie set. Do you know what that could do for us, for our future?"

Just like that, Eva turned to putty in his hands. "Oh, Niki, darling." She pulled him closer. "Sì, sì. For our future, you may do whatever you need." She leaned across the bar, and wrapping her arms around his neck, kissed Nicola in a way that would normally make his toes curl. And while his body did respond as would be expected, his mind was thinking about the creator of the pamphlets.

Over the course of the afternoon, Alex learned that Marta had been brought up on the vineyard and knew by the age of ten that she wanted nothing to do with it.

Nicola, on the other hand, always had a fondness for it and spent much of his youth helping his grandparents with the business and learning about making wine. He could tell a good reserve from a cheaper stock by the bouquet alone by the time he was twelve. Longing for a more exciting life for herself, Marta attended university in Florence, met her husband there, and never left. When Nicola returned from school and saw that his grandfather was beginning to fail, as were most of his long-time employees, he invited his Florence cousins to come work with him at the vineyard. They had been there ever since, living in the homes that Nicola had helped them to purchase. It was Nicola who insisted that his youngest cousin, Maria, go to college, and he helped her through school and then hired her to manage the vineyard. Alex was amazed that she did not know all of this, but Marta was not.

"Nicola is quite humble and does not trust easily. He is a businessman, but he has a good heart. And he is still a dreamer. He sees this old place much differently than I do." She laughed. "He believes it will be a famous vineyard someday with wines in demand all over the world."

"I think it can be," Alex said. "Why not? Nicola knows what he's doing. He has the education as well as the love of the vineyard and all that it stands for in his mind. Maria is a whiz at management, and I hope I can contribute as well. The vineyard's logo is perfect, but it's not universally recognized. We need to use it more. I've designed some brochures that I think will make it stand out and be remembered." Alex stood and walked to the kitchen counter. Picking up one of her designs, she went back to the couch and handed it to Marta. "I need to take some more pictures, but it's a start."

"This is good," Marta said as she carefully assessed the brochure. "It is very good. You took these?" She pointed at the pictures.

"I did." Alex nodded her head. "The print quality isn't as good as it should be, because we did them in house, but once we have them professionally printed, I think they'll look very nice. Nicola took several with him to Eva's, hoping that some of her guests might use us in the future."

"I bet Eva will love that," Marta said, under her breath. "The pictures, they have good composition, nice lighting. They look very professional. Do you have training?"

"I do," Alex said and saw Marta in a whole new light. "I took classes in college. It was part of my major."

Marta looked at Alex with surprise. "What did you study?"

"Fine Arts," Alex said sheepishly. "I know, it doesn't sound like a real major. Believe me, my mother told me that a hundred times, but I just love all of it— photography, art, music." Alex stopped speaking when she noticed the way Marta was looking at her. The woman smiled and grabbed her hand.

"You and I, we are kindred spirits. I, too, love them all. My parents did not understand either. Michelangelo already painted the Sistine Chapel, Puccini and Vivaldi already composed musical masterpieces. What did I think I could do that has not already been done?"

Alex laughed and then had a thought. "The photographs on the wall in the vineyard. Are they yours?"

Marta chuckled and nodded. "From a long time ago. My father told me that if I was going to dream such silly dreams, then he should reap something from them."

"I admired them the very first day I came. I was trying to achieve the same effects in mine."

"We will go out this weekend and take pictures, sì?"

"Sì," Alex agreed.

"So, tell me, has the elusive Eva been here much?"

"Eva? No, not really. But elusive? Why would you think that?"

"She is always elusive when I am here. You will see. She does not care for me, I believe."

"How could she not like you?" Alex was amazed. Marta seemed so wonderful.

"Because she is not right for Nicola, and she knows that I know that. But it is his decision. Who am I to tell a grown man how to live his life?"

Alex was surprised that Marta felt that way and even more surprised that she shared her feelings with a stranger, but they didn't feel like strangers. Maybe it was because Marta looked so much like a younger Isabella, or maybe they truly were kindred spirits. Whatever it was, Alex felt an instant connection to the woman and suddenly felt sorry for Eva. She changed the subject and asked about Marta and Nicola's father. Marta was delightfully animated when she talked about her husband and their life in Florence.

When Alex showed Marta the journal and explained how she found it in the barn, Marta took the book carefully into her hands and caressed it with care. Gingerly opening it, she read a page and wiped away a tear began to trail down her cheek.

"She was such a wonderful woman," Marta said as she reached for a tissue in the box on a nearby end table.

"She was," Alex agreed. "I would have been lost without her." Alex looked away and hoped that Marta wouldn't press her for more information. She wasn't sure she was ready to confide in Nicola's mother about her own tragic family story. As if sensing that Alex would rather talk about Signora, Marta made no comment about Alex's family or her past. Instead she apologized.

"I should have gone to her funeral," she said, her words filled with melancholy. "I loved her so much."

Instinctively, Alex reached for Marta's hand. "I'm sure she understood." Alex offered a small smile. "She had a way of always seeing into a person's heart." Marta smiled back.

"You have a good heart yourself, Alex. I can sense it, and I am sure that my aunt could as well. Tell me about Zia Isabella. How did you meet her?"

Alex proceeded to tell Marta about the time she spent working for Signora, and Marta laughed at Alex's stories and shared many of her own.

The women were still lost in conversation when Nicola walked in that evening. Maria had already come in to say goodbye, and the two women had moved to the living room, then eventually back to the kitchen for a late afternoon snack of coffee and cookies. Bored and lonely the night before, when Nicola was squirreled away in his office, Alex had decided to bake. She was feeling lonely and longed for one of the comforts of the States, so she made good, old-fashioned chocolate chip cookies. Though she had to improvise on a few of the ingredients, she was pleased with their outcome, and Marta raved over how wonderful they were and how much they reminded her of her own time in America.

"Mamma," Nicola said warmly as he hugged his mother. "Have you told Alex all the family secrets?"

"Not all of them," his mother teased and winked at Alex.

They spent the evening together, and Nicola thanked his mother for the excuse to miss Evangelina's party.

"You could have gone. Why did you not?"

"I would rather be with you." Nicola smiled.

"Is that so?" she said with a conspiratorial glance toward Alex that caused the young woman to blush and look away. Marta then suggested they go out for the evening, and Alex was happy for the change in subject.

The weekend was a blur of activity. Marta and Alex spent a lot of time together taking pictures of the vineyard and getting to know each other better. Nicola worked in the fields and the office but found himself looking out the window quite often. He knew that his mother and Alex would become friends. He hated to admit it, but Alex reminded him of Marta from the start. He hesitated when his mother suggested she come for the weekend, but he had been avoiding Alex all week and was feeling guilty. She needed to feel like she belonged and had someone other than Maria to lean on, and he didn't know if he was capable of being that person for her. Yes, he was capable, he admitted, but it was impossible.

When Nicola told Eva that he wasn't staying for the party, she became furious. She was having a conniption that Alex was living at the villa and was pushing Nicola to move onto the Lombardi family estate with her. It was a move that he was not ready for, and he couldn't help but ask himself why. It did seem to be the obvious solution, and they had been talking about marriage for a while, but there was something about moving in with Eva that gave Nicola an uneasy feeling in the pit of his stomach.

He shook away his thoughts of Eva and watched Alex as she crouched down with her camera to get the right angle. His mother was talking and pointing, giving instructions like she was a master. He smiled at the way Alex frowned when she looked at the camera's screen and her determination to keep shooting until she had the shot right. With her auburn hair pulled back from her face, and the tank top and shorts that she wore, she looked no more than eighteen. Nicola found that endearing and forced himself to turn back to the paperwork in front of him.

On Saturday evening, Nicola invited Eva to have dinner with them.

"But darling," Eva cooed into the phone, "why does Alex have to be there? We should have your madre to dinner here at the estate, and let Alex enjoy time to herself."

"Mamma likes Alex, and they have been working on new pictures for the vineyard."

"Stop," Eva commanded. "I do not care what they have been doing together. Your madre should be spending time with me."

"Then come over tonight. Mamma wants to teach Alex a special recipe—"

"Basta!" Eva interrupted. "That is enough! If anyone is going to learn a special recipe from your madre, it is me."

Nicola tried to suppress his laughter. "Mio tesoro, sweetheart, you do not cook."

"Then I will learn tonight." Eva hung up the phone, and Nicola stared at his cell in disbelief. Dinner was going to be quite interesting.

"Ahi!" Eva cried out in pain and pulled her hand away from the hot pot and raced to the sink. She ran her palm and fingers under cold water and watched a bright, red mark mar her perfect skin. Marta and Alex exchanged a look.

"Eva, dear, you must use a potholder to take the pot off of the stove. The handle gets very hot." Marta smiled at Eva. Alex thought Marta looked genuinely concerned and gave her a lot of credit. She recalled what Marta had told her the previous day about Eva not being right for her son. Alex tried to picture these two women sharing Nicola, but it was hard to imagine. Eva didn't seem like the type to share anything.

"Sì, sì, you could have told me that before I touched it." Eva didn't attempt to hide her own feelings as she let the cold water run over her fingers. "One would think that the handle would be made to stay cool so that the pot could be easily lifted from the stove."

"We are almost finished. You can sit down while Alex and I put the food on the table."

"I think I will find Niki," Eva said before turning off the water and hastily retreating from the room, grabbing a stream of paper towels and wrapping her hand as she went out of the door.

Alex couldn't help herself. She burst into a fit of giggles. "I'm so sorry. Truly, I am. I know I shouldn't laugh, but, but…" She took a deep breath and tried to stop laughing. "Oh my gosh! First, she cuts her finger with a knife, a tiny cut at that, and it was as if she needed to go the hospital. Then she burned the biscotti, and to top it off…" Alex began laughing again. "I'm such a horrible person." She held her belly and put her hand over her mouth to stifle herself.

"Shh." Marta put her finger on her smiling lips when they heard Nicola and Eva's voices growing louder. Alex turned to the sink and held her breath as she drained the water from the pasta, using a potholder to hold the pot.

Unbelievably, Eva took credit for most of the meal, including the dessert which Alex managed to salvage by scraping the bottoms of with a knife, much like she used to do in college when using their ancient and unreliable toaster.

After she left, Nicola turned to his mother and Alex. "So," he began, the corners of his mouth twitching and his eyes sparkling. "Eva turned out to be quite the cook?"

Alex smiled at Marta. "Oh, she was 'quite the cook' all right."

"Sì," Marta agreed. "Quite the cook."

"Is there something, some story, I do not know?" Nicola was clearly amused, no doubt his imagination running wild at the thought of Eva cooking.

"Oh, don't worry," Alex told him. "When you're married, I'm sure you will be amazed by Eva's culinary skills." She winked at Marta and took a seat on the sofa. "Shall we?" she asked as she picked up the journal.

"Sì, I am very curious to hear what Nicola thinks about the journal." Marta gently took the book from Alex and turned it over in her hands. "I do not remember ever seeing this. You never saw it, Nicola?"

"No." He shook his head. "Not until Alex showed it to me. She found it in the loft."

"Si," Alex agreed. "As I told you earlier, I found it when I first arrived. Nicola and I haven't gotten very far, but it's fascinating. We've really only just started reading, but I already see that there was so much about Signora that I never knew."

"Zia Isabella," Marta said wistfully. "How I loved her."

"You knew her well?" Nicola asked in surprise.

"Very well. I have been to her home in Baltimore. When I finished at university, Nonno and Nonna sent me to stay with her for a little while so that I could see some of the world. I almost stayed…." She closed her eyes and sighed, a slow smile curling on her lips. Alex had the impression that there was something Marta was not sharing.

"Why did you come back?" Nicola asked, and Marta quickly opened her eyes as if she'd been startled into coming back to the present.

"I was to marry your papà. He was waiting for me. And Florence is where my heart is, where it has always been."

Alex thought she noticed something in the way Marta answered, a look in her eyes, or a catch in her voice. She couldn't quite put her finger on it.

Marta returned her attention to the journal and smiled. "So, Zia Isabella has not told any family secrets has she?"

"Not yet," Alex said. "Unless you count her secret love for Roberto."

"Oh, that is not so secret. Zia Isabella was married to Zio Roberto for a very long time. I think it was only secret because of the war. Zia was very young, and she did not know if Roberto would return, so she did not tell. Love is a very serious thing during a war." Marta looked at Nicola. "And even when there is not a war."

Nicola looked away, but Alex noticed a red flush creep up his neck toward his face. Trying not to make things uncomfortable, Alex decided it was time to leave Nicola and his mother alone. She bid Nicola and Marta a good night and retreated to her room.

"She is beautiful, no?" Marta asked after Nicola watched Alex go upstairs and disappear into the dark, upper hallway. "Inside and out."

Nicola shrugged. "She is pleasing to look at and be around." Marta looked at her son for several seconds, but she remained silent.

"Tell me about Papà," Nicola said. "Is he well? I wish he could have come with you."

"So do I." Marta sighed. "I will make him come with me the next time. He cannot spend his entire life working in his uffizi."

Marta and Nicola talked for a little while longer before saying goodnight and heading to bed.

On Sunday, the family dinner was held at the villa, and Alex and Marta went all out with their scrumptious meal. Eva begged off, saying she was worn out from the previous night. Smiling, Nicola ended the call and shook his head. He had to admit that it was probably for the best. His mother got along with Alex better than she ever had with Eva. For some reason, the thought amused him. When he walked his mother to her car after dinner, he found himself glad that Eva hadn't returned for another dinner, though he couldn't explain why.

"It could be like this every day, my son." Marta motioned to the cheery sounds coming from the house. "Maria says that you and Eva may be talking marriage."

"Mamma, stop," Nicola told her. "Eva and I are talking about the future, but I do not know when we will get married."

"So, you are planning on marrying her." It was a statement rather than a question.

"Si, when the time is right."

"And when will that be? You've been seeing each other for a very long time."

"I do not know, Mamma. I am so busy now trying to build the business. I am teaching Alex what to do, and I do not have time to plan a wedding."

"Nicola, you and I both know that Eva has had her wedding planned since the day she was born. I do not think there would be much for you to do. Or perhaps, there is some reason you do not wish to marry Eva?"

Nicola looked at his mother. "What do you mean? I have many reasons. I am a busy man. Eva will want lots of parties before the wedding and then a honeymoon. I do not have time for that now."

"And your feelings have nothing to do with Alex?"

Nicola knew that his mother was always able to see through him. He could never hide anything from her, but this time, she was wrong. He didn't have any feelings for Alex other than as a friend and partner.

"I am glad you like Alex, and I am fond of her, but as you see, she is my business partner, nothing more. You said yourself, I have been with Eva for a long time. She is right for me."

"I do not see what you see," she told him. "Sì, you and Eva have been together for quite some time, but that does not mean that she is right for you. Ask yourself, my son, who you want to wake up next to each morning, who is going to care about you and your life, your business, your family? Be sure before you make up your mind."

"Thank you, Mamma, for your concern. I am quite certain what I want," he said before changing the subject. "I am very happy you came. Please give my love to Papà."

"Sì, figlio mio, lo farò" she said. "Yes, my son, I will." She sounded defeated, and Nicola felt a pang of guilt.

He kissed her goodbye and closed the door after she got into her car. He watched her leave then turned back toward the house. The night sky was clear and abundantly filled with stars. He could hear the laughter coming from the house and wondered, just for a moment, what it would be like to raise his children here on the vineyard with Alex by his side as his mother seemed to be suggesting. Guiltily, he pushed the thought from his mind. He was a planner, an organized man who saw his entire life laid out ahead of him. He knew nothing about Alex and everything about Eva. Maybe that was the problem. Alex was new and intriguing, while Eva was the same girl he had always known. Certainly that caused some unrest in his mind, some wandering thoughts about the unknown. But he could change that. He would get to know Alex, and once she was no longer a mystery to him, he could get back to normal.

January 8, 1943

For a week now, I have wrestled with my feelings. I am conflicted about what I have done, the promise I have made. Who is this boy who has gone off to war? Does he truly believe in what the Germans and Italians are doing, or was he commanded to go? Who is this man to whom I have promised my heart? I feel as if he's a ghost, an elusive creature I cannot feel or touch or take measure of. I do not know what I have gotten myself into. I have become like a ghost myself, thin and pale, pacing the house at night, unable to rest.

"How sad," Alex said.

It was Monday evening, and Nicola was no longer avoiding her, at least not this night. The weekend seemed to have broken the ice, and Alex was happy to be back by his side, reading Isa's words from the past.

"I can see her worry," Nicola said. "She really does not know this man, but she is drawn to him. Does she love him or the idea of him? Will he come back, and what will he be like when she gets to know him better? What are the things she does not know about him? It is very confusing."

Alex turned and looked at Nicola with curiosity. Why did he not sound like he was talking about Isa and Roberto?

Nicola seemed to read her thoughts. "It was a very confusing time for everyone, the War and what havoc it would bring."

Alex thought about that. "How did the Italian people feel about the War? Did they want to fight alongside the Germans?"

Nicola shook his head. "Many, perhaps most, did not. In fact, when the Italian soldiers heard that Mussolini was deposed, most of the men laid down their weapons and went home." He looked at her to be sure she understood. "I mean, they laid them down, in the streets, in the fields, and went home. They were done."

"Wow," Alex said. "I had no idea. Was that at the end of the War?"

"Oh, no. It was in the middle and just the beginning of the War here in Italy. In the summer of 1943, the Italians just stopped fighting. Hitler ordered the German soldiers to enter the country and take it over. It was a dangerous time here for everyone. The Americans and British did not know whom to trust. They bombed the cities. There was a great deal of effort made to preserve the antiquities, but it did not always happen, and the Italians refused to help identify buildings and items of importance at first because they did not know who they could trust.

"The Germans were telling the people that the Americans wanted to destroy the cities and steal the art, and the Americans were saying the same of the Germans. Alas, we know now what the truth was. The Nazis butchered whole towns and cities and took the treasures with them. A great resistance took place, but in the German occupied cities, the resistance fighters were in great danger. We are very lucky to still have the treasures and buildings that we have. Many of our cities, including Florence and Pisa, were devastated by the American bombings and by German explosions. A few cities were completely destroyed."

Alex couldn't imagine such devastation. She was a child when 9/11 took place, and that was limited in its destruction. She couldn't fathom widespread bombing of entire cities the likes of New York and Washington.

And to think that ancient cities, like Pisa and Florence, were not spared was appalling.

"Do you think any of that affected Isa? Why did she leave? Was it because of the War?"

"As I have said, it is not something that my family talked about. Perhaps we will find the answer." He motioned to the journal and turned the page.

January 10, 1943

Papà is up to something. I do not know what. Unable to sleep at night, I find myself at the window a lot, sometimes staring at the stars, other times watching for Roberto to return, to beckon me to the loft. Last night, I thought I saw him coming out of the barn. My breath caught in my throat, and I nearly threw open the window and called out to him. Then I saw that it was not Roberto, and he was not alone. Papà came out of the barn with a group of men. Some of them I know from town, but others I did not recognize. What were they doing in there in the middle of the night?

At breakfast, I asked Papà if he had slept well last night. He looked at me strangely and then turned back to his newspaper. As I finished eating and got ready for school, I saw him looking at me again. Had he seen me in the window last night, hiding behind the drapery in the dark? Does he know that I saw him? I feel it best to let it go and not ask him again, but I know that is not in my nature. It will eat at me until I discover the truth.

Chapter Seven

The following week was a busy one. Alex immersed herself in learning about grapes, proper harvesting, and wine making. The small grapes hung in beautiful green clusters throughout the vineyard. Alex and Nicola walked up and down the rows, stopping here and there for Nicola to show Alex the subtle differences between each type of grape. Though some of the grapes would hold their green hue, most of them would turn red as the months went on and the fruit ripened. Of the red, there were three different types of grapes that would be blended to create the Amarone, and their quality was dependent upon the soil and the climate. These were all things that Nicola insisted Alex not only know but fully understand.

During the day, when they weren't going over information about the grapes or the harvesting and wine producing process, Alex worked on the brochures, handouts, website, and other areas of marketing. At night, if they weren't too tired from the business and from the heat, and Nicola was not with Eva, they read from the journal. Most of the entries dealt with Isa's everyday life—her last year of school, her life on the vineyard, her fears about the War, and her confusion about Roberto. Some entries were long and detailed, and others were brief and concise. The ones Alex and Nicola spent the most time on, discussing and analyzing, were the ones about the War.

January 20, 1943

There is still no word from Roberto. I do not know where he is, whether or not he is alive and well, or even what his beliefs are about the war or anything else. I guess I cannot blame Roberto for going off to war. It is how we are raised. Boys go to war, girls get married and have babies. Mamma tried to satisfy the rule, but giving birth was hard for her, and only Paolo and I lived. Mamma worried for many years that she and Papà would be in trouble with the Blackshirts for not having at least five babies as Mussolini insisted, but Papà always promised her that his medical records would show that she had tried her best.

You see? I try to sleep, but my thoughts ramble on and on and continue to keep me awake. And I cannot stop thinking about Papà's strange behavior. I saw Papà with those men again last night. Their meetings seem to be growing more frequent, and I am about to burst with curiosity. He says nothing in front of me, but I know that Mamma must know what is going on. I have tried to drop hints, but she acts like she does not hear me. The next time I see him go into the barn at night, I am going to follow him.

"You are very quiet tonight." Eva stroked Nicola's leg under the table as they ate.

"It is very loud in here. It is hard to talk." Nicola took a large gulp of wine and tried to ignore Eva's hand as it moved higher up his thigh. It irritated him that she would do such a thing in a public place.

"We can leave whenever you like, Niki. Papà is away on business. If you are not in the mood to talk, we can do other things." She smiled and rubbed her fingers against him. "I know how to make you say the things I like to hear."

"I am not feeling well, tonight, Eva." He smiled and tried to maintain control over his mind and body. "I do not think it would be wise for me to be that close to you. You might catch something."

Eva snatched her hand away, yanked the napkin out of her lap, and threw it on the table.

"You seem to be feeling ill a lot these days. And right now, I am feeling ill, too. I am tired of your games. I will find my own way home." Eva stood and turned from him, but Nicola reached for her arm.

"Mi dispiace, Eva. I do not mean to make you upset. I am tired. It has been a long and hot day, and I am worried about the heat. It can be bad for the grapes. Please, do not go."

Nicola tried to look remorseful. Eva glared at him for a few seconds more and then shook her hair out and lifted her nose as if to regain her dignity. She stood.

"Pardon. I will be back."

Nicola watched her go and breathed a sigh of relief. How could he explain to Eva what he was feeling when he honestly didn't know himself? His plan to get to know

Alex better so that he could get her out of his head was not working. Every day she amazed him with her knowledge, her talents, and most of all, her unselfish, unmasked, honest and sincere kindness. She seemed to be growing from an insecure girl to a mature woman right before his eyes, and her innate goodness just seemed to grow as well. Unlike Eva, she never complained, never put off work on others, never shirked any responsibility, and she cared for everyone around her with a gentle and loving spirit that often left him without words.

As if on cue, Eva returned. "I have decided to forgive you, but only if you do something for me," she said in her matter-of-fact way. "You must come away to the coast with me. We need time alone."

Caught completely off guard, Nicola just stared at Eva.

"Well? Am I to forgive you or not?" Nicola could see the sparks in her eyes and was reminded of the sparks in Alex's eyes on the day she moved into the villa and refused to leave.

"I will see what I can do," Nicola said. Eva seemed to take that as a yes.

The next day was like most of the others before it. There were many days full of work with little rest, but Alex was content to work beside Maria and Nicola and saw no reason to complain. Hearing a noise outside, Alex looked up from the computer to see a delivery truck pull up in front of the villa. She was used to trucks arriving at the vineyard with new barrels or crates of wine bottles, but she had never seen one pull up to the house. She went outside to redirect them, but Nicola beat her to it. As she approached, he motioned to the house and then ran to the front door and held it open for them. Alex watched as several men used a trolley cart to haul a large, and obviously very heavy, piece of furniture into the house. It was covered with fabric and tied tightly with rope. Alex watched the men maneuver it and wondered what it was when it suddenly struck her that the shape was wonderfully familiar.

With a spring in her step, Alex ran to the villa and stormed into the room as the men heaved the instrument into place. She waited patiently as Nicola thanked them and handed one of the men a tip. Biting her lip and holding her breath, she watched Nicola cut away the rope and give the fabric a strong tug. Alex squealed with delight when the glossy, black piano was revealed and ran to Nicola, wrapping her arms around him.

"How? When?" She couldn't even form a complete sentence.

"It was not me," he said with a shake of his head, though his twinkling eyes and large grin betrayed his involvement. "Mamma sent it as a thank you gift for making her weekend here so pleasant."

Alex didn't know what to say. Tears sprang to her eyes, and she couldn't decide if they were tears of joy at the beautiful, thoughtful gesture or tears of pain that her own mother would never do anything quite so wonderful. She closed her eyes and shook her head as she lost control and tears gushed as if from a broken dam. Nicola's grin disappeared, and he grabbed her arms, looking at her with concern.

"Mia bella, what is it? Do you not like it?"

Alex took several breaths before she could speak. She looked up at Nicola and whispered through tears, "I love it."

Without thinking, Nicola enfolded her in his arms and let her cry. After a few minutes, she regained control of her emotions and pulled back from his embrace.

"I must call her," she said as she wiped away her tears, and before Nicola could say anything, she was gone, but the feeling of her in his arms remained.

That evening, over a dinner that they cooked together, Nicola told Alex that Eva had gone away for a few weeks to her family's home on the coast. Alex seemed surprised when Nicola said he would not be going with her.

"She asked me to, and I am afraid that she is very angry that I declined."

"You will visit, I assume. You don't have to worry about the winery. Maria and I can handle things inside, and Giovanni and Luigi will tend to the vines."

"Sì, I know that it would be okay, but I do not like to go to the coast. There are too many people there now, and Eva will do nothing but lie on the beach all day. I would be very bored. I have assured her that we can go after the wine production, for Christmas perhaps." Their discussion had not been that easy, nor had it gone well. Eva presented Nicola with an ultimatum, and she expected an answer as soon as she returned.

Thankfully, Alex dropped the subject and offered to play the beautiful, new piano. When they finished doing the dishes, she sat on the bench and tentatively touched the keys. It had been a long time since she played, she explained, since before Signora died. She did a few exercises with her fingers and then began to play. She sounded rusty at first, and acted slightly embarrassed, but as she went on, her fingers began to fly across the keys, and Nicola watched as she became lost in a rapture that he assumed few people could comprehend. He was entranced as he watched her sway to the music, her hands, feet, and the piano blending as one. She played for over thirty minutes, and he was riveted. When she was through, she turned to look at him, a wide smile on her lips.

"I have never heard anything like it," he said quietly, and Alex blushed.

"Come on," she said. "I'm not even that good. I had classmates who played at Carnegie Hall."

"I am happy having you play here," Nicola said quietly.

Alex felt a ripple of sensations go through her as she looked at Nicola. He looked at her with admiration, fondness, and perhaps, she thought, desire. Alex wasn't sure what to think. She was overwhelmed with emotion and had been since the moment she saw the fabric fall away from the piano. She knew that Marta must have spent a small fortune on the beautiful Fazioli upright, and Alex felt blessed. But she realized that her swell of emotions also had to do with Nicola. For the first time, it hit her that her feelings for him had progressed beyond the friendship and partnership that they were building. She wondered if Nicola felt the same, but she knew that he was committed to Eva, and she feared that such an admission on her part would cause their relationship to collapse. Instead of exploring her feelings further, Alex rose from the piano bench, bent down, and picked up the journal from the table. She held it up questioningly, and Nicola patted the cushion next to him on the couch.

February 1, 1943

I am a spy. Worse yet, I am spying on my own father. Night after night I have watched him, and now I find myself following him, hiding behind doors, and listening from above his head, unseen and unheard. I fear that last night will not be the last night I do so.

I had a feeling that they would meet. It had been three days since I last saw them, and Papà was not himself at dinner. After the house was silent, and the night was dark, I sneaked from the house and climbed stealthily into the loft. I took Roberto's blanket from where I hid it beneath the little bench under the window where I have sat and looked out at the fields since I was a child. I wrapped myself in the blanket, but the added warmth did not stop the frigid air from enveloping me in spite of my thick nightclothes and wool socks. I curled up in the hay and waited.

It was not long before I heard them. First there were just two voices, unfamiliar ones, and then Papà's voice joined them, and finally a voice I knew as well as I knew Papà's. It was Padre Lorenzo. The priest asked, "What's the news?" and Papà told them that the Allies are gaining ground all over Europe. He said that several major cities have been bombed, including Berlin, and some of the German soldiers have surrendered. One of the men asked, "What does this mean for Italy?" Papà said that there are rumors that Mussolini is losing power and that it may be only a matter of time. Padre Lorenzo seemed to have read my thoughts, for he asked, "And then what?" "I do not know," Papà said with such worry in his voice. One of the men asked if the Italians will keep fighting, but Papà did not know the answer. "What will happen to my boy?" a voice asked. Papà said he was sorry, but he just did not know.

The barn suddenly became eerily quiet. I held my breath until I heard them all leave. I felt colder than ever and longed to go back to my bed, but I was afraid to move until I knew that Papà had gone to bed. It felt like hours before I got up, and my body was stiff with cold. If I were smart, I would not do such a foolish thing again, but alas, I know I will.

Maria and Alex spent Saturday in Verona. Alex said she felt the desire to do some shopping, and Maria was more than happy to help her update her wardrobe and give it some Italian flare. When she returned home, Nicola laughed at all of the packages that Alex carried into the villa.

"Did you buy every dress in Verona?"

"No, but I did buy more clothes today than I've ever bought in my entire life. I almost feel guilty, but we were having so much fun that I couldn't help myself. I'm sure Signora would approve."

"Have you sold her house yet?"

Though they didn't talk about it much—talking about her inheritance with Nicola seemed to make Alex uncomfortable—she had shared with him that she was thinking about having the house and its contents appraised for sale.

"No, but my brother left me the patent to his computer software, and I was able to sell it to a friend of his. I consulted your great-aunt's lawyer, Peter Owen, and he helped me negotiate the sale. So I'm not destitute after all."

"Congratulations," Nicola said and wondered why his feelings were hurt that she hadn't talked to him about the sale or about her brother's death. Having checked her out thoroughly not long after she arrived, Nicola knew all about the murder, but it was not something they had ever discussed. The enigma that was Alex O'Donnell continued to intrigue him.

"As far as Signora's house and belongings," Alex continued. "I've decided to hold on to it for a bit longer. Just in case."

"In case of what?" Nicola asked.

"In case this doesn't work out. Don't look so surprised. I do have a backup plan," she said casually, and Nicola had come to know her well enough to know that she was lying. Alex rarely seemed to have a plan.

"Of course," Nicola said, but in spite of his belief that she didn't have any other plans, he felt as if he'd been punched in the gut. The thought that Alex might actually leave some day had not occurred to him for weeks now, not since he first wished it would be so. Now he couldn't imagine her going away.

He watched her take her purchases upstairs and wondered why it had never before occurred to him that she might leave. After all, she did have a house halfway around the world. What was to stop her from deciding to return to America? For the first time since she came, Nicola realized that he didn't want her to leave.

After dinner that night, Nicola suggested that they read from the journal. He was beginning to look forward to sharing his evenings with Alex as they read his aunt's words. It was something he could never see himself doing with Eva.

February 8, 1943

I do not know my father any longer. I am told that when he married Mamma, he moved into this house, my grandfather's villa on the vineyard. He wanted nothing to do with the growing of grapes or the making of wine. He was a doctor, and he was much too busy to work in the fields or slosh in the grapes. Mamma loved him with all of her heart and was proud of him and what he did. And though he was much higher in class and stature than anyone else in the family, he loved them all and treated my mother like a queen, even when he came home to find her hands and feet stained purple and smelling of sweat and dirt. Together they tried to make a good life for Paolo and me, until the war came. They were babies of war themselves, born just after their fathers returned from fighting for the Italian army in the Boxer Rebellion in China. But with Mussolini's rise in power, and worries about the future of our country, things were hard for us, even with Papà being a doctor.

I know that Papà does not care for our leader. He scoffs at the things they teach us in school. He cried when Paolo went off to war and said that Mussolini and Hitler would get all of our young men killed. He salutes the German soldiers in public and treats them when they are sick or injured, but he ridicules them at night when only Mamma and I can hear. I have always known that he does not like the way our country is ruled, but I never suspected this.

My papà is part of a secret resistance. He told me so himself. Last night, I kept still as I listened to the men talk of ways to go against our government, of secret meetings, and messages sent to the Allies. When they were gone, I waited, as I did the other night, for Papà to go to bed. When I could not stand the cold any longer, I crept down the ladder and out of the barn. But when I went out into the yard, my papà stepped out from behind the door and grabbed my arm. He pushed me back into the barn and told me that I was putting myself and our family in grave danger. I told him that he was doing the same, and he looked at me for a long time. "What are you doing here?" he asked, and his voice was filled with sadness. "I want to help," I told him. Before he could argue, I reminded him that I am not a child anymore. After a moment, he shrugged and sighed. "So, you want to be part of this." I eagerly nodded. "Then we will see what you can do." That was all he said, and so I wait.

Alex had a hard time concentrating on work the next day. Sleep had not come easily the night before, and when she did sleep, she was plagued with the most realistic dreams. In her dreams, she watched as Nicola went off to war and listened to her own father in the barn. She saw her brother, Chad, alive and well but wearing a Nazi uniform. She was cold, in spite of the July heat, and she awoke several times calling out for Chad, her body soaked with sweat but shivering as the air from the ceiling fan swirled around her.

Nicola was nowhere to be found when she went downstairs that morning, and he hadn't made an appearance inside the winery by the time she and Maria were locking up at the end of the day.

"What does he do all day in the fields?" Alex asked, gazing out the window at the long rows of green vines.

"He makes sure that the birds and the insects are staying away, that there is not rotting on the grapes, that the plants have water, but not too much water. But,"

Maria thought for a moment. "I think he is staying outside today for another reason."

Alex wasn't sure what Maria meant and turned from the window to face her. "What other reason?"

"I think that he is staying away from you."

Maria's tone was matter of fact, not teasing, not accusing. Alex wasn't sure what she was implying.

"Have I done something wrong? Is he angry with me?"

"I think he is angry with himself."

"Maria, you are talking in riddles. What are you trying to say?" Alex did not try to hide her irritation. She folded her arms across her chest and gave Maria a look that demanded answers. Maria shrugged and sighed.

"I think that he does not know what he feels. He is confused by you. He is trying to work with you, but his feelings get in the way. Eva has wanted him for years, and now they talk about marriage, but then there is you. He does not know how to feel or what to do. It makes him feel, I think, not in control. He was always in control with Eva, even if she thought she was making the rules, but now, things are different. Eva will be gone for a while, and you are living across the hall from him. He has not even tried to sleep with you, no?"

Alex shook her head. "Of course not. He's practically engaged."

"This means nothing. Men are pigs. Even my cousin is still just a man."

"Is that a good thing? That he hasn't tried?"

"Good? I do not know. Telling? Sì, it is very telling."

Maria picked up her purse and walked to the door. Alex stood by the window trying to process what Maria had just said.

"Wait," Alex called as Maria opened the door. "I don't understand. Nicola is not a pig. He is a gentleman. He would never betray Eva. What makes you think he would even be interested in me?"

Maria shrugged. "Maybe I am wrong."

"And, by the way, I'm not trying to make any rules or be in control."

Maria smiled, "Amica mia, I think you have been in control since the day you walked in this door." Maria left the building and closed the door as her parting words washed over Alex. She was filled with both fear and exhilaration, not to mention guilt. She began to wonder what she should do next.

By the time Nicola finally came into the villa, it was almost dark. The table was set, the wine poured, and the aromas of balsamic vinegar and garlic filled the air. Alex began to make the plates while Nicola washed his hands in silence. After they were seated and said grace, a heaviness began to settle around them. They ate without speaking, and Alex was sure that Maria had completely misread Nicola's mood. Something was wrong, but it had nothing to do with Alex. Finally, Alex couldn't take it anymore.

"What is it, Nicola?" she asked in Italian.

Nicola pushed his dinner around on his plate but didn't look at her. She watched as his jaw tensed.

"Have I done something wrong? Are your parents okay? Did we lose a buyer? What on earth is bothering you?"

Nicola met her eyes, a look of surprise on his face. "What makes you think something is bothering me?"

"Oh come on." Alex rolled her eyes in frustration. "Do you not think I've gotten to know you after all of these weeks? Something is bothering you, and as your partner and housemate, I think I have a right to know what it is."

"Okay, as my partner, maybe you do." Nicola spat out the words, and Alex wondered why he was so angry with her all of a sudden. "Our orders for wine are not good, and tourist season is here. We should be selling much more."

Alex looked at Nicola and tried to read his expression and tone. "We can fix that," she said hesitantly. "I have ordered a lot of new marketing materials, and the website looks great. We'll catch up."

"There you go. You think you can just come in here and fix everything." Nicola picked up the napkin from his lap and threw it on the table. He started to stand, but Alex would not allow him to have the last word.

"I'm trying to help. This is my business, too. And I thought you appreciated what I'm doing. You said you liked all my designs, the changes I've made, the website."

Nicola started walking away, but Alex stood and went after him.

"Don't you dare walk away from me." She raised her voice. "We're not finished. Something is going on here, and you're acting like a child. Tell me what the hell is making you behave like such a jerk."

Nicola turned around to face Alex, and she recognized the same fiery Italian temper that he displayed when she first arrived at the villa, but mixed into his expression was a bit of confusion. It was if he didn't seem to know what to think or how to respond to her.

"You say you know me, then you should know when I do not want to talk. Good night." Alex could see Nicola fighting to keep control, but she wasn't willing to let it go.

"We're going to talk whether you want to or not. What has gotten into you?" she demanded.

Suddenly Nicola turned and walked back to Alex. He put his arm around her and drew her to him until there was not a breath of air between them. With his other hand, he grabbed her auburn hair and pulled it back so that she was forced to look up at him. Alex wasn't sure whether to scream and kick him away or sigh and melt into him. They stood there, each gasping for breath, staring into each other's eyes. Alex thought that she could feel both of their heartbeats thumping in rhythm with each other. Her eyes shifted to his Adam's apple that moved up and down as he swallowed, then she slowly lifted her gaze back to his warm, melted chocolate eyes. Hot chocolate was more like it, no—steaming, hot chocolate. His eyes were literally clouded over as if filled with steam.

Without warning, it was Alex's body that felt like it was melting, or rather, it was falling, quite literally. She made a great effort to steady herself without the pillar of Nicola's body holding her up and had to grab onto the nearby banister of the stairway. She watched the front door as it slammed shut after his hasty departure. She exhaled deeply and sunk onto the ground. Maria was wrong. Alex was most definitely not the one in control. She would surrender everything to him if he asked, and that scared her more than anything she had ever felt in her life.

Chapter Eight

"Daddy!" Alex screamed and sat up in bed. It had been another restless night, and the few periods of sleep she managed to have were interrupted by nightmares. She closed her eyes and tried to catch her breath, but before she could stop them, the tears came. Alex leaned forward, put her face in her hands and cried. Without looking at her phone or thinking about the calendar on the wall in the winery, she knew what today was. It had been exactly two years since what was left of her world had been ripped to shreds. Alex was no longer in her bed in Italy but in the back seat of a car covered with glass, bleeding from cuts both seen and unseen.

A knock on the door brought her back to the present. As she looked up, the door opened, and a wide-eyed Nicola poked his head into the room.

"Mia bella," he said as he rushed to her side. "For two nights, I have listened to you call out in your sleep. And then this morning, I hear you crying. What is it? Please forgive me if I have hurt or scared you." He sat on the bed, a worried look was on his face, and he seemed unsure about whether or not to touch her.

Alex shook her head. "No," her voice was small and weak. "It's just…" Her words failed her, and she found herself crying into her hands again. This time, Nicola put his arms around her and pulled her into him. Just as she had done when the piano was unveiled, Alex allowed herself to cry in his arms.

"Stai bene, sono qui," he soothed. "You're okay, I am here." Nicola repeated his words over and over and smoothed her long hair until her sobs quieted down.

"I'm sorry," Alex whispered into his tear-stained t-shirt. Nicola leaned back, took her chin between his fingers, and tilted her face up toward his.

"No, I am sorry. My behavior last night…"

Alex blushed and averted her eyes. "Mine was no better," she said. "I shouldn't have pushed you, especially since your problems are none of my business."

"No, no," he insisted. "I was not myself. You were right. We will work together to make things better for the vineyard."

The vineyard was the last thing on Alex's mind as she curled back onto his chest and nodded. Nicola held her close, and Alex fought the urge to look back up into his eyes. Leaning against him, his arms around her, while she was still in her long nightshirt and he on her bed, felt so intimate, so right. Alex wanted to stay like that forever, while at the same time, she was petrified that if their eyes met, they might become even more intimate; and that little voice in the back of her head reminded her that he was taken.

Finally, Nicola pulled away and spoke in a quiet voice. "You called for your papà. Do you want to tell me what happened?"

Alex shook her head. The answer was both yes and no. Yes, she wanted to tell him, but no, not like this. "I would like to, but," she hesitated, "could I, could we…" she shifted uncomfortably, even though she was actually quite comfortable, and pulled the covers more tightly around her body.

As if he could read her mind, Nicola said, "Oh, sì, sì, mi dispiace. I will meet you downstairs when you are ready." Nicola let her go and stood. For a moment he just looked down at Alex, seemingly lost in thought, forgetful already that he was supposed to be leaving. Then he shook his head slightly as if to clear it and hurried from the room. Alex sighed heavily and leaned back on her pillows. Suddenly the villa didn't seem quite as big and roomy as it had the day she moved in.

Alex descended the stairs to the smell of fresh cappuccino and toasted pastry. When she entered the kitchen, Nicola turned and smiled. Alex offered an uneasy smile and took the seat he offered her.

Once they were both seated and eating, Nicola began speaking. "Before you begin, I will tell you what I know. I found, online, news about your brother and your father. I am so sorry. I cannot imagine how it felt, how it feels."

Alex swallowed a mouthful of coffee and put down her cup. She was slightly taken aback by the thought that

Nicola had looked her up online, but then she remembered how she had done the same thing before coming to Italy. "I don't want to sound mean, but you're right. You truly can't imagine how it felt or how it feels." She closed her eyes and went back to the day that they received the call about Chad. "He was so smart." She smiled. "And sweet. He would do anything for anyone, and of course, that was his downfall."

Alex relayed the story to Nicola, how his friend, Melissa, showed up at his door early one morning, begging for his help. Making a long story short, and leaving out all of the details about Melissa's two years in hiding, Alex explained how Chad had helped his friend disappear in order to escape a hit man hired by the Vice President, who was revealed to be her mother's rapist and Melissa's father. The story had been covered by reporters worldwide, but Nicola gave no indication that he had heard it. Using the computer skills that caused the tech community to refer to him as 'The next Mark Zuckerberg,' Chad secured for Melissa several new identities and instructed her on how to stay off the grid. After loaning her some clothes, an untraceable laptop, and all the money he had in his flat, he watched Melissa leave and went on about his day.

Everything Alex knew about what happened next was based solely on speculation. Piecing together Melissa's testimony, police reports, and the confession of one of the most powerful men in the world, it was believed that Chad's killer entered the flat within less than a day after Melissa left, killed Chad, stole his car, left the vehicle in an alley, and dumped Chad's body into the Delaware River. It took over three weeks for the police to take his disappearance seriously, and by that time, identifying the body was almost impossible.

Alex was a Freshman at Loyola University in Baltimore at the time. Being the closest in proximity to the crime scene in Philadelphia, and wanting to spare her parents the pain, she volunteered to take on the gruesome task. The police would not allow her to look at what was left of the body, so she identified her only brother using a digital reconstruction of his face and confirming the medical and dental records that the police had obtained.

"How terrible it must have been for you," Nicola said as he reached his hand across to covers hers. Alex sat to the right of him at the table, Nicola at the head. She nodded.

"I thought, at the time, that my life couldn't get any worse than it was at that moment. Then…" She looked away, and a tear escaped from her eye and trailed down her cheek. She sniffed and blinked before continuing. "Then we had to go through the funeral where my mother collapsed at the gravesite and was taken to the hospital. She was suffering from exhaustion, from dehydration, and from the pain of loss. But most of all, she was beginning a spiral into such a debilitating depression that it took over a year for her to even be able to appear normal. When she seemed almost herself, Dad decided that we needed to get away, to try to be a family again. We went on a road trip to New England just before my junior year of college."

Alex stopped and closed her eyes. She scrunched her face and shook her head as if to clear a memory or an image. "We were almost back home in Chicago when a drunk driver hit us head on. There was nothing Dad could have done to stop it, and there was nothing the doctors could do to save him." More tears came, and Nicola tightened his hold on her hand. Alex gave him a half-hearted smile and finished. "My mother and I haven't spoken since just after his funeral when she told me to get out and never come back. She blamed me for Dad's wanting to take the trip. I'll never understand it, but that's the way it is."

Alex pulled her hand away and stood up. She picked up her dishes and walked them to the sink and then gazed out the window. "I received just enough money from the insurance settlement to pay for the rest of my college education and for rent on the townhouse I shared with my friend, Sandra. I returned to Baltimore and haven't been back home since." She turned back to Nicola and gave him a genuine smile. "I met Signora that winter, and she loved me like my mother hadn't in almost two years. Though I worked for her, she was my friend, my confidant, my advisor, but most of all, she was my family."

Nicola stood and went to her. "Sì, she was your family, and now you are our family." He took her hands and looked deeply into her eyes. "This is your home, and sono qui per te, per sempre, I am here for you forever."

Alex looked up at Nicola, and time seemed to stand still. The room was suddenly smaller, so small that Alex could hear his heartbeat. Neither moved nor spoke until they heard the front door close. They quickly jumped away from each other. Alex, her face hot and red, reached for the dishes she had put in the sink and turned on the water. Nicola hurried to the table to retrieve his own dishes.

Maria walked into the room and surveyed the situation. A small "O" formed on her lips, and she blushed. "Mi dispiace, I thought perhaps Alex was alone. Nicola, you are not in the, oh, mi dispiace." She turned to go, but Nicola forced a laugh.

"It is okay, Maria, we are just finishing breakfast."

"Come on in," Alex called, trying to sound normal. "Nicola was just leaving." She gave him a look that told him to get out, and he obeyed.

"Ciao," he called as he slipped out the back door.

Maria went to the sink and stared at Alex. After a moment, Alex turned to look at her. She felt her face go red again at the questioning look on Maria's face.

"What?" She tried to sound casual.

"You look, you look like you have a secret, like you did not sleep last night, and like, well, you know what you look like."

"No, I don't know what I look like," Alex said, shaking her head as if Maria's words were nonsense. After all, if Alex understood her implication, it was nonsense.

"Why is Nicola so late going outside?"

"We had a late breakfast. We were *talking*," she emphasized when Maria cocked her head and looked at her with disbelief.

"And Nicola is in a very good mood this morning," Maria added, her eyes burning into Alex's profile as Alex tried to ignore her and finish the dishes.

"Oh, for Heaven's sake, Maria. We had a, well, a breakthrough, I think. I told him about my past, about my brother and my father's death. It was not a romantic conversation." *Though it did feel romantic in the end, didn't it?* She pushed the thought away. "Everything is fine between Nicola and me, and you and I have work to do."

She turned off the water and headed toward the stairs. "I'll be over as soon as I brush my teeth," she called, leaving Maria to think whatever she wanted to about her and Nicola. It wasn't as if anything was ever going to happen between them.

Alex was tight-lipped all day, and she could tell it was killing Maria. She hated keeping her in the dark, but there was nothing to tell. Nicola acted no differently than he did on any normal day. He neither avoided Alex nor sought her out. The three of them met after lunch to go over some business strategies, and, as far as anyone of them could tell, nothing was happening between Alex and Nicola other than business.

"Tours? No," Nicola said emphatically. "I think you both know how I feel about that. Besides, the last time I gave a tour, a stranger ended up being my business partner."

"Oh, come on," Alex prodded. "You were so good at it." Nicola gave her a wary look.

"I mean it. You were really good at it. I left feeling like I actually learned how to make wine. Granted, I forgot most of it before I got back to Verona because I felt so bad over the way it all went down, but…" She looked sheepishly at the two cousins.

Maria rolled her eyes, "Even with the way the last one turned out, I think Alex is right."

"You what?" Nicola looked at her with surprise. "You have never thought it was a good idea."

"I have always thought it was a good idea. You…" She poked Nicola in the chest. "…were always against it, so I said nothing."

It was settled then. It was two to one, and even though Maria's opinion didn't legally count, Nicola knew it might as well have. He was outnumbered, and the tours would take place.

"Fine, but I am not giving them," he declared.

"I don't know why not," Alex challenged. "You *are* good at it, and you are fluent in four languages."

"My Spanish is mediocre at best."

"I don't want to hear it. You can speak and understand more than enough to get by. And I can do the English tours if you want."

Nicola raised an eyebrow, and Alex playfully swatted him. Maria watched the exchange without a word. The dispute was soon resolved. Maria would do the Italian tours, Alex would do the English tours, and Nicola would grudgingly do the rest. Alex began updating the web site right away, and Maria called the tourist agencies in the area to let them know that the vineyard was now open to the public and that literature would soon follow.

That evening, Pietro joined them for a night on the town to celebrate. It was Alex's idea, and though Nicola acted like he didn't want to go, neither of the ladies bought it.

"The gentleman doth protest too much, methinks," Alex whispered to Maria.

"He is not the only one," Maria countered, but Alex ignored the comment.

Exhausted and feeling a bit tipsy, Alex went right to bed when they returned to the villa that evening. For the first time that week, she slept soundly through the night without any nightmares, although she certainly had her fill of dreams.

Nicola was pleased with the results from his grape picking and analysis the next day.

"The sugar is just right, and the acidity is low. It will be a very good year," he told Alex at dinner.

"How do you know that already?"

"As long as temperatures and rainfall are as predicted, it will be good. We have pruned the vines, but the hottest part of the summer is still to come, so it is a delicate balance now between sunlight and shade."

They discussed the state of the vineyard while they ate and did the dishes and then settled down on the couch. Neither mentioned the events of the previous morning, both acting as if nothing had happened. Of course, Alex constantly reminded herself, nothing, in fact, had happened. She settled onto the cushion next to Nicola and listened as he read.

February 10, 1943

Word has reached us that a new General has taken over the American Forces here in Europe. Papà woke me before dawn this morning and told me the news and said that I needed to leave early for school so that I could deliver something for him. I could tell by his tone that the task he was entrusting to me was not an ordinary errand. I dressed, ate quickly, and went outside. My bike was already by the front door. Papà handed me my satchel and told me that I was to deliver mother's meat order to the butcher on my way to school. It was in my bag, he said, rolled and tied with a black ribbon. I was not to open it under any circumstances. I nodded and left for school.

All the way there, my heart pounded in my chest, and I found myself to be very alert, watching for someone to come and push me off of my bike and empty the contents of my bag in search of the rolled paper. When I reached the butcher shop, there were two soldiers standing nearby smoking cigarettes. I tried to ignore them as I parked my bike. My hands shook as I reached for my satchel, and I feared that they would notice. Their laughter felt like blows to my body as I averted my eyes and walked into the shop. My voice shook as I told Signor Lombardi that I had mother's order. He nodded and looked around before taking the paper that I slipped from my bag. He told me to come back after school to retrieve her meat, and I practically ran from the store.

I could barely concentrate on my studies as I watched the clock tick by all day. If my teachers noticed my distraction, they did not say. Perhaps they, too, had secrets of their own that they hid and hoped nobody would discover. After school, I headed back to the shop, relieved to find no soldiers this time. The butcher handed me a sack of cheesecloth. I could feel the heavy meat inside. "Go straight home," he told me. "Speak to no one. Give this to your father right away." I nodded and raced home as fast as my bike could carry me. It was off-balance with the heavy package in the basket, but I made it all the way without falling over. Father was waiting for me when I arrived. He was working less and less in his medical office these days, and I wondered how we were going to pay the ever-growing price of food. He took the package and hurried into the house before I could even dismount from my bike. By the time I got to the kitchen, the beef was opened on the counter, and Mamma was preparing it for dinner. Papà and whatever else was in the package were gone, his office door closed.

"Lombardi?" Alex asked Nicola.

"Sì, it is how the family made their fortune," he answered.

"In meat? How on earth did they make a fortune as butchers?" Alex asked incredulously.

"It was a different time. Everyone needed food, and beef has always been an important food in Italy."

"What does the family do today? I can't imagine Eva butchering a cow." Alex tried to suppress a grin.

"Ah, you have not been to Eva's estate. They own cattle, many, many cattle. While Eva plans parties, her brothers raise and slaughter the beef cows and sell to the local markets. It is, in fact, very lucrative."

Alex made a face of disgust and pointed to the journal. "Let's keep reading so that I can get that image out of my head."

Nicola continued.

March 1, 1943

For weeks, I have been a courier of unknown information between Papà and Signor Lombardi. I have tried in vain to find out what messages are contained in the packages I risk my life to carry between home and the shop, but I am not brave enough to go against Papà's orders and try to peek at the hidden notes. It is not the soldiers I fear but Papà. If I do not follow his orders, he will not trust me anymore, and even though I know not what I deliver, I know that I am helping my country.

Today, however, Papà called me into his office after dinner; his voice had a tone I did not recognize. "I have something for you," he told me, and he held out a stained paper, folded into a small square, with my name neatly printed on it, Signorina Isabella Abelli. I slowly reached for the paper and tried to take it, but Papà's grip on the paper remained firm. I looked at him, and his eyes were like marble. "I do not know that I approve of this," he said sternly. "Sì, Papà," I told him even though I had no idea what he was talking about. "It is one thing for you to go behind my back, but it is another altogether for this route of communication to occur. It could endanger our whole operation." I apologized and waited. It seemed like hours before Papà loosened his grip and handed me the note. I asked to go, and he nodded.

With my heart racing, I ran to my room and carefully opened the note. It was a letter! From Roberto! I could hardly believe my eyes, but there it was in my own trembling hands. How he knew to send it to Signor Lombardi, and why he didn't send it through the mail, I did not know. At that moment, I did not care.

My dearest Isa,

I write to tell you that I am well. It is hard trying to be like one of the others, but I try and must be succeeding. Your Papà will understand and may explain it to you someday. Please know that you are ever in my thoughts and in my heart. Hold fast to its key, for only you can unlock it upon my return.

Faithfully yours,
Roberto

"How beautiful that she taped it here like the other note," Alex said wistfully. "How hard it must have been for them both."

"They barely knew each other," Nicola reminded her.

"But they knew," was all she said, and he silently told himself that it was like his feelings for Eva. She was right for him, and he knew it. But that nagging voice in his head reminded him that it wasn't Eva who was now always on his mind.

Chapter Nine

The week went by quickly as the winery was spruced up and made ready for the first tour. Nicola was relieved that the debut tour was for an American couple. He was confident that Alex could handle it just fine. He smiled to himself when he thought about the irony of the situation. Two months ago, he learned that an American college student, with no knowledge of the wine industry, had inherited half of the vineyard, and now she was not only his partner, but living in his house, and giving a tour of their business. He shook his head in disbelief.

"Buongiorno," he said into his cell, and his smile widened. "Mamma, how are you?"

Nicola's face fell when he heard his mother's reply. A lump caught in his throat, and his eyes began to fill with tears. He told her that he would be there right away and pressed the end button on the phone.

Nicola stood among the grape arbors and closed his eyes. His emotions swelled up inside of him until a torrent of agonizing sobs ripped through his chest, and he fell to his knees in the dirt. Hearing his cries, Giovanni ran to him, and Luigi went to the winery. In minutes, Giovanni moved over, and Alex was by his side, wrapping her arms around him. In a reversal of roles, she held him while he sobbed in her arms over the loss of his father.

Alex had dreamt of Florence her entire life, but she never imagined that her introduction to the grand city would happen this way. She walked with Luigi down the aisle of the Basilica di Santa Maria Novella and slid into the pew with Marta and Nicola. Maria, Pietro, Giovanni, Adrianna, and Marco sat behind them. Surprisingly, Eva was not in attendance. What kind of woman didn't show up to her fiancé's father's funeral?

Alex was captivated by the stained-glass windows, larger and more vibrant than any she had seen before, and by the magnificent frescos depicting the lives of the saints, most notably St. Phillip the Apostle. If Alex's memory served right, this was one of the many architectural feats of Giorgio Vassari, one of Florence's most famous architects, known primarily for the famed Vasari Corridor over the Ponte Vecchio.

As she tried to concentrate on the Italian Mass and Homily and not get lost in the art and architecture that surrounded her, Alex felt Nicola's hand slide into her lap and reach for her hand. Neither turned toward the other, but Alex knew that Nicola was trying to hold himself together for his mother. His hand trembled, and Alex felt his body shaking with grief. Like her Nonna, Marta tried unsuccessfully to have more children, but the Lord must have had his reasons for not granting her wish. She had only Nicola to comfort her now that her beloved husband had passed on. Alex knew that Nicola would need to be his mother's rock through this ordeal.

When the service was over, the family followed the casket out of the church and into the magnificent piazza. The heat instantly soaked through Alex's black dress as if a warm bath had been poured over her as they walked into the daylight from the cool basilica. After the burial in the cemetery, Trespiano, the family gathered in Marta's small studio apartment for a dinner provided by her neighbors. Unlike the American funerals that Alex had attended, only the family gathered for the meal, though many of Marta and Nicola' friends attended the funeral and paid their respects after the Mass. Over dinner, Alex heard stories about Nicola's father as well as about Nicola, who spent most of his youth in Florence.

"Nicola, where is your beautiful girlfriend?" Maria's mother asked.

"She is away," Nicola said. "It was too difficult for her to get to Firenze. The roads are so crowded this time of year."

Alex noticed the look that Marta gave Nicola and the way he turned away, seemingly too embarrassed to face his mother's questioning gaze.

Alex, Maria, Luigi, Giovanni, and the few other relatives who attended the service were returning home the next morning, but Nicola was staying to help his mother finalize the funeral costs and to go over his father's estate. Alex was packing her things when Nicola knocked on her hotel door. At one time, the family owned a house in Florence, but houses in the city were expensive, and with Nicola gone, his parents had moved to a small apartment. Nicola was staying on his mother's sofa, but Alex and the rest of the family had stayed the night in a hotel near his mother's home. Alex opened the door to find Nicola standing in the hallway. Her heart broke when she saw the pain in his eyes. She opened her arms, and Nicola went into them like it was the most natural thing he had ever done. Alex held him tightly until he pulled away.

"I'm almost ready," she said, "but I didn't expect to see you. I thought I was riding back with Luigi, Maria, and Pietro."

"That is why I am here," he said. He looked into her eyes, and Alex saw the pain, but she saw something else, too. She looked at him questioningly. "Please stay."

Alex's heart leapt, and she tried not to read too much into his request, just as she had tried not to read into his holding her hand at the funeral. He was in mourning, and he just needed to lean on her.

"Are you sure? I don't want to be in the way. I'm sure you and your mother already have many things to handle."

"Please," he said, and Alex could hear the anguish in his voice. "I need you to stay."

Alex's eyes filled with tears, and she tried to blink them away. She had spent the past several days reliving every minute of her brother and father's funerals, and she knew just what Nicola was going through. She longed to hear her mother call for her, ask for her help, ask her to stay, hug her, or simply reach for her hand the way Nicola had done in the church the previous day. The least she could do was to do for Nicola what her mother had never allowed her to do for her. Alex reached for his hand and squeezed it. Then a thought occurred to her.

"What about Eva? Surely she should be the one to comfort you."

"She is not here. Please, for me."

Alex was torn. On one hand, she was very uncomfortable standing in for Eva, especially when Eva already thought of her as 'the other woman.' On the other hand, she and Nicola were practically family. If he needed her, then she should be there for him. She nodded.

"Okay, then, I will stay. I will do whatever you need me to do. I can run errands, cook, whatever you or your mother needs..."

"Right now, you are all I need. Come with me," Nicola said and grabbed her hand.

"Wait." She tugged at him to stop. "Let me grab my purse and my room key. And I'll need to let the front desk know that I'm not checking out."

"I already did," Nicola said, and with that, Alex let him lead her out of the room, down the stairs, and onto the streets of Florence.

Nicola could not explain what had gotten into him. Yes, he was furious with Eva for refusing to leave the coast to attend the funeral, claiming that she hated funerals and would comfort him in 'her own way' when they both returned home. Even the thought of that seemed inappropriate to him under the circumstances. It proved once more just how selfish she was. But his desire to have Alex stay with him was more than a need to replace or even get back at Eva. He knew in his heart that she would make him feel better, make him forget the sadness for a short time and have fun. Several hours later, he had no regrets. In spite of the reason for their stay in Firenze, Nicola almost felt lighthearted as he sat with Alex on the steps in front of the Pitti Palace, home of the Medici family during the Renaissance and an art gallery and museum today.

"I had no idea gelato was so good," Alex said as she wiped her mouth with her napkin. "It's better than ice cream."

"It was one of the things I missed the most when I studied in America." Nicola licked the last spoonful of his ricotta stregata, 'bewitched ricotta,' and smiled as he watched Alex finishing off her bacio, chocolate and hazelnut.

Nicola was scheduled to meet his mother at her apartment for lunch around two, so he and Alex filled the morning with sightseeing. Nicola took her to the famous Duomo, the Cathedral of Santa Maria del Fiore, and its Baptistry. From there, they walked to the Piazza della Signora where Alex got her first glimpse of the Palazzo Vecchio where the replica of Michelangelo's David stands at the entrance.

"Someday," Nicola promised, "I will take you to see the real one inside Il Galleria dell'Accademia. We will call Mamma's friend, Antonella, who gives tours, and she will take us in without waiting in line."

"I can't imagine that the real one is any more spectacular than this," Alex said in amazement.

"Come," Nicola said, "and I will show you the famous statues, along the Uffizi, of Firenze's most celebrated citizens."

They rounded the corner and stopped at each of the statues—Dante, Michelangelo, Galileo, Machiavelli, and at least a dozen more—that lined the most famous office building in all of Italy, once the office of the Medici family and now an art gallery. Nicola explained to Alex that the wait to get inside could be as long as five hours. The line of tourists extended the entire length of the building, and Alex marveled at the number of people waiting in the excessive heat to get a glimpse of Botticelli's *Birth of Venus* and DaVinci's *Adoration of the Magi*. In spite of the long wait and the agonizing temperatures, she felt a pang of jealousy and hoped to be able to come back to Florence soon to see the great works of art.

Continuing on, under the famed Vassari Corridor, they headed to the wall that stretched along the length of the city and looked down at the Arno River.

"There." Nicola pointed to the row of buildings lining a bridge crossing the river. "…is the Ponte Vecchio."

Alex couldn't believe she was here. Even after all of these weeks in Italy, it hadn't sunk in that she was in the city that gave birth to the Renaissance. She stared at the bridge and almost had to pinch herself to believe she was truly seeing the famed structure.

"No wonder," she breathed.

"What?" Nicola asked as he, too, gazed at the bridge.

"No wonder that German soldier didn't have the heart to bomb it."

"You know the story?" he asked.

"Of course. Every art student knows that when the Germans were told to destroy the bridges to stop the advance of the Allied armies, one man refused to detonate the charges under the Ponte Vecchio. And there…" She pointed to the windows above the bridge. "…that's the Vassari Corridor where Hitler and Mussolini met to discuss their war plans."

"I am impressed," said Nicola. "You do not need me to be your tour guide at all." He smiled at her, and her heart melted.

"There's a huge difference between reading about these places and seeing them with someone who grew up here. Please, show me more."

They walked down the sidewalk beside the Arno and up onto the Ponte Vecchio. Nicola pointed out the Ponte Santa Trinita, a bridge considered by most to be even more beautiful than the Ponte Vecchio but not spared during the War. Rebuilt in 1958, the bridge is considered one of the highlights of Florence. It was here that they stopped to enjoy the gelato near the Pitti Palace. Afterward, they made their way across the Ponte Santa Trinita toward Marta's apartment near Santa Maria Novella.

After lunch, Nicola went to meet Marta to go over paperwork while Alex, using Nicola's directions, walked to the San Lorenzo marketplace. She ran her hands over the leather bags and purses and bargained with the vendors as she looked for the perfect purse for herself and even one to send home to her mother. Every now and then she sent a card or a small gift, hoping for a response. Perhaps this time…

Dinner at Quattro Leoni was an experience like no other Alex had ever had. In spite of the circumstances of their trip to Florence, Marta treated Alex and Nicola to an evening of fine wine, scrumptious food, and delightful company. The three of them sat in the restaurant for hours talking, laughing, and enjoying each other's company. On the walk back to the hotel, Marta looped her arm through Alex's.

"You make Nicola very happy," she said with a smile. "I wish his father could have met you. We always thought there would be time." Marta wiped away a tear, and Alex leaned toward the woman who seemed much too young to be a widow. Alex didn't respond because she wasn't sure what Nicola had told his mother nor exactly what her relationship with him was at the present time. She didn't know herself, and once again, she felt guilty. How would Eva react when she heard about their day together? Certainly, Nicola would tell her, and Alex was not looking forward to seeing Eva when she returned from the coast.

After bidding them both 'arrivederci,' Alex watched Nicola and his mother walk away. For the first time in a long time, she looked forward to going to bed and dreaming, but she was so exhausted and slept so deeply, that she remembered none of her dreams the next morning.

Chapter Ten

When Alex and Nicola returned home the following
day, Alex felt as if everything and nothing had changed
at the same time. She and Nicola had clearly made a
connection in Florence. Not only had he held her hand
during the funeral, but he held it off and on throughout
their tour.

Does that mean something, or was it just a friendly gesture?

Alex couldn't quite figure out where things stood.
And there wasn't time to figure it out once they were
back at the vineyard. Alex quickly put her bags in her
room and grabbed a bite to eat before heading to the
winery to check on Maria. Alex knew that Maria's hands
had been full while she and Nicola were in Florence and
Maria had to cover all of their daily jobs as well as
rescheduling and getting ready for the tours.

"You have two English tours scheduled for
tomorrow," Maria told her. "Do you need the afternoon
to get ready? Because the brochures are ready to be
picked up from the printer, and we have an outgoing
delivery today. The men will all be busy doing some
trimming and hydrating—"

"Whoa, slow down," Alex said. "Take a breath. I'll
go get the brochures and prep when I get back. I

prepared what I'm going to say before I left, so I'll be fine. Just let me run next door and grab my purse."

"Not so fast," Maria stopped her. "What happened in Firenze? When Pietro and I were checking out, Nicola came in and told the clerk not to check you out. Then he told us to have a safe trip back, and he disappeared into the elevator." Maria narrowed her gaze at Alex. "And you never answered my texts. And now you are blushing. What did I miss?"

Alex shrugged and headed toward the door. "Oh, nothing." Maria looked at her skeptically. "Nicola just wanted to show me around Florence, and Marta wanted to have dinner. It was very nice. I didn't have time to text you back." *Nor did I know how to answer your questions.* "We just walked around and saw the sights. We had some gelato and a nice meal. We couldn't get into any museums because it was too late to get tickets, but Nicola said that next time—"

"Ah ha!" Maria exclaimed and pointed at Alex. "You said 'next time.' So there will be a next time for you and Nicola to go to Firenze?"

"Of course," Alex said with exaggerated exasperation. "I'm sure that we will have business reasons to go back, and of course, there's Marta."

"Do not try to fool me. There is something different about you. There is more that you are not telling me."

Alex blushed and looked away then turned back with a frown. "I don't know what to tell you. He held my hand some of the time that we were together, but that's all. I don't think anything has changed between him and Eva."

"Uffa," Maria scoffed. "She did not even come to his father's funeral. What kind of fiancé is that? Mi madre had quite a lot to say when we drove her home that morning, and she was right. How could her holiday be more important than Nicola?"

"I don't know," Alex agreed. "She's supposed to be gone for another week, so we'll have to wait and see what happens when she returns." She sighed. "You know, it was an emotional few days, with the funeral and helping his mother settle his father's estate. He may have just needed a day to have some fun, and I just happened to be there."

"Nicola has many friends in Firenze. He could find others to have fun with. He chose you."

"As I said, we'll see," Alex said. "For now, I'm just going to act as if nothing has changed. It's his call as to what happens next. I'm not going to come between him and the woman he claims he wants to marry. I've got to go. I'll be back soon."

Maria watched Alex go and couldn't keep from smiling. There was certainly a change in Alex. Things are going to be even more interesting around here, Maria thought. She chuckled to herself and thought about how far Alex had come in the short time she'd been there, and how far Nicola had come as well. Tours, fancy brochures, Nicola falling in love—she was sure of that. Maria never thought she'd see this day, and she loved having a front row seat to it all.

It was late by the time Alex and Nicola sat down to eat, and they were both exhausted. Nicola looked so tired that Alex thought he was going to fall asleep at the table. His eyes were heavy, and he yawned almost continuously. His first day back at work, along with the emotional toll of his father's death and burial, had left him exhausted.

"Why don't you go up to bed, and I'll clean up," Alex told him. Instinctively she went behind him and began rubbing his shoulders. Rather than relax, she felt his muscles tense and she quickly pulled her hands away.

"No, please," Nicola said tiredly. "That feels so good."

Alex smiled and continued kneading his shoulders and neck. "It's payback for when you consoled me on the date of my father's death. I haven't felt that…" Alex almost said 'loved' but stopped herself. "…cared for in a long time."

"It was my pleasure," Nicola said, but the words were quiet and slurred. His head slumped, and his shoulders relaxed. Alex kept massaging for a few more minutes until she heard his shallow breathing and noticed how limp his body had become. She smiled and gently nudged him.

"Go to bed, Nicola," she whispered. "I'll see you in the morning."

Nicola stood and staggered up the stairs. Alex smiled as she watched him go. Yes, she thought, the same yet different. But it was all good.

March 15, 1943

Papà is sending me on a dangerous mission, and I'm not sure whether to be frightened or proud that he trusts me so. Tomorrow, I will board a train to Firenze. I will go alone, though Mamma worries about this. Papà assures her that I will be fine. I wished to take Gabriella with me, but Papà said that would only endanger her, and I cannot put my dearest friend in harm's way. Papà will take me to the train early tomorrow morning, and I will deliver a letter to a church. That is all that I know for now.

"How scary," Alex commented the following night as they read the journal. She was leaning against Nicola as he read, their bodies touching and sending pulses through Nicola unlike anything he had ever felt. He resisted every urge to kiss the top of her head or to turn her toward him and take her fully into his arms. Living in the same house and sharing the intimacy of his great-aunt's haunting story were becoming increasingly harder for him. He told himself that it was only because

Eva had been gone for so long. He was lonely, but he wasn't going to take advantage of Alex.

"I cannot imagine how she felt," Nicola said honestly. "I only wish I could have asked her. I never even tried to see her or get to know her."

Alex turned her head to look up at him. "You would have loved her," she said quietly. "I can picture her, a younger her of course, as you read. I can see how she became the woman I knew her to be. She was strong, smart, confident, all of the things I wish I could be." Alex looked down and sighed.

"But you are, mia bella, you are, and you do not even see it." He stopped himself from leaning over and skimming the top of her head with his lips. Before he allowed his emotions, and his body, to take over, he propped the book back up and continued reading.

March 16, 1943

I am so tired I can barely put my words on paper, but I must write down the events of my day before it all seems more like a dream than what is real. Papà took me to the train early this morning. I had to awake before the sun rose, but I was filled with excitement and did not feel tired at all. Of course, once I was alone on the train, my excitement turned to fear. There seemed to be soldiers everywhere. I had no way of knowing if one of them might ask me where I was going or what I was doing there. The letter was hidden inside the seam of my coat, my mother's handiwork in the late hours of the night. My hands were cold inside of my gloves, and my boots did little to stop the cold from settling into my toes. I coughed when the doors opened and tried to hold my breath to stay quiet and not draw attention to myself.

When I finally reached Firenze, the city was just waking. There were very few people on the streets as I walked from the Santa Maria Novella station. I passed by the Basilica and nodded to the sisters on their way to daily Mass. I had to hurry, or I would be late. I had been to Firenze before but never alone. I tried to follow Papà's directions, but they were not written down as he made me commit them to memory. I had to stop myself from running through the Palazzo Strozzi. I was out of breath by the time I reached Chisea di Santa Trinita. I went inside, dabbed my finger in the holy water and blessed myself before sliding into a pew about halfway up the aisle. I knelt down and barely finished my prayers before the priest began his ascension up the aisle to the altar. The Mass seemed to drag on forever, and in spite of the cold outside, I began to perspire under my heavy coat, but I was too afraid to take it off in case I needed to run quickly away. After Communion, while I prayed, I quietly and carefully pried open the seam inside my coat and slid out the envelope containing the curious letter. I waited for the church to empty before slipping into the Confessional. I began to say, "Bless me Father, for I have sinned," but I remembered that I was supposed to use the code that Papà told me, and so I asked for pardon and gave the code. The priest opened a small door in the wire between us, and I slid the paper into his hands. I prayed that this was the right person and not a trap. Father thanked me and blessed me and then prayed for my safe return home.

After Mass, I hurried from the church without looking back. I still do not know if the letter made it to its intended receiver, but I followed my papà's instructions, and made it to Firenze and back safely. Now, I lie here and pray that I was successful and that Papà will send me again. Aside from the night in the barn, I have never felt such a thrill in my life.

The vineyard was busy the rest of the week and into the weekend with tours, the filling of orders, and general care of the vines. On Sunday, Alex complained that it was all she could do to drag herself out of bed in time for church. Nicola smiled, but he didn't tell her that she hadn't felt exhaustion yet. Just wait until harvest began. She fell asleep in the car on the way home from Giovanni and Adrianna's, and Nicola felt his heart tug as he watched her sleep. They'd had little time alone since they returned from Florence. Even the evenings had been busy getting ready for the extreme heat the end of July and the month of August would bring.

Nicola quietly exited the car and walked to the passenger side. He opened the door and cautiously unbuckled Alex's seatbelt. Gingerly, he scooped her out of the seat and used his hip to close the door. Alex snuggled up against Nicola's chest without ever opening her eyes. Somehow, Nicola managed to open the front door and get into the house, but that was as far as his arms and back would allow him to carry her. Gently laying her down on the couch, he stood over her and watched her curl up onto her side. Nicola picked up a blanket from the nearby chair and draped it over her sleeping body. Kneeling beside her, he leaned over and brushed the hair from her face and resisted kissing her on the cheek. He smiled.

He noticed the smell of her hair, the same strawberry and vanilla scent he remembered from the day they met, and her skin was as soft and smooth as the skin of a grape. Her lips were the color of a rich rosé, and her skin glowed with the tan she had been building up as they worked in the fields and walked the streets of Florence. He resisted the urge to cover her mouth with his and stood quickly before he did something he would regret. Closing and locking the front door, he gave her one last look before heading upstairs to bed.

Alex opened her eyes. Her lips curled into a sleepy smile as she pulled the blanket up tighter around her shoulders. She felt just a tiny bit guilty about pretending to stay asleep when Nicola lifted her from the car. Being enfolded in his arms as he carried her into the house felt too much like being carried by an angel through the gates of Heaven. Besides, she reasoned, she was awfully tired. She snuggled down into the cushion where they usually sat reading the journal, closed her eyes, and drifted off to sleep.

In the morning, Nicola was treated to a delicious breakfast before heading to the fields. Alex spent the day giving tours and working on marketing materials that they were sending to restaurants throughout the region. Both continued acting as if their day in Florence had never happened.

"I don't understand," Maria prodded. "Are you seeing Nicola or not?"

"Of course, I'm seeing him. I see him every morning and every evening and any time he comes inside, plus church, family dinners—"

Maria cut her off. "You know what I mean. Are you two...?" Maria gave Alex a curious look.

"Heavens no," Alex said as she playfully pushed Maria away. "That would just complicate things. He's still with Eva, and besides, I'm not like that." Alex blushed and looked away.

"Not like what?" Maria waited, but Alex did not answer. Her face reddened even more deeply, and Maria suddenly understood. "Wait. Do you mean—?"

"So, what do you think of the modifications to the web site?" Alex quickly changed the subject.

"Mamma mia! You're an American! How can this be?"

"Just because I'm an American doesn't mean—my goodness. What kind of American movies have you been watching?"

"It is understood that American women are—"

"Now wait a minute," Alex said emphatically.

"No, mi dispiace. I did not mean—"

The phone rang, and Alex breathed a sigh of relief. She busied herself with a few final tweaks on the web page and hastily scribbled a note for Maria before the phone conversation ended. She headed to the villa for lunch, grateful to be able to get away before any more was said about her relationship with Nicola or about her lack of experience. She'd had this conversation with her girlfriends, not to mention Patrick, too many times in her life and wasn't about to rehash it. She wasn't going to be just another cow giving the milk away for free.

That evening, Alex and Nicola had a simple dinner of paninis made with fresh tomatoes, mozzarella, and basil. It was simply too hot to cook anything else. Instead of sitting inside, they sat on the chairs on the front porch. Alex curled her legs under her and melted into the chair. She sipped her wine and closed her eyes as Isa took her back in time.

March 24, 1943

Papà says that the War is becoming more intense and that it is only a matter of time before the Allies reach Italy. I do not know if this is good or bad. What will happen to our towns and cities when the fighting is on our land? I fear for my family, my friends, and Valpolicella. We hear of many Jews throughout Europe being taken from their homes and put into work camps. Papà says that not allowing this to happen in Italy is the only good thing that Mussolini has done in this war. Papà says that if that changes, our little group will have a much more difficult job—to somehow hide, or smuggle from our country, our Jewish friends and neighbors. This both frightens and excites me. I so wish that I could do more.

April 1, 1943

I have delivered perhaps the most important document that I've handled so far. I was leaving school today when Signor Lombardi called to me and asked me to pick up an order for my mother. Confused, but guessing the meaning of this sudden directive, I went inside the butcher shop. I hurried home with the meat wrapped in paper and wondered, not for the first time, if we were lucky recipients of free meat, or if he and papà had a deal in which Papà's secret correspondences included payment for the meat. But back to the letter. Papà called me into his room a few minutes ago to tell me that if all goes as planned, we will have a new leader within the week. He refused to tell me any details, but it seems that the resistance, thought by many to have faded into the background, is alive and well and being led by Pope Pius XI himself.

Nicola stopped reading, and Alex felt a shift in the air. She realized that even across the porch, she could feel his movements and mood changes. She opened her eyes and looked at him as he shook his head in confusion.

"What is it?"

"This has always been suspected. History tells us that the Italian resistance did not exist during the War and that Mussolini remained in power until the middle of the summer. And Pope Pius was seen as aiding the Nazis by not speaking out against them. I have heard that there was more to it, but I have never known for certain."

"Perhaps the rumors were true. Could this be the beginning of the end? Maybe the end of his reign began in April and was finalized during the summer."

Nicola shook his head again. "Non lo so. I am not sure what is right."

"Then keep reading, my man. Let's see what happens next."

Nicola feared that the journal might turn out to be a work of fiction, a projection of his aunt's thoughts but also her imagination. Having never actually met the woman, Nicola couldn't vouch for her sanity nor whether she had a penchant for not telling the truth. He worried that these writings would give Alex a false impression of the history of Italy as well as his family. But he felt a thrill at the possibility that the resistance did exist and that his family and the Pope were a part of it. He read on.

April 8, 1943

Alas, the plan was foiled, and not one word of it was uttered on the radio or in the papers. The government controls every piece of news, and they continue to act as if the resistance does not exist, as if every Italian man and woman are in full support of our so-called leader and this War.

Papà believes that the Blackshirts heard of the plot and warned Il Duce, thus allowing him to leave the country. It is reported that he met with Hitler yesterday in Austria to further their plans for the War. Uffa! I never thought I would wish for someone to die or that I would be a part of a group planning to kill one of the most powerful men in the world, but I do believe that there is a God and that he will not allow us to suffer through this much longer. Papà says that all is not lost. Il Papà is working with priests throughout Italy and Germany to stop Hitler. Other lay people like us are carrying the messages. I pray that we are successful. God, please forgive me for my thoughts and for my words. Please forgive those of us involved for our lies and secrecy and especially for our part in what may happen. I do not know how to live in this world any longer without losing myself, my soul. If only Paolo and Roberto would come home. Then perhaps, the world could be right once again.

"Wow," Alex said. "There certainly seems to be a whole part of history that the world does not know. How do you know that there was no resistance to the War in Italy?"

"It is what we have always been taught, or at least, it is always what we were led to believe, but as I said, there have always been rumors." Nicola became quiet.

Alex leaned toward him and took the journal from him, turning it over and laying it gently in her lap.

"Isa was a good person, Nicola. I know she was. Signora was a remarkable woman who loved her country and her family. Whatever she did, whatever she was involved in, she truly believed it was the right thing."

Nicola nodded. "I know you are right, and it truly does shed a new light on the actions of the Pope." He smiled a small, half-hearted smile and turned toward

Alex. "You knew her better than I." He hesitated. "If she loved it so much, why did she never return?"

Alex looked at him affectionately. "I don't know, but perhaps she will tell us." He nodded, and Alex thought it best to leave him to his thoughts. "I'm going to bed now. Good night, Nicola."

He looked at her then, and her heart leapt as she saw in his eyes the reflection her own affection. "Goodnight, mia bella. Sleep well."

Alex smiled at him before getting up and going into the house.

Once in bed, she had a hard time going to sleep. Her thoughts ran free like a horse out to pasture, and she let them gallop, unbridled. Flashing through her mind were the scenes she pictured of a young Isa lying in this same room, writing in her journal; an older Signora, proud and regal, talking about her country and all of its treasures; the atrocities unleashed on the world by the two dictators for whom Isa rightfully held so much disdain; and finally, Nicola, his loving touch, his warm chocolate eyes, the kiss that she longed to taste. At last, her mind quieted down having run itself into exhaustion, and Alex drifted off to sleep thinking of Nicola and hearing Isa's words floating through the room like whispers on the breeze.

Then perhaps, the world could be right once again.

Chapter Eleven

A light, steady rain fell on the grapes, just the kind for which Nicola had been hoping. Growing grapes for wine was a delicate balance of heat and rainfall. Too much or too little of either one could be devastating. He stood at the window watching the drops fall onto the wide, green leaves, and drip down into rivulets that ran in the soil. The sound of the gentle rain on the roof was a welcome one, and he smiled at his good fortune—a healthy crop, a growing business, a savvy new partner, *who would have thought?*, and just the right person with whom to share it all. Of course, his father entered his thoughts several times a day, and Nicola regretted not making the short trip to Florence more often over the past few years. Never did he imagine that his healthy, jovial father would suffer a sudden, fatal heart attack. It was simply unthinkable. But time is fleeting, our lives all too often end without notice, and it is up to each one of us to make the most out of what we've been given without squandering it.

"Alex," Nicola said suddenly, turning from the window. "Let us take a ride."

Maria and Alex both looked at each other with raised eyebrows.

"Nicola, we have work to do."

"No, we are good. The tours have been cancelled. I cannot work in the fields. Maria can answer the phones." He looked at his cousin who nodded and smiled.

"Allora, go and leave me in peace. There are too many people inside this room today for me to concentrate."

"Where are we going?"

"You will see," Nicola promised. "Let us go."

Alex ran to the villa to retrieve her bag, a fine leather purse stamped "Made in Italy," and Nicola started his car. Managing to stay mostly dry, Alex climbed in and asked again where they were heading. Nicola just smiled and put his silver Fiat 500X into drive.

In less than an hour, Nicola entered a small, quaint city. Once parked, he walked around the car with an umbrella to shield Alex from the rain which was falling a little heavier now.

"Where are we?"

"Treviso, the closest place to us that the War came."

Alex tried to look around as Nicola led her through an empty piazza to a church that was quite modest compared to those she had seen in Florence. Once inside, he left the umbrella by the door and proceeded to a small window where he bought two tickets. Alex read the sign beside the window—Museo di Santa Caterina.

"I've never even heard of this place," she said as Nicola took her hand and led her inside.

"It is not on most tourist lists. It was once a church but is now an art museum. I thought you would like to see it on this rainy day best suited for indoor adventures."

Alex looked at Nicola and smiled. He seemed to know her so well. "Thank you," she said and walked beside him through the cloisters, decorated with vivid frescos by the artist Tommaso da Modena. Nicola told Alex the history of the artwork as well as the building.

"I can't believe you know so much about art and history. I'm constantly amazed by your knowledge," Alex admitted.

Nicola smiled. "Marta," he said. "Do not forget that she is much like you."

Alex nodded. "Ah, sì."

They continued their stroll through the gallery and then moved on to the archaeological section where Nicola translated whatever signs Alex could not read. He was impressed by how much she understood without translation, as was Alex. She hadn't realized how easy it had become to recognize words, phrases, and sentence structure.

When the museum closed at mid-day, Nicola took Alex for lunch and panna cotta.

"If you keep feeding me these desserts, I'm not going to fit into any of my clothes."

"Sì, I will need to put you to work in the fields."

"Wait? What are you trying to say?" Alex wasn't sure how to take his comment until he started laughing. She took another bite of her creamy dessert while trying to decide whether or not to be insulted.

Alex and Nicola walked around the town for the rest of the afternoon, huddling under the umbrella and jumping over puddles. They hardly noticed the rain.

On the drive back to Belle Uve, Alex thanked Nicola for the day.

"It was wonderful, but you never told me what you meant about the War? What happened in Treviso?"

"It was bombed by the Americans."

"Oh," Alex said quietly. "I'm sorry."

Nicola shrugged. "It happened, and it is over. The Allies freed us from the Germans. It was not all good, but it is over, and we go on."

"Were many people killed?"

"Around a thousand, I think. It was worse in other cities. Thankfully, the vineyard was not destroyed nor any of the other homes or small towns in our countryside."

"I can't imagine what it was like. I don't remember 9/11, so I can't really compare it to anything."

"I do not have anything to compare it to either." Nicola said. "Perhaps Isa will enlighten us."

When they arrived at the villa that evening, they settled on the couch in the parlor, and the last of the rain played light, staccato music to accompany their reading.

April 10, 1943

Father is displeased with me again, and I know I should be happy, but I weep with sorrow and fear.

My Dearest Isa,

My world is growing darker every day without you in it, and the fighting is more than I can sometimes bear. The Russians have assailed us night and day, and we are no match for them. I have seen many of my friends and brothers die. So few of us remain, and I fear that the Russians will close in on us any day. I am writing to you during the harshest winter I have ever experienced. I pray that I will return to you with all of my limbs, but I fear that I, too, will suffer the frostbite that seeps into the fingers and toes of so many around me and eats at them until they cry in agony and beg to have the appendage cut away from their body. I pray that I will return to you alive. I do not know how much longer we can hold on.

Always know that you are the light I seek in the darkness, the candle in the window that beckons me to come home.

Yours,
Roberto

"Winter?" Alex wondered out loud. "How long do you think it took for the letter to reach her?" She gently fingered the wrinkled, tear-stained paper, yellow and cracking with age.

"My guess is he was referring to the battle in Stalingrad, in January I think, so three months' time. If I remember correctly, many of our men were captured there. Most of them never came home from the Russian battles along the borders and in the Alps. It was no better in the South. Mio nonno, Paolo, was sent somewhere in Africa and was believed to be dead for many months. He spoke very little of his time in the war. It was a very sad time for Italy."

"How old was your grandfather when he went to war?"

"Young, very young, eighteen, the same as Roberto."

"I don't mean to pry, but…" Alex thought about how to phrase her question. "Wasn't he kind of old to be your grandfather? I mean, my great-grandfather went to war as a young man, and they served in the same war."

"Sì, it took many years for Nonno to find true love. The War, it changed him, I am told. It took a very special woman to find the good in him." Nicola smiled.

"I'm glad she did," Alex said quietly. Realizing she was giving away too much insight into her own feelings, she shifted slightly so that there was a bit of space between them. She looked down at the worn paper and the water stains on the page of the journal.

"I can't begin to imagine what she went through. What either of them went through."

"It was a miracle she received his letter. Whoever this group was, they were very clever." The reverence in Nicola's voice was notable, and Alex wondered what else the secret resistance did during the War.

"Shall we?" she motioned to the journal.

Nicola nodded and turned the page.

April 20, 1943

There are so many rumors, but our government does not permit us to know what is happening outside of Italy, so we rely on our missives and put our trust in the unknown people who risk their lives to send us the news. The Americans have been under heavy attack by German submarines, but they are making gains in Tunisia, pushing the Germans farther north. There is no more fighting between the Russians and the Italian 8th Army as most of our men have died or been captured. We have been told that the Russians are sending many of them home because they are sick or dying, and the Russians do not want to deal with them, but we have not heard any more from Roberto. Papà has tried frantically to locate him as well as Paolo, sending me on almost daily missions to Signor Lombardi, but none of Papà's inquiries have been answered. Though we have heard twice from Roberto, albeit not lately, there has been no news from Paolo, and we fear that he was captured or killed in Tunisia. My heart breaks for my brother and my parents but also for myself.

After an easy dinner of leftovers and bread bought in Treviso, they settled back on the couch to discuss what they had read earlier that evening.

"Paolo." Alex spoke the name quietly. "How long did they believe he was dead?"

"I do not know, but I am sure it felt like an eternity."

"You were very close to him. Your grandfather."

"Sì, very close. It is because of him that I have such great love for this vineyard. This was my home more than the city."

"I can see why. Florence is a beautiful city, and I look forward to going back, but out here…" She paused. "Out here, there is quiet and peace and something magical in the way that the moonlight shines on the grapes, the fruit of the gods."

Nicola looked at Alex, and, not for the first time, he realized how alike they were. Had Prozia Isa known that? How could she? She only knew Nicola from letters and phone calls and perhaps things his grandfather and mother told her. What had they told her that prompted her to introduce this woman into his life?

Nicola realized he was staring at Alex and that she was staring back. He reached over and laid his hand gently on her cheek. He curled his fingers and caressed her smooth skin with his knuckles and felt her sudden intake of breath. For several moments, his hand lay still on her soft cheek just beside her lips, and they looked into each other's eyes. Nicola watched Alex swallow and followed her motion with his eyes, noticing the glowing tan of the skin that trailed down into her t-shirt. He lifted his gaze back to her face, stopping at her lips and longed to touch them with his fingertips, his mouth, his tongue.

"I think it is time for bed," he whispered.

"Sì, time for bed," she agreed without moving.

With the restraint of all the saints and angels in Heaven, he looked away and took his hand from her face.

"Goodnight," he said quietly as he stood and walked away without looking back. In his mind, he could still see her sitting there, the desire in her eyes, the blush on her cheeks, and her rosè lips. Did they taste as sweet as wine? He took the image of her with him as he climbed into bed and held onto it, knowing in his heart that it was not enough. He knew that tomorrow, everything would change.

By mutual consent, the following morning, they decided to take a break from reading for a few days. Eva was coming home, and Alex knew that Nicola was anxious to see her; though her heart sank at the thought of their reunion after the intimate moments she and Nicola had shared the night before. They grew closer each day, but Nicola remained at a distance, and Alex knew that it was because he belonged to someone else. Her thoughts went to one of her favorite musicals, *Wicked*, and the haunting ballad 'I'm Not That Girl' that Elphaba sings when she realizes that she will never be the one Fiyero chooses. Of course, as all love stories go, it was Glinda who sang the song's reprisal after Fiyero listened to his heart and chose Elphaba instead.

"Fiction," she mumbled to herself. "It's based on a work of fiction. It's always the Evas and Glindas of the world who are chosen in real life."

Nicola hurried through his work on Friday, filling orders and rushing through tours, much to Alex and Maria's dismay, and left as soon as the last tour was over that afternoon.

Nicola pulled back from their kiss and gently removed Eva's arms from his neck. He felt her body go rigid and saw the familiar sparks in her eyes.

"So, this is the way it will be, then, no? You kiss me like a brother and push me away, and I am to just smile and say goodbye?"

"Eva, I'm sorry."

She held up her hand. "No. You are not sorry. You are wretched. You used me for all of these years, and then you cast me aside when someone new arrives."

"Eva." Nicola reached for her, but she backed away and turned from him. "Please, listen to me. I always imagined us together. I believed it was right, but I never felt…" He hesitated, not wanting to hurt her more. "It is that you and I are very different. We want different things. You want someone to take you away from your father's house and spoil you with lavish gifts and trips to the coast. I want to spend my life on my vineyard, raising children who will love my work as I do. I have traveled, and I am content to now be at home and work until I die of old age, as mio nonno did. You would never be happy with that life."

"And I suppose she will be?" Eva spat the words at Nicola as if they contained venom.

"I do not know. I hope so." Nicola sighed and looked at Eva.

"Then you do intend to go to her?"

"Sì, if she will have me. I have not always been kind to her, but she has been nothing but kind to me."

Eva rolled her eyes. "Do not lament to me about your failures and her virtues. She will not satisfy you the way I do. You will see."

Nicola did not respond. Eva had satisfied him in many ways, but he had only recently realized that none of them were the ways that counted. He thought it better not to add insult to injury.

After a few moments of silence, Eva waved her hand at Nicola in dismissal. He was amazed at her composure. He had expected shouting and the hurling of objects at his head. He supposed that when he cancelled the plans to join her on the coast, she knew what was coming.

"Go, then. Be with her. She will never make you happy like I could. And like your nonno, you *will* have to work until you die. She will never be able to give you a life of comfort. You will come to regret your decision in time."

"Perhaps it is so," Nicola said. There was no use in trying to explain to Eva that all of the riches in the world, all of the luxuries she could have provided for him, would never add up to the wealth he believed he could have with Alex nor the inheritance they could leave to their children. It was the kind of wealth and inheritance that Eva would never know or understand.

"Ciao," was all Nicola could say as he turned to leave. The heaviness in his heart was not for his own loss but for Eva's. He knew that she would never truly be happy the way he knew he would be.

Alex awoke on Sunday with a heavy heart after thinking about the journal for the past two days as well as wondering what torrid things Nicola had been doing with Eva to welcome her home. She had not seen Nicola at all on Friday night or Saturday and assumed he was with Eva. He returned to the villa late Saturday night, just as Alex was falling asleep. She hated that her thoughts turned to him as soon as she awoke.

Rather than hurrying to get dressed and head downstairs, Alex stayed in bed until she heard the kitchen door slam and knew that Nicola had gone outside. She was surprised that he had even come home both Friday and Saturday nights. On Friday, Alex and Maria had gone to see a movie—Maria told Alex it would help with her Italian, and truthfully, it did. When she returned to the villa, Nicola' car was in the driveway, and she assumed he had gone to bed, though she thought that it was odd that he was home early on the day that Eva returned. She had no idea where he was all day on Saturday, but she assumed he was with Eva.

On Saturday, Alex had a stroke of inspiration. She looked up a favorite recipe of Isa's and headed to the market. She spent the day making Nonna's Salse Marinara, a homemade red sauce that Alex and Signora made together one day the previous summer. The aroma of boiling tomato sauce still filled the house, and Alex wondered if Nicola had tried any when he arrived home late that night.

She reached for her laptop and checked her personal email and the news from back home. Killing time, she opened her web browser and navigated to Facebook for the first time in weeks. The app's inbox was full of messages from people, who were never truly her friends, insisting that they missed her and would love to come visit. Apparently word had gotten around about her inheritance. Alex closed the browser without answering any of them except for the one from her friend, Cindy. She tried to keep up a correspondence with the only friend she retained from childhood. It was a quick note to say hello with the promise of writing again soon.

Too hot to stay in bed, Alex threw off the covers and headed to the bathroom. Knowing she needed to get ready for church, she took a much longer shower than she had a right to. Her thoughts were a jumble of misgivings about and yearnings for Nicola, irritation with the people who assumed she would welcome into her world when she was never welcomed into theirs, longing for her mother and a real family, sorrow for Isa's family and all that they went through, and a nagging feeling that she was there for a reason and had no idea what that might be. Alex stood under the spray of water, her head bent and eyes closed. She cradled her forehead with her hand and sighed. Reaching for the wall with her other hand, she let the water wash over her until it ran cold and she was forced to turn it off and face her day. Certainly, God wouldn't give her any more than she could handle on this, already, oppressively hot and perplexing day.

The church was cool, the music was soothing, and before long, Alex began to relax and push aside all of the negative thoughts that had haunted her all weekend. After Mass, she and Maria headed toward Maria's car, arm in arm. Maria's boyfriend, Pietro, walked and chatted with Nicola, who had not said a word on the entire ride to church, prompting Alex to tell him that she wanted to ride home with Maria. Just as Alex reached for the car door handle, someone grabbed her arm.

"Scusami," said a familiar and unfriendly voice. "May I have a word with you?"

Alex turned to see Eva standing next to her. She was fashionably dressed, as Alex suspected she always was, and she was glaring at Alex with a look that could only be described as pure hatred. Alex stepped several feet away from the car with a feeling of foreboding, and Maria watched over the hood. Was Eva in church? Alex didn't see her in her family's pew, and she hadn't sat with Nicola and his family.

"What do you want, Evangelina?" Alex asked. Though she tried not to sound unfriendly, her words and tone were frosty. Truth be told, she was actually frightened by the look on the woman's face.

"Why are you here?" Eva asked.

"I'm here," Alex stated with what she hoped was annoyance and not fear, "because I own half of the vineyard and am going to help Nicola run it."

"Niki never needed help before. And you know nothing about running a vineyard." Eva's tone left no doubt as to how she felt about Alex.

"You know nothing about me," Alex raised her voice, unaware that people were beginning to stare.

"I know everything about you," Eva said in a low and all-knowing voice. "I know that your brother was murdered, your father died in an accident, and you and your mother do not speak. I know that you have been trying to claim Nicola as your own. And I know that you befriended an old woman who was not in her right mind and convinced her to leave you everything. I would not be surprised if you poisoned her so that—"

The slap was fast and hard. Eva's head snapped to the side, and Alex felt a throbbing in her hand. If not for that, she might not have believed that the action taken was her own. Eva let out a string of words that Alex recognized but would never dare repeat. In an instant, Nicola appeared by her side, and with his hand on her back, led her to the car. Without saying a word, he opened the door and helped her slide onto the seat. Alex sat in shock and watched as he spoke to Maria in Italian, giving instructions to Maria to take her home.

As they drove off, Alex turned and watched as Nicola unleashed his fury on Eva, and she wished she could hear what he was saying.

"Mi dispiace." Nicola apologized when he entered the kitchen some time later. "I do not know why Eva did that to you, and in front of so many people."

"Ha," Maria scoffed. "You do know, and so do I. In fact, Adrianna and Alex know, too," she said, gesturing to the other women in the kitchen. "She wants to be the woman living here, not Alex. Better yet, she wants you to be living with her, spending all of her father's money. She has always wanted that. The whole world knows that you're to be married, but you lead Alex on like she has a chance. It is not fair to either of them. You are the one who should be slapped, and by both of them."

"I made it perfectly clear to Eva a few days ago that I want nothing to do with her and that Alex belongs here."

Alex looked at Nicola in surprise. Maria stood speechless, her mouth agape.

"What?" Nicola demanded.

"No more Eva?" Maria asked.

"No more Eva," Nicola affirmed.

"I don't understand," Alex said. "A few days ago? When? How?"

Nicola sighed in exasperation. "Eva returned on Friday. We were to have dinner, but when I arrived, I told her that it was over. That is all."

Alex thought back on the past couple of days. She and Nicola spent Thursday in Treviso, and that was the night she felt it, that Nicola had finally recognized the obvious connection between them. Friday was a busy day at the winery with tours to give and orders to fill. She and Maria were out that night, and Nicola was gone on Saturday. Alex's assumption that he had been with Eva had been wrong.

"But why?" Alex asked. "I thought..."

"It was not right," he said. "Eva is not interested in the life I want, and I am not interested in the life she wants. It is better this way." He looked around the room and then asked in Italian, "Where is everybody? I am hungry."

Maria went to the kitchen door and called for everyone else to come inside. The men walked over from behind the house with drinks in hand. It was apparent to everyone that they had cleared out when Nicola drove up and were waiting for their cue to come inside. Alex and Adrianna hastily put the food on the table, and they all tried to pretend that nothing had happened, but Alex's head was spinning with the news, and she replayed Nicola's words over and over, trying to figure out why he had broken off his engagement. Could he possibly have feelings for her? Was she reading too much into the way he had looked at her and touched her face that night? She tried hard to avoid catching his eye throughout the meal, but she felt him staring at her several times and had to force herself not to look back.

That evening, though it had been a long day, Nicola asked Alex if she wanted to read together, but Alex could not push away thoughts about her encounter with Eva.

"I must ask you something first," she said. "Does she really hate me?"

"Who? Oh, Eva? No, but she does hate me," Nicola replied with a wave of his hand.

"I'm so sorry," Alex said. "It's all my fault."

"Mia bella," Nicola said, looking at her. "It is her own fault and mine for leading her on. She will move on, and so will I. We, you and I, have a business to run and," he hesitated, "a journal to read." He smiled at Alex, picked up the book, and opened the front door to the porch. She wished he would say more, but it was obvious that the subject was closed, at least for now. She imagined him taking her into his arms and telling her that she was the reason he had ended things with Eva. When he said nothing else, but just stood holding the door open for her, she walked onto the porch with a smile. "Sì, we have a journal to read," she said casually and took a seat in her usual chair.

May 14, 1943

News has come at last, and it is good, and bad. We learned that Paolo has been in North Africa. Yesterday, our troops there surrendered to the Allies. Though they are now prisoners of war, we believe (is it too much to believe?) that they will be treated more humanely than those in Russia. There are still many in Italy who do not trust the Americans, but those of us who have been working underground trust them more than the Germans. We do not know when Paolo will be able to come home, but at least he is no longer engaged in the fighting. We are trying to learn more, but word from the front comes slowly here. We pray that everyone returns home soon.

May 26, 1943

Sicily has been bombed. The war has arrived in Italy. Though it is many hundred kilometers from here, I am afraid. The stories we hear from other countries are so bad. Entire cities are destroyed. People have been taken from their homes, not just Jews, but Catholics, too. No place is safe, it seems. Will this never end?

Alex wiped away a tear. "I feel so sad just listening to this. I can't begin to imagine what they were all going through."

"Sì. It is hard to imagine the fear that they all had to live with every day."

"I visited the Holocaust Museum once." Alex turned toward Nicola. "That's in D.C." She paused and shook her head. "The piles of shoes, eyeglasses, and other personal items that were just discarded. It's unbelievable that human beings could treat other human beings with such disregard. The faces of the children in the photographs." Alex shuddered. "I don't even want to think about their fear."

Nicola wrapped his arms around Alex, and the two of them sat in the dark, lost in their own thoughts of sadness and despair.

The next morning, Alex and Maria found themselves hard at work in the kitchen. Flour dusted their clothes and clung to their hair while piles of cookies surrounded them.

"I had no idea we were going to be baking this many cookies when you told me that we had to bake for the festival." Alex blew the hair from her face that had fallen from her ponytail.

"I told you that feast days are very important in Italy. We are to celebrate the feast day of St. Valens, our Patron."

"I know, you've told me a dozen times. St. Valens was the Bishop of Verona, and he established Our Lady of the Roses Parish. I get that it's an important date, but really, five pounds of flour? Won't there be other food there besides our cookies?"

"Sì, but everyone likes our cookies the best. My nonna always told us—"

Alex chimed in, and with her best Italian accent, said with Maria, "This is a family recipe. If you make it, you will win a prize."

The women were laughing when Nicola walked in. "What is going on in here? I thought you two were going to be working hard." Nicola grinned and reached for a cookie.

"Do not think about it." Maria said as she slapped his hand.

"Ahi," Nicola said. "That hurt. And I think I deserve a cookie since I gave you both the day off."

"Excuse me?" Alex glared at Nicola. "You gave *me* the day off?"

"I mean, I agreed that you could help Maria," Nicola said as he backed out of the kitchen.

"You should stop while you're behind, Nicola," Alex called to him as he disappeared into the next room.

"Stop while he is behind?" Maria asked.

"I'll explain later," Alex told her. "Let's just get these cookies baked."

Later that evening, after all of the cookies had been packaged and the kitchen cleaned, Alex and Nicola returned to their reading.

June 1, 1943

Roberto is home, but he is not well. I have not been allowed to see him. His younger brother appeared on our doorstep just now with a message, not even a handwritten one, for Roberto is unable to write. He is sick and hurt and may not live. I want to go, but Papà says no. It is too much for me, he says. He is going over there, and I must wait.

Papà has returned. He and Mamma talk, and I wait still. They speak in hushed tones, and I cannot hear what they say. My heart is being wrenched in two.

June 2, 1943

The pain is too unbearable to put into words, but my pain is nothing compared to Roberto's. Mamma pleaded with Papà. If he is to die, she told him, she must say goodbye. And so Papà made the return trip to Roberto's home, taking with him my mother's healing soup, a bottle of Amarone, and his heartbroken daughter. The wounds are so deep that I almost did not know the face of my beloved. His hands and feet are bandaged. He has lost almost all of his toes and three fingers to the cold. Part of his face is gone and covered over with the hopes it will heal. He is malnourished and thinner than a grapevine. I wanted to hold his hand, to rub his cheek, to kiss his lips, but alas I could not touch him for fear of pain or infection. I tried to speak to him, to assure him of my love and faithfulness, but all that came were tears, and as it was, it didn't matter. He only sleeps, lulled into a deep, death-like place where he should feel no pain, but still, he cries out when he is touched the doctor, even though he does not wake.

I want to smash something. I want to scream like a banshee. I want to tear down walls and claw my way out of my imprisonment. But then I remember that my prison is one of mind, and his is one of body. My mother tried to comfort me when we returned, but there is no comfort. There is only pain and the smell

*of death that will never leave my hair or my clothes. He is more
lost to me now that he is home than he ever was at war, for I know
that the next time we say goodbye, it will be forever.*

Alex covered her mouth and swallowed the sobs that
threatened to push their way up and be released into the
quiet night. Her tears streamed down her face, one after
another, in an unceasing stream.

"Oh, God," she whispered into her palm. "Isa,
Signora, I never knew…"

"As I have said, it is not something they talked about,
the pain of the War. It took Nonno many years to get
over it." Nicola blinked back his own tears, and Alex
noticed a slight tremble in the hand that held the journal.

"I wonder how long he was sick. I've only seen
pictures, but he looked…normal," Alex said.

"Ah, but what is normal after war? I can only
imagine what he saw or did and how he felt, not just in
body…"

"But in mind," Alex finished the sentence and
thought about the grief that they both must have felt.
"How does someone recover from that? Not just the
frostbite and the malnutrition, but the mental torture?"

"There is a word for it, Post Terror—"

"Post-Traumatic-Stress-Disorder. Sì. It is what my
mother is diagnosed with. And she's never even been to
war."

"Ah, but it is her own kind of war, no? She lost her
son to violence and her husband to an accident that was
someone else's fault. Perhaps she fights her own war and

cannot rid herself of the pain and smell of death, like mi prozia."

Alex was silent. Could her mother be going through the same kind of thing, the same kind of feelings that Isa went through during and after the war—the loss of the life she knew, the death of friends and family? In the end, Roberto survived, and Paolo returned. But her mother would never have that relief, that gift of her loved ones returning. They were all gone except, of course, Alex.

"I think I will write to her. Again," Alex said. "I need to tell her…" Her words trailed off and she blinked back her tears.

"Let us retire," Nicola said as he closed the journal. "You have your thoughts to tend to, and I have mine."

"I'm so sorry, Nicola, you must be hurting, too. You've just broken up with Eva, and you're reading this sad, sad story about your family. Perhaps we should stop,"

"No," he insisted. "We will keep reading, but not tonight. Tomorrow, we will hope that all things will begin to get better."

Alex wondered about his words, but her thoughts returned to her mother. She said goodnight and went upstairs. She was in bed without even knowing how she got there, her teeth brushed and clothes changed. Yes, she would hope that tomorrow all things would begin to get better. She couldn't stop thinking about her mother and about Isa. She drifted off to a fitful sleep once again, and in her dreams, she saw her mother, but she heard Isa.

I want to smash something. I want to scream like a banshee. I want to tear down walls and claw my way out of my imprisonment.

Nonna's Salse Marinara

Isa, the best time of year to get the ingredients is July or August. You should jar enough for entire year. The below ingredients will make twelve 16oz mason jars of pasta sauce.

1 bushel fresh San Marzano plum tomatoes: find long and thin ones that are plummy - very red will mean more tomato meat inside rather than water/tomato juice. Ask people in store which tomatoes are best. If they are nice, they will tell you, but do not tell them why you are asking so you do not have to tell them your sauce recipe. Remember, this is family secret.
2 white (medium) onions - chop small or long
(if you chop long and someone doesn't like them
in sauce, they can pull them out)
12 cloves of garlic
parsley & basil to your liking
3 cups of olive oil

Wash tomatoes and paper towel dry them.
Cut tomatoes in half (take seeds out with spoon or your fingers if you have gloves). Then cut tomatoes into fours.
You should cook one bushel in two halves. Take half bushel and boil them with one cup of water for 10-15 minutes.
Strain and grind tomatoes through machine (it's called a mouli legumes there, I think) - put foil on side so skins and outside of tomato do not get everywhere.
Add onion and garlic to paste and cook for 1 hour
(1 onion, 6 cloves of garlic).
Add parsley and basil and cook for another hour and half.
Add olive oil at end (1½ cups), and cook for another half hour
(3 hours total).
*Add salt to the sauce throughout to your tasting,
DO NOT PUT TOO MUCH!

Chapter Twelve

Alex was groggy the next morning, but the dread from the previous morning's scene with Eva and the sorrow she felt last night were both gone. She was going to do what Signora always told her to do when she was anxious or sad.

"Stop fretting over your life, and live it," she would say. "If I can wake up every day and face whatever life throws at me, then so can you."

Alex never quite understood the meaning of her words before now, always attributing them to Signora's old age and frail body. Signora went through so much, but she never felt sorry for herself. She was a fighter, so full of confidence and wisdom. She took everything she faced, all of her suffering, and turned it into a reason to celebrate the fact that she was still alive. How many times had she told Alex that she needed to appreciate the life she had and not dwell in all that she had lost? When Alex lamented about her mother, Signora told her to be patient, that there would come a day when the time would be right, and her mother would return to her. Hadn't Isa spent what must have felt like an eternity waiting for Roberto and Paolo to return? She didn't even know if they were alive, yet she believed.

After a shower and breakfast, Alex called over to the winery and told Maria that she would be in late today due to a personal matter. She would share her plan eventually, but for now, she wasn't one hundred percent sure of it herself. She spent over an hour on her computer trying to figure out the details. When she felt like she had everything worked out, she went to the fields to look for Nicola.

"It sure is hot today," she said when she found him inspecting one of the arbors.

His smile came easily as Nicola took the cap from his head and wiped the sweat off of his brow with his arm. "Sì, fa molto caldo."

"I know you're busy, but can we talk for a minute?"

His smile disappeared as he replaced his cap and noticed the seriousness of her voice and expression.

"Sì. Va tutto bene?"

"Sì, everything is fine. It's just…" she hesitated and wished she had something to lean on. She suddenly felt like she needed extra support. "I need to go home," she said quickly.

"Che cosa?" He looked stunned as he uttered, "What?"

"Not for good," she rushed to clarify. "I need to see my mother."

"Sì, sì, ho capito."

"I knew you would, grazie." Though she thanked him for understanding, she still felt that she needed to explain. "I need to tell her that I understand. Well, not that I do completely understand, but that I'm still here if she needs me, and that I miss her." Alex looked at Nicola and blinked back a tear.

"Mia bella, of course you do." He took her hand and looked at it, seemingly at a loss for words.

"I'll be back," she assured him. "And in time for the harvest."

He raised his gaze and looked into her eyes. "Not until then?" Alex thought she heard a catch in his voice.

"I will return as soon as I can." She squeezed his hand before pulling away and turning to go.

"When do you leave?" Nicola called to her.

Alex turned back toward him and gave him a weak smile. "Today," she told him. "I must leave today."

Nicola watched her go and felt like a case of wine had been dropped on his chest. He certainly hadn't felt this way when Eva left for the coast. It was further confirmation that he made the right decision in ending their relationship. Alex wasn't even gone yet, and he knew already that nothing was going to be the same until she came back.

Fifteen hours and two planes later, Alex landed at Chicago O'Hare Airport. It was only 4:30 in the afternoon in Chicago, but it was 11:30 at night back home. She smiled at the thought—Belle Uve had become her home, and she felt like a complete foreigner in Chicago. She had debated over just taking a taxi out to her childhood home or renting a car. She finally gave in to the convenience of being able to get around on her own. She had no idea what kind of vehicles might be at the house or what kind of shape they might be in.

It was past six when she stepped out of the car in front of the house where she lived until she was eighteen. Not much had changed as far as the house went, but the bushes were overgrown, the grass was dead, and there were no flowers adorning the gardens that were once the showcase of the neighborhood. She took a deep breath and almost choked. She could almost taste the pollution in the air and already felt a longing for the clear, dry air of Belle Uve, filled with the aroma of grapes and the passing scent of olives when the breeze blew in the smells of the neighboring fields. Grabbing her bag from the back seat, she made her way to the front door. Should she knock or just walk in? She hesitated before trying the knob, but it was locked, so the choice was made for her.

Alex felt like a guest standing in front of her family home, an unwanted guest at that, and suddenly all of the misgivings she kept at bay began to assail her. Maybe she acted too hastily and made a rash decision. She was looking around as if she needed to find an escape when the door burst open. Looking much older than her years, with no makeup and wearing an old sweat suit, Annie

O'Donnell stared at her daughter as if she were a stranger. The silence was deafening, and Alex began to perspire in the heat of the August evening.

"Mom?" she said tentatively.

"Alex?" Her mother breathed her name in a way that sounded like talking was foreign to her.

"Sì. I mean yes, it's me, Alex. Mom, can I come in?"

Annie hesitated, and Alex waited, fully expecting the door to be closed on her as literally as it had been figuratively when her mother told her to leave and never come back. But after a minute, Annie simply opened the door, and Alex went in.

The house looked the same but felt like a different world than the one Alex knew and loved a long time ago. The furniture was the same as it had been when Alex left home for college, but now, the blue striped sofa was faded, and the white stripes were a dingy beige. The room was dark, the curtains closed tight, and the musty smell was overwhelming. Alex didn't smell any lingering alcohol, for which she was glad. She had always wondered....

The room grew darker when her mother closed the door, and Alex had to wait for her eyes to adjust to the dim light from the solitary lamp.

"I don't have much for dinner," her mother said as she made her way to the kitchen. It wasn't 'welcome home,' but it was a start.

Alex followed her into the slightly brighter room with the familiar Formica counters and the oak table where the four of them had shared many meals, stories of their day, and laughter; there had always been laughter. Alex ran her fingers over the grain as she stood in the room that seemed so much smaller now. She looked up to find her mother staring at her.

"You look good," Annie said. "Healthy and tan. I guess you're finally spending some time outside."

Alex grinned, "Some, yes." Her mother had always tried to steer Alex toward sports—running, swimming, field hockey, anything to get her out of the house, but Alex always had too many books to read, paintings to finish, photos to edit. Though she played tennis in high school, she gave it up for theater in college. She simply couldn't devote the time needed for both and keep up with her schoolwork.

"Good," Annie nodded. "The fresh air is good for you." She turned to the refrigerator and opened the door. "Salad?" she asked. "It's about all I've got." She peeked over the top of the door and gave Alex a weak smile.

"Salad is fine, Mom." Alex smiled back even though her stomach was growling, and she could practically taste a nice, generous bowl of linguini with pesto and sun-dried tomatoes. Tomorrow she would go shopping and make her mother a nice, hearty, Italian meal. That is, if her mother let her stay.

She watched her mother throw together two plates of salad and was grateful when she opened the cabinet and took out a fresh-looking loaf of bread.

"Toasted?" Annie asked.

Alex shook her head. "No, thanks. Do you have any olive oil?"

Annie gave her a quizzical look. "I don't know. Maybe." She began rummaging through the cabinets.

"Butter is fine. Thank you," Alex said. "But I need to use the bathroom first."

"Oh, sure. You know where it is?" Annie asked, as if Alex was a visitor.

Tears came to her eyes as Alex nodded and headed down the hall.

When she was done, she made a right and went to the room at the far end of the hall. The door was closed but unlocked. Alex imagined a sewing room or office, but what she found was the room of an eighteen-year-old girl, turquoise walls covered with artwork and photographs, framed art and photography awards on the shelves, and the teddy bear Chad won for her at a carnival when she was ten. She walked around the room and ran her fingers along the shelves and the many books that lined them. It was as if she had fallen asleep and woken up in another time. There was no dust on anything. Her mother seemed to have kept it neat and tidy and ready for her teenage daughter to return at any moment.

Backing into the hallway and closing the door, she started toward the kitchen, but she hesitated halfway down the hall. Taking a deep breath, she turned the knob and opened the next door. Not quite as decorative as her own room, Chad's room bore little resemblance to the room he lived in before moving to Philadelphia. Most of his belongings were gone, having been moved to his flat after he graduated from college and left home for good. But the furniture was the same, and some of his posters still hung on the wall. Alex walked over to his desk and picked up the framed photograph. It had been taken when they were four and ten. At an age when most boys would have been trying to get away from their little sisters, Chad treated Alex like his own little princess. He doted on her, and she looked up to him like the hero that he was.

"I still miss him every day." Annie's words cut through the silence, and Alex jumped at the sound of her mother's voice. She turned to face the woman who had cut her own daughter out of her life.

"So do I, Mom. So do I." Alex paused. Was she really ready to do this? "I miss you, too," she said, leveling her gaze at her mother and holding her stare.

"Things are different now," Annie said. Alex nodded.

"Yes they are," she agreed. "But not everything had to change."

"But it did," was all her mother said before turning and leaving the room.

Alex's shoulders slumped. She felt defeated. She was exhausted. Her back ached from the flight, her head was beginning to pound, and all she wanted was to go back to the turquoise room, shut the door, crawl under the old, multi-colored comforter, and squeeze the teddy bear to her chest. Instead, she went to the kitchen and sat in front of the plate of salad. She drank the entire glass of iced tea in one giant gulp and reached for the pitcher. It was stifling in the house. She ate the salad, glancing across the table at her mother now and then. She was relieved to see that the food was fresh, and her mother was eating, though she was much too thin and needed more than a salad for dinner each night.

Neither of them spoke, and when she was finished eating, Alex cleared her dishes and her mother's, washed them by hand, and put them away as she had become accustomed to doing. Her mother sat in silence and watched her.

"I'm going to bed, mom. Will you be here in the morning?"

"I have to be at work by ten, but I'll be here before then."

Alex was surprised that her mother had a job. She was curious but too tired to ask about it and relieved that her mother wasn't protesting Alex's stay overnight. "Goodnight then. I'll see you in the morning."

"Goodnight," Annie said. "Alex," she called, and Alex stopped and turned around in hopeful anticipation. "There are clean towels in the bathroom."

"Thanks," she mumbled before retrieving her bag and heading down the hall.

Nicola sat in the kitchen alone and ate his breakfast. The villa seemed so empty. No, it was downright lonely.

Amy Schisler

Had it always felt this way since his Nonna died? He had never noticed it before.

He washed his dishes and gazed out at the fields. Harvest was about a month away. That seemed like a very long time. The good news was that with harvest time nearing, Nicola was going to be very busy hiring the temporary workers and preparing the vats and barrels for the first round of grapes.

"Buongiorno." Maria smiled when Nicola walked into the winery.

"Is it?" he asked. "I am not feeling well today, and I have much to do. I will be in the office if you need me."

"Nicola." Maria's caring tone halted him, and he turned toward her. "She will be back."

"Will she?" he asked. "I am afraid that she does not know, that I have not told her…"

"She knows, Nicola. And yes, she will be back."

Nicola nodded and went into the office, shutting the door quietly behind him.

By three in the morning, Alex was wide awake. If she were at home, there it was again—the thought of Italy as home—if she were there, she would be checking emails, answering the phone, compiling orders. She and Nicola would have had breakfast already and discussed their plans for the day. Maria would be telling her a story about Pietro or lamenting that he was never going to propose. There were tours scheduled for that afternoon, and Alex felt bad about not being there to handle them. Nicola would do them, and he probably wouldn't even complain about it. He denied it, but Alex could tell that he enjoyed giving them. He loved Belle Uve, its selection of wines, its beautifully maintained arbors, and he loved talking about the plants, the process, and the vintage. He delighted in seeing people's reactions when they tasted the samples he poured for them, and Alex smiled as she lay in bed and remembered the way he looked at her over the glass as she took her first sip of Amarone. It may have been at that precise moment that she fell in love with him. The warmth of his brown, sparkling eyes, his smile, his quiet but enthusiastic way of describing the properties of the wine. It was hard to say which she fell in love with first—the wine or him.

Alex reached for her phone on the nightstand. She hadn't looked at it since it died on the way to her mother's, but it had restarted at some point during the night and was fully charged. After the "Welcome to the US" texts rolled in, and the messages relating to roaming costs flashed on the screen, she saw the message from Maria, *He misses you.* Alex smiled and held the phone to her heart as she closed her eyes and thought about what Maria was actually saying in those three small words. She didn't reply. Maria could read her like a book. There was no need to send the obvious, *I miss him, too.*

Alex switched on the lamp, got out of bed, and tiptoed to the closet. She pulled out a photo album, the very first one she ever put together when she was six and scrapbooking was all the rage. Settling on top of her covers, she turned the pages and looked at the faces of her family, so familiar yet unfamiliar at the same time. Who were those people? The happy, smiling faces in the professional portrait her mother had let her have, of the perfect family—a mom, dad, son, and daughter—looked out at her like the ones you see in the frames when you first buy them from the store. She always wondered if the people in those pictures were real families or just models. That's what the family in the album looked like, models of what the perfect family should look like if they actually existed. The other photos were less than amateurish, the folly of a six-year-old just learning how to use a camera and set up a shot. Heads were cut off, and the focus was off, but Alex relished each one, remembering happier times when her family was all together.

Alex went from one album to another-her elementary school years with photos of ponies and birthday parties; middle school days with awkward, metal smiles, and several firsts—first school dance, first crush, first boy who ever broke her heart; high school friends and clubs, jobs, and college acceptances. Those pictures were half in the albums and half in the boxes on the floor of the closet—abandoned for boyfriends, sleepovers, and AP homework. Before she knew it, the sun's rays were haloing around the drawn shade like the eclipse Alex had once watched with her science class. She picked herself up off the floor, to which she had migrated to go through the boxes, and stretched her arms and back. She wondered whether or not her mother was up and prayed that there was coffee in the house.

By the time the aroma of Folger's House Blend filled the kitchen and made its way down the hall like a welcome friend, Alex had managed to find some eggs and a small bit of ham which she fried on the stove.

"Ah, the smell of Heaven," her mother said from the doorway. "I didn't know you drank coffee." She slipped into the small space beside Alex and reached into the cabinet for a mug.

"There's a lot you don't know about me, Mom," Alex said quietly. "But I'd like to change that if you're willing."

Annie poured her coffee and pressed her lips together. "You seem different, more confident," Annie said.

"I've grown up, Mom. I was barely twenty the last time you saw me, only halfway through college, with absolutely no idea what I was going to do next. Now I'm almost twenty-three, not much older, I know; but I live abroad now, and I own half a vineyard. I'm helping to run a successful business, and I'm using my skills to market our products. I'm not the same person you knew." She looked at her mother. "And I don't think you are either."

"I don't know if I can go back, Alex," Annie said after a moment.

"Then let's not go back," Alex offered. "Let's go forward."

Annie didn't answer. She sipped her coffee and watched as Alex finished cooking breakfast. They ate in silence. Alex wasn't sure what more she could say, and it broke her heart when her mother rose, put her dishes in the sink, and left the room. It was all Alex could do not to run from the house in tears. She finished eating, washed the dishes, and went to her room. She stayed behind her closed door until she heard her mother leave for work and wondered why on earth she had come back.

When Annie returned from work that evening, the little house was filled with aromas of Italy. Alex prepared the same meal that she had made for Nicola and his family when she first arrived in Italy, and she even managed to find a bottle of Amarone at the local wine store. It wasn't Belle Uve, of course, but she couldn't resist buying it. She hoped that she might be able to break the ice with her mother the way she had done with the others.

Annie pushed the pasta around her plate, taking small bites here and there, and she buttered her bread even after Alex suggested she try the olive oil Alex bought at the store earlier that day. It was as if Annie purposely resisted every move Alex made. The wine left a bitter taste in Alex's mouth, not a testament to its quality, but rather a reminder that it was not the wine that Nicola had produced. Annie didn't touch her wine but drank her unsweetened tea as she nibbled at the food.

Alex was tempted to ask her mother if she liked the meal. Would it be so hard for Annie to compliment her? Alex would rather find out that her mother hated every bite than sit in silence, but both women seemed to be at a loss for words. By the time Alex finished eating, she was exhausted, both mentally and physically.

"I'm going to bed. Don't worry about the dishes. I'll clean everything in the morning. I bought groceries, so help yourself to whatever you want for breakfast. There are fresh cheeses and fruits, and I put some pastries in the cabinet."

Alex waited for Annie to reply. When she did not, Alex sighed and left the room.

Awake much too early again the following morning, Alex began going through her dresser drawers. Why had her mother kept these things? An old t-shirt from a Hilary Duff concert, an ugly sweater with a cat on it that had been a present from her father, a pair of jeans that her mother always hated because they had holes in them, but which Alex loved to wear around the house. Alex shook her head as she sorted through the clothes, abandoned when she left for school and forgotten, for good reason, when she left home for the last time. She looked around the room and decided that she would spend the day cleaning, not just in here, but throughout the whole house.

Throwing on an old t-shirt and a pair of shorts, she appraised her appearance in the mirror. What she imagined she would see was a much younger self, a throwback to her high school years. What she saw was a woman wearing child's clothing. Though she had maintained the same body, in spite of the pasta, wine, and desserts, she knew that she was not even close to being the same person. Even as she pulled her hair into a ponytail, she realized that she would never again be that girl, so unfocused and lacking in self-confidence.

Alex wasn't sure if it was her early entry into adulthood after the death of her father and rejection by her mother, the hard work and long hours she put into college, her time with Signora, the responsibility of owning a business, the months spent living in a foreign country, or falling in love with Nicola that created the woman she now was. She supposed it was a combination of all of these things. Things that she never saw happening, never felt changing her, but which were leading her on a journey she didn't even know she was taking.

She remembered a class she once took in school. She couldn't remember the name of the course, but every book they read had the same theme—*The Adventures of Huckleberry Finn, Great Expectations, The Odyssey, To Kill A Mockingbird*—all 'coming of age' books. Alex cocked her head and looked at her reflection. She hadn't saved a slave by rafting down the Mississippi. She hadn't taken care of a grieving widow during the Industrial Revolution. She had not returned from war by way of an epic adventure nor watched her father defend an innocent man being tried more for the color of his skin than for any crime he may or may not have committed. Still, Alex had lived through a lot, and every event, every tear shed, every triumph hailed, had brought her to this moment. For the first time, Alex saw herself as a capable young woman rather than a lost and scared child. Perhaps she was finally seeing what Nicola had seen all along.

Alex sipped her coffee as she watched Annie dump too much sugar to be healthy into her own mug. Annie stirred the liquid without speaking, and Alex wondered what was going through her mother's mind. Alex turned and gathered some utensils from a drawer before reaching into the cabinet for bowls and sitting them on the table. She placed fresh yogurt, sliced fruit, and pastries on the table and took a seat.

"I've been thinking about what you said yesterday," Annie said quietly as she spooned some yogurt into her bowl. "I don't know if I know how to move forward. I seem to be, stuck, I suppose. I don't know where to go from here, but I can't find a way to stay behind, to go back to a time when we were all together." She looked at Alex, truly looked at her, for the first time since Alex arrived.

"You have a job," Alex said. "You must have found a way to make that happen."

"It's not much. I'm just a salesclerk at a shop in town. My therapist found it for me, to be honest. She said it would be good for me. I guess so. At least it gets me out of here for a few hours each day." Annie looked around, and Alex followed her gaze. Everywhere she looked, she saw Chad and her father. It must have been ten times worse for her mother, living with their ghosts all of these years.

"It's a step," Alex said.

"Yes, that's what my therapist said. She said I just have to take one step at a time until I'm not thinking about how to walk anymore."

Alex thought about that, about the comparison to being paralyzed and learning to walk again. She supposed that's what her mother had been—paralyzed. Maybe not physically, but certainly mentally.

"So where are you with your steps?" Alex asked.

Annie looked puzzled. "What do you mean?"

"How far have you come? Are you far enough to be a mom again?" Alex didn't mean for it to sound cruel, and she hoped that her mother would hear pain in her voice rather than anger.

"I, I don't know," Annie whispered. "I'm, it's not that I don't want to." She looked pleadingly at Alex.

"Okay," Alex said, "but can you at least think about it?"

Annie nodded. She stuck the spoon into the half-eaten bowl of yogurt and stood. "I'll try," was all she said before leaving the room to get ready for work.

After her mother left, Alex took down all of the curtains in the house. She washed and rehung them and was happy to see that it made a noticeable difference in every room. While they cycled through the wash, she scrubbed the walls and the floors and cleaned the windows. Before she knew it, her mother was home.

Annie stood in the living room and looked around. "It's awfully bright in here, don't you think?"

Alex tried to see what her mother saw-freshly washed curtains, clean floors and windows, the trash taken out, and the furniture dusted off. Alex had left the curtains open so that the sun shone in, and even without the lamp on, the room sparkled with light.

"I figured I should help out while you're at work. I'm sure you don't have time to."

"Are you saying I can't take care of my own house?"

"Of course not." Alex swallowed and closed her eyes.

Memories of being fifteen and clashing with her mother came flowing back, and Alex had to remind herself that she was an adult now and not a teenager with an attitude. She took a deep breath and laid out the argument she had rehearsed. "I always had chores when I lived here as a child. Why should it be any different now? With you at work, I might as well earn my keep. Is there something else you'd like me to do?" Alex squeezed her lips between her teeth and hoped that her mother wasn't about to kick her out. Again.

"Well." Annie paused. "I suppose it does feel better in here. If you really want to keep going, I'm okay with it."

Alex tried not to smile too broadly or seem too relieved. She felt like Galileo must have felt when he discovered the moons of Jupiter. A major breakthrough had just taken place.

The next morning, Alex decided to try a new approach. "I've been thinking," she began. She noticed the way her mother stiffened, and she had to push herself to keep going. "I understand that you're not quite ready to be a mom again. So I've been thinking—what about being a friend?" Alex offered. "With no pressure or strings. Can we start there?"

Annie pressed her lips together, and it occurred to Alex for the first time that they both shared this habit. She watched her mother bring her coffee mug to her tight lips and hold it there. The steam rose from the cup, leaving behind its warm, moist presence on her upper lip in the form of small beads of condensation.

"Maybe," she said, and then smiled a small, shy smile like a toddler meeting a distant relative for the first time. "Yes, I think I would like to try being friends."

An hour later, Annie appeared in the kitchen doorway, freshly showered and dressed. Alex noticed that her mother wore another cute, up-to-date outfit and asked about her new wardrobe, a far cry from the sweats Alex had found her in when she first arrived.

"It's from work. I get a discount." And then, after a moment, she added. "You could come by today, if you're not busy."

"I'd love to," Alex said, careful not to let her exuberance show too much. They were still in the 'new friend phase,' after all.

"Okay, then," her mother said. "I'll see you later. You know how to get there?"

"You told me the name, so I can find it," Alex assured her.

"Okay, then," Annie said again. "I'm off to work." She smiled and reached into the hall closet. For the first time since being home, Alex noticed her mother's purse, a beautiful leather bag that was stamped 'Made in Italy.'

Alex looked from the purse to her mother's face. "It's a present," Annie said with that same, shy smile. "From a friend."

Before the end of the day, Alex went into the little suburban town to see her mother's place of work. The boutique was adorable, filled with designer clothes of which Alex couldn't even imagine the cost. It was one of those places where there were no price tags, and Alex was astonished that her mother could afford the clothes, even at a discount. She suddenly felt a ripple of pride go through her. It had taken several years, but Annie was slowly returning to the woman Alex had known and loved. She prayed that their 'friendship' would last and would grow into something deeper. Alex longed to have her mother back in her life more than she had ever realized.

Over the course of that week, Alex's body adjusted to the time change, but her heart was not adjusting to being away from Nicola. She thought about him every minute of every day. She wondered if he was thinking about her, or if his life had resumed as normal, just like she'd never been there. What worried her the most was whether or not he had seen Eva since she'd been gone. But every morning, she awoke to a text from Maria reminding her that Nicola missed her, was asking about her, and was wondering when she was coming home. He hadn't made any attempt to contact her personally, but Maria let her know that her presence was still being felt and that he was looking forward to her coming 'home.'

Later that week, Alex did some poking around in her mother's desk and discovered bank statements that sent her reeling. Chad had left his mother a software patent as well, and the amount of money she made in the sale was staggering. Give your house to charity, buy a whole new wardrobe, and live the rest of your life bouncing from one cruise ship to another kind of staggering. No wonder her mother could afford the fancy clothes. Alex looked around the house with its outdated furniture and the old-fashioned box television set and marveled at the fact that her mother was quite a wealthy woman.

"Well, good for her," Alex said out loud. "Good for her," she repeated and meant it. Obviously Annie wasn't running around spending the money like an overzealous lottery winner, but she would be able to purchase nice clothes for work even if she did spend all of her free time in worn out sweats, and she would be comfortable for the rest of her life.

"Speaking of comfort," Alex said. "Let's see what I can whip up for dinner." She stopped and looked in the mirror over her mother's dresser. "And is it bad that I'm now talking to myself?" she asked her reflection. At least she didn't wait around for a reply.

By the time Sunday rolled around, Alex and Annie were more comfortable with each other, and Annie seemed to be okay with the small changes Alex was making around the house—new pillows for the old sofa, new rugs at the doors, flowers on the front porch and back deck, and the bushes trimmed to a reasonable size.

"Mom, do you want to go to church?" Alex asked that morning when the aroma of coffee lured Annie to the kitchen. Annie stopped in her tracks, a look of horror crossed her face.

"Church?"

Alex recognized the signs of a panic attack about to occur. She had suffered through her fair share throughout her high school and college years.

"Mom, it's okay. I'm just asking because I'm going this morning and thought perhaps... You don't have to go. I just thought that if you were going, we could go together."

"It's just that... your father... I haven't gone since..."

...*the funeral,* Alex mentally finished the sentence. "It's fine. I'm going to go, but you can stay here."

"Thank you," Annie whispered. "Someday..." Alex nodded. She was nervous herself. She hadn't been to their parish church since that day either.

As she sat alone in the pew, Alex looked around at the building, a late 1990s style church with white walls and clear glass windows. There was stained glass above the altar, but the church, though nice, was quite bare compared to Our Lady of the Roses. Alex glanced at her watch. It was four in the afternoon at home. She wondered which house the family was gathered at today, was there a soccer game on, was Pietro there, was Eva? Alex stood for the entrance song and tried not to picture Eva at the dinner table.

When the phone rang that evening, Nicola couldn't answer it fast enough.

"Ciao," he said and then felt a guilty letdown.

"Not her," his mother said. "No word?"

"No, nothing. I do not think she is coming back." Nicola walked to the sofa, their sofa, and sat down on the too-large-for-one-person cushion.

"She said she was coming back, Nicola, and it has only been one week."

"One week?" He looked over his shoulder through the window where only his car sat in the driveway. Certainly it had been longer.

"What does Maria say?"

"That she misses me but that her mother is doing better, and she needs to stay longer."

"Ah," his mother said. "Perhaps you should call."

"I do not want to be a nuisance. She wanted time with her mother, so I must wait for her to want to come back to..." He looked around the lonely villa, the one place he had always felt content and at home.

"To you," his mother said.

"Si," he admitted. "To me."

When they ended their call, Nicola picked up the journal and held it in his hands. He smiled as he ran his fingers along the leather front.

"Prozia Isa, you did know me, more than I imagined."

His cell rang again, and Nicola picked up the phone although he didn't recognize the number.

"Ciao."

"Ciao," said the most beautiful voice he had ever heard. "How's my vineyard doing?"

Nicola laughed, "Your vineyard? I think *il nostro vigneto.*"

"Sì." She laughed. "It is our vineyard." The line went quiet for a few seconds, and Nicola feared the call had been dropped.

"Alex?" He panicked.

"Sì, Nicola, sono qui."

No, you are not here, you are there.

"Allora, I thought the cell...How are you, mia bella?"

"How are you, mia bella?" They were the most beautiful words in the Italian language.

"I'm well, Nicola, but I miss home." *And you.*

"When are you coming home?" Alex smiled at the affection in his voice, or was it her imagination?

"Soon, I promise. My mother is doing well. In fact," she smiled, "we are both doing well, together."

"Oh, Alessandra, I am happy to hear the news."

Alessandra. It was the first time Nicola had used the Italian form of her name, and the sound of it on his lips was like a choir of angels to her ears.

"One week, Nicola, and then I will be home."

"One week, Alessandra, until we see each other again."

"Sì, Nicola, but I must go."

"So soon?"

She both loved and hated the sadness in his voice.

"Sì, but one week more. Ciao."

"Ciao, mia bella."

The call was short, but it was all she needed to make it through another week.

Over the next several days, Alex stayed busy by cleaning out closets and drawers. Annie was surprisingly receptive to the idea of decluttering once Alex had gotten started, and Alex was happy to help her mother make the transition back to the realm of the living. While keeping herself busy in the States, Alex's heart and mind often crossed the Atlantic, her thoughts always taking her to Italy. If she closed her eyes, she could hear the sound of the summer breeze as it swept through the leaves, smell the fragrance of the grapes, and feel the warm sun as it shined down on the field as she and Nicola walked hand-in-hand, feeding each other a grape here and there. She and Nicola began calling each other every other day, for just a few minutes at a time, and Alex could feel the miles between them, both elongating and melting away at the same time.

The week was nearing its end when Alex's cell phone rang. Smiling as she reached for the phone, she expected Nicola to wish her a good morning. Instead, she heard Maria's frantic voice.

"Alex, grazie a Dio." Alex's heart skipped a beat, and she clutched the phone tightly.

"Maria, cosa c'è?" Alex asked what was wrong as a sudden panic gripped her.

"È Nicola. È ferito. Era sul tetto e lui è caduto. Siamo all'ospedale."

Alex tried desperately to understand, but Maria was speaking so fast, and many of the words were ones that Alex did not know. As Maria continued to talk at a breakneck pace, Alex's mind swarmed with possibilities. All that she knew was that something was wrong with Nicola.

"Maria, prega, slow down. Non capisco."

Annie walked into the room and sat down on the couch next to where Alex had unconsciously collapsed. She reached for her daughter's hand and tried to follow the conversation that floated back and forth between English and Italian.

"Sto arrivando." Alex promised to head home and ended the call. Her eyes filled with tears.

"What is it?" Annie's eyes and voice showed her concern.

Alex shook her head. "I don't know any details, but Nicola is hurt. I think Maria said he fell off of the roof." She furrowed her brow in confusion. "She was talking so fast, and my Italian is still pretty lame. I had to keep asking her to slow down and to say it in English, but she was having a hard time finding the right words." Alex turned to look at her mother and grasped both of her hands. "I need to go."

Annie nodded. "Of course you do." She squeezed her daughter's hands and offered a feeble smile. "You love him," Annie said quietly.

The tears fell in a steady stream from Alex's eyes as she nodded. "I do," she admitted, and for the first time in many years, Alex's mother pulled her into a warm and comforting embrace. Annie smoothed Alex's hair and gently shushed her cries. After a few minutes, Alex pulled away and gave her mother a weak smile.

"I'll help you pack," Annie offered as she stood and pulled Alex up from the couch. She wrapped her arms around her daughter in the loving embrace that Alex had missed so much.

"Thank you," Alex whispered. "For everything."

Chapter Thirteen

After a tearful call to her mother to say another goodbye, Alex boarded her plane. It was bad enough that her mind and heart were a jumble of irrational thoughts and tear-provoking emotions; but in addition, the turbulence on her trans-Atlantic flight was a series of jarring dips and turns that left her stomach in knots and her head pounding. The storm that seemed to hold the plane in its grasp for the entire last part of the flight also slowed down its descent and made its landing the stuff of which daredevils can only dream.

Nearly missing her connection in Frankfurt, Alex ran through the concourse and yelled for the attendant to hold the door at the gate. Once in her seat, she reached for the inhaler that she hadn't used in ages and calmed her exercise-induced asthma before the plane alighted back into the dark cloud from which Alex had just descended.

Several hours later, Alex stood by the conveyer belt in baggage claim, impatiently tapping her foot and continuously glancing at her phone for updates. There were none. Was Nicola okay? Awake? Mildly hurt or seriously hurt? Critically? No, she couldn't go there.

After what seemed like an eternity, she spotted her suitcase slide down onto the turnabout. She grabbed the bag and heaved it up and onto the floor. Without pausing, she pulled up the extendable handle and raced for the door. Thankfully, she still had the presence of mind to locate her car, but only because she snapped a photo of the space and aisle numbers before she left.

Alex followed the directions on her phone app and made it to the hospital in Verona in less than the fifteen minutes that the GPS originally calculated. She swung into a spot and sprinted into the building. Thankfully, Maria had received her text and was waiting in the lobby. The two women embraced.

"What happened?" Alex searched Maria's face for clues about Nicola's condition.

"E' stata rapida. Era sul tetto, e poi e' scivolato,"

"Maria, please, I've been gone for almost two weeks, and you're speaking so fast."

"May I help?" A nurse with a British accent came toward them.

"Yes, please," Alex implored. "My, uh—"

"Her boyfriend, my cousin," Maria managed to say.

Alex blushed, but there was not time to explain. "Sì. I mean yes, I mean Nicola Giordano, can you tell me what happened to him? Is he okay?"

"Let me check." The nurse went to a nearby desk and typed into the computer. "Ah, I see," she said, but Alex still didn't see. She was desperate to get answers but waited patiently for the nurse to finish reading the information.

"Okay," she looked at Alex and Maria. "Your name?"

"Alex, Alexandra O'Donnell." Alex's patience was wearing thin.

"Very good, you are on the list." The woman smiled and continued. "I am not a doctor, but I can explain what happened and how he is. Mr. Giordano apparently fell from a roof at a vineyard." Maria nodded in agreement. "He sustained multiple rib fractures, a broken leg and arm, and has a concussion. He is heavily sedated." The nurse looked up, and Alex feared that she was going to tell them to go home, but her expression softened. "Of course, you may go see him, but he probably won't know you are there."

"He will know," Alex said, feeling confident that Nicola would somehow feel her presence. The nurse nodded.

"I'm Jacqueline, and don't worry. It looks like he's going to be fine. I'll take you to him." Alex thanked her and followed her closely through the double doors that led into the cavernous bowels of the hospital.

When they came to a stop outside of the room, Alex looked through the glass window at the unrecognizable man lying in the bed. His face was barely visible behind the oxygen tube, and his head was wrapped in white gauze. One arm was raised into the air in a sling that hung from the ceiling. A leg in a white cast peeked out from the blanket and rested in a similar sling. Tears welled up in Alex's eyes, and Maria put her arms around her friend. Sensing their presence, Marta turned toward the window and stood from the chair.

"Can he breathe?" Alex managed to choke out the question.

"Yes, but he is in a lot of pain, and we need to be careful that the ribs don't puncture anything. The oxygen helps him breathe easier," Jacqueline said quietly.

Marta closed the door behind her and wrapped Alex in a warm embrace.

"I came as soon as Maria called."

"I knew you would. He needs you." Marta turned back toward the window, and Alex followed her gaze.

"You can go in if you want to." Jacqueline touched Alex's shoulder.

"Si, go in," Marta said, releasing Alex and moving away from the door.

Alex carefully opened the door and tiptoed into the room. She hesitated by the foot of the bed, the beeping and pulsing of the machines causing her heart to skip a beat. Slowly, she moved to the side of the bed and gently took his hand in hers. The bandages around his chest and torso stopped below his collarbone, and his arms were bare.

"Nicola, it's Alex," she whispered and hoped for a reaction, a flicker of an eyelid, the twitch of his hand, but Nicola remained still. Alex wiped away a tear with her other hand and sniffed. She let go of his hand just long enough to settle in the chair and drop her purse onto the floor as she sat down. She took his hand in both of her hands and began to pray.

Maria, Marta, and Jacqueline watched from the window.

"They are very much in love?"

"Sì, sono molto innamorati," Maria said.

"Then it is good that she is here."

Maria and Marta looked at each other and nodded. It was good.

"Alex." Whether it was her softly spoken name or the gentle nudge, Alex was awakened a few hours later by Jacqueline, the nurse. Her mouth felt like cotton, her neck and back were sore from leaning over in the chair with her face on her hand, and the imprint of her knuckles and fingers was pressed into her cheek. She blinked a few times and registered the sounds and sights of the room, of Nicola still motionless in the bed.

"I'm leaving and thought I would check on you. Visiting hours are almost over."

Alex looked at Nicola and wondered how she could leave him. His mother had gone back to the villa to rest and fix dinner, but Alex wanted to stay as long as possible.

"Thank you." She turned to the nurse and whispered with a ghost of a smile.

Jacqueline nodded and patted Alex's hand. "He's going to be fine. It looks much worse than it is."

Fighting back tears, Alex gave a quick nod and rose from the chair. She leaned toward Nicola, wishing she could find a place on his face to leave a gentle kiss. She gave his hand a squeeze and reluctantly whispered goodbye.

"I'll be back tomorrow," she promised.

As she headed back through the halls of the hospital, she saw people weeping and heard moans and cries from various rooms. She thought about Roberto and realized just how lucky they were.

Though Marta was at the villa, a feeling of loneliness hung over everything like a shroud. Alex put her purse on the chair in the front parlor and headed toward the kitchen. The house was silent. Alex expected the scent of Italian food to waft through the air when she opened the door, but the kitchen was clean and empty.

She quietly walked up the stairs and peeked into the extra bedroom, Nonno and Nonna's room, that was now used by Marta and presumably other guests. Marta was wrapped in a blanket on the bed, her steady breaths were the only sound in the house.

Alex tiptoed back down the stairs and began to hunt for something to eat. By the looks of the empty shelves in the fridge, it seemed that Nicola had not done much shopping while she was gone, and Marta must have eaten out since arriving the previous afternoon. If the circumstances had been different, Alex might have been annoyed that Marta had neglected to call or text her to bring home food, but Alex knew that Nicola's accident, right on the heels of losing his father, must have been quite a blow to the poor woman asleep upstairs. What would they all do if they had lost Nicola when he fell off of the roof of the winery?

Alex suddenly shut the door to the refrigerator and gasped. Nicola had been in the process of fixing the roof and hiring the temporary workers for the upcoming harvest. Her heart began to pound as the realization sunk in that Nicola would not be able to help, probably would not even be there to make the final decisions about staff. He wouldn't be able to do all of the things he normally did to ensure a smooth and successful harvest. What exactly did he do? This was Alex's first fall on the vineyard, and she was now in charge, and Nicola would be counting on her. She could not fail him.

She reached out and placed both hands on the refrigerator to steady herself. Of course, Maria, Luigi, and Giovanni would know what needed to be done, but were there decisions that only Nicola made? What were her responsibilities going to be now that she was the only owner of Belle Uve available to make them?

She opened the fridge back up and took out the bottle of wine she had seen moments before. Pouring herself a glass, she hunted for bread and olive oil, or anything else to stop her stomach from protesting its emptiness. She sat at the kitchen table and ate bread, a handful of olives, and a hunk of cheese. By the time she finished off the wine, it took everything in her to make the climb up the stairs, dragging her suitcase behind her, unmindful of the noise she was making. She used the bathroom and brushed her teeth, but she didn't even change out of her clothes before collapsing onto the bed and giving into exhaustion.

"Grazie mille." Alex hung up the phone in the office and breathed a sigh of relief. Marta reported that Nicola had slept peacefully through the night. There were no signs of further damage from the ribs, and the latest tests did not reveal any swelling or bleeding in the brain. He was still sedated and would probably not be taken off of the medication until later that day. She had time to focus on the vineyard. Though she wanted to be there when the doctor made his morning rounds, she knew that once Nicola woke up, he would want a report on the winery. Thankfully, Marta was there to meet with the doctor and assuage Alex's fear that there might be more damage than they had originally been told. Nicola had been able to move his hands and feet when he was brought into the hospital, his spine was intact, and his reflexes were good.

"I need to see everything that Nicola was working on before the accident." Alex walked into the front room where Maria was going over their inventory of the recently delivered bottles, labels, and cases.

"You mean, other than the roof," Maria said with a raised brow.

"Yes." Alex rolled her eyes. "Other than the roof."

Maria spent the next hour going over with Alex every aspect of Nicola' work from the past two weeks. Alex read his notes, asked questions, and made decisions that had been left unanswered. Then she walked outside to continue the needs assessment with Luigi and Giovanni. She spent most of the day tying up loose ends and handling everything that seemed most pertinent while she gave orders to Luigi and Giovanni to choose which of the applicants would be called back. There were still questions to be answered and plans to be made, but she hoped that Nicola could take care of those when he came home, even if it meant setting up a temporary office in the villa.

At 3:00, Alex told Maria that she was leaving for the hospital. She wanted to be there when Nicola woke up, and the doctor estimated that it would be close to four when he was expected to start rousing from the medicine-induced sleep. There were further tests and more x-rays to be done once he was awake, but Alex wanted to be there when he opened his eyes.

"Is he still asleep?" she asked Jacqueline as soon as she spotted her.

"He is. Ordinarily, I wouldn't know since he's not my patient, but I did check in on him a few minutes ago. I knew you would probably be in soon, and I thought it might be easier for you if I helped with any translation needs."

Alex felt an instant release of tension in her neck and shoulders. "Thank you so much. That would be wonderful."

"Is his mother still here? I didn't see her when I was up there."

"She should be. Perhaps she stepped out for lunch."

They walked toward Nicola's room and chatted idly about the weather—it was hot, of course, Verona—it was beautiful but very touristy at this time of year, and Jacqueline—she met her husband, an Italian businessman, while vacationing in the South of France.

"I'll leave you alone." Jacqueline motioned to Nicola when they reached the door to his room. "But here is my cell phone number." She handed Alex a piece of paper. "Text me when the doctor arrives or if you have any questions or need anything before then."

"Thank you." Alex took the paper and smiled at Jacqueline, hoping that the woman knew just how much it meant to Alex to have her there.

Alex walked into the room and took Nicola's hand.

"I don't know if you can hear me," she said quietly. "But I'm back. I was hoping you would open your eyes and tell me that you're glad I'm home." Alex tried to smile and keep her tone light, but her voice caught on the word 'home,' and she had to choke back her tears. Then, she felt it, a slight twitch, the smallest of movements, then the light squeeze of her hand. Or had she?

"Nicola, can you hear me?" She raised her voice just a notch louder and held her breath. A few seconds passed, and then she felt it again. There was no other sign that he was awake, but Alex knew that Nicola had just squeezed her hand.

She couldn't contain her tears as she leaned closer. "Nicola, I'm here. Can you open your eyes? Please," she begged. And then she saw the movement, the rippling of an eyelid, so subtle, but there nonetheless.

The beeping beside her increased, and Alex turned to see that Nicola's heart rate was beginning to rise. She felt a moment of panic before the doctor entered the room.

"È buono." He smiled. "Lui sì sta svegliando." Alex had no problem translating the doctor's news. Nicola was waking up.

Marta rushed into the room, a cup of espresso in her hand. "What is happening?" she asked Alex.

"I think he's waking up." Alex went to Marta and took her hand. The two women watched in anticipation as the doctor examined Nicola.

Alex let go of Marta and reached for her phone. She sent a quick text to Jacqueline as she watched the handsome doctor check Nicola's vital signs. Though Marta was there, Alex wanted to know that she fully understood everything that the doctor told them. She observed the doctor gently lift an eyelid and shine a penlight into Nicola's eyes.

When Jacqueline came in, she smiled at Alex and Marta. "Good timing," she said. "I just finished giving my patients their medication." Jacqueline turned to the doctor and explained why she was there.

"Very nice to meet you. I am Doctor Graziani," he said to Alex in a thick accent. "I can speak English, but it would be faster and easier for me to explain to Jacqueline, if that is pleasing to you."

Alex turned to Marta who nodded her head in agreement.

"Sì, por favore. Grazie," Alex said and then quickly added, "He squeezed my hand. Just now. Nicola squeezed my hand."

Dr. Graziani nodded and smiled before turning to Jacqueline. He spoke for a few minutes and then turned to Nicola and folded his hand around Nicola's hand.

"Nicola, riesci a sentirmi? Se riesci a sentirmi, spremere la mano."

Alex watched and waited, and then just as he had done with her, Nicola slowly squeezed Dr. Graziani's hand.

"Ottimo." Alex understood, "Very good."

"Nicola, sì può aprire gli occhi?"

Alex watched as the rippling behind Nicola's eyelids began again, both eyes this time, and held her breath in anticipation. Jacqueline took her hand, and Alex could feel the nurse holding her breath as well.

"Nicola, apri gli occhi."

It seemed so painfully slow to Alex, but she watched through tears as Nicola managed to lift his eyelids halfway. He closed them, and then opened them again and blinked twice.

"Bentornato." Dr. Graziani smiled as he welcomed Nicola back to awareness. "Qualcuno vorrebbe vederti."

Alex needed no prompting. Yes, she did want to see him, as Doctor Graziani told Nicola, but she turned toward Marta for permission. Smiling with understanding, Marta motioned for Alex to go to Nicola. Tears streamed down Alex's face as she took his hand and looked into his open eyes.

"Ciao," was all she managed to squeak out before wiping away her tears with her free hand and beaming at Nicola.

He tried to speak and then seemed to notice the tube in his throat. For a moment, he looked panicked.

"No, no, va bene," the doctor reassured him.

Alex let go of his hand so that Dr. Graziani could move closer and speak to Nicola.

"He is explaining to him why he has the tube," Jacqueline told Alex. "Once they are sure he can breathe normally without too much pain, they will remove it. I am guessing that they will remove the tube from his mouth and use nasal tubes. They will be much more comfortable." Alex nodded. "He is telling Nicola that he will be taken for some tests and that it might hurt, but that they need to assess his injuries."

Dr. Graziani pushed the call button on the wall above Nicola and turned and spoke to Jacqueline.

"You are welcome to wait here," Jacqueline said as a nurse came in and began unhooking some of the machines.

Nicola reached out from the blanket, and instinctively, Alex went to his side and took hold of his hand. Marta followed her.

"We will be here when you come back," Alex told him. Nicola looked from her to his mother and gave a slight nod before being pulled away and letting go.

When he returned to his room thirty minutes later, his face was pale, and his breathing was heavy.

"Lui è nel dolore." The nurse let them know that Nicola was in pain before she began hooking him back up to the machines. A second nurse entered the room and gave him dose of pain medication through his IV.

"Dormirà," the nurse told them, and the women knew they had only minutes before the medication would take effect. Marta leaned over her son and kissed his forehead before telling him goodnight. Alex then went to his side and took his hand. Holding it between her palms, she kissed the tips of his fingers.

"Andare a dormire, il mio amore." "Goodnight, my love."

Nicola closed his eyes and went to sleep.

Early the following morning, Alex and Marta walked, arm in arm, out to Marta's car.

"Are you sure, Marta? It's your house, and Nicola is your son. You are more than welcome to stay longer."

"Grazie, Alex, I know that I am welcome in your home." Alex's heart did a flip at the sound of Marta's words and her acknowledgement that the villa, and all that came with it, was more than just a house to Alex.

"Nicola is improving, and he is in good hands. I must return to Firenze. I have only been working at the Uffizi for a week, and I must not let them replace me so soon." Marta smiled at Alex and embraced her tightly before kissing her on each cheek. Alex knew how excited Marta was about her new job at the iconic museum, and she couldn't imagine how torn she must have been to have to choose between her job and her child. "Take care of our Nicola."

Alex's eyes misted as she answered, "I will. Please tell him that I will be in to see him later."

Marta nodded and hugged her, pulling her into a tight embrace.

Alex watched as Marta drove down the driveway and was grateful for Marta, for her friendship, for Marta's knowing, even before Alex knew, that her love for Nicola was strong and true. Though neither woman mentioned it, and Nicola and Alex had yet to profess it, Alex was sure that all parties involved could see what Signora had seen all along.

Chapter Fourteen

Alex was at the hospital before Dr. Graziani arrived. She wanted to fill Nicola in on what was happening at the vineyard, if he was able to stay awake, and she had several questions for him.

"Buongiorno, Nicola." Alex smiled brightly when she saw Nicola awake and without the tube in his mouth. Smaller oxygen tubes rested in his nostrils and curled around his head.

"Mia bella," Nicola said, his voice hoarse but his smile wide. "You just missed Mamma."

"Sì. I waited so that you could have some time alone." She hesitated before leaning in to kiss him lightly on the cheek, careful not to touch his bandaged chest.

"Only one side?" Nicola teased.

Alex felt a light blush rise onto her cheeks. "Yes, unless you want to set back the healing of a rib or two," she admonished. "How are you feeling?"

"You are a lady. I cannot say in front of you." He winced as he tried to get more comfortable.

"Well enough to answer some questions?" She held up some of the paperwork he was working on before he fell.

"Sì. It will feel good to do some work."

Before they could get started, Dr. Graziani arrived.

"Buongiorno, Nicola, Alex. Come stai oggi?"

Nicola told the doctor how he was feeling, where his pain seemed to be the most intense, and how he slept the previous night. The doctor checked his vitals and examined his injuries as best he could through the wrappings and casts.

"Ciò mi rallegra," he said to Nicola before turning to Alex. "I am pleased. His progress is good. A few more days, and I think he will go home."

"Grazie mille, Dottore." Alex smiled.

"I want to do one more tomografia computerizzata," he looked at Nicola for help.

"The scan for the brain?" Nicola asked Alex.

"Sì, a CAT scan."

"Sì, sì, e CAT scan. Grazie. After that, we will know for certain how long until he will leave. Questions?"

Alex wasn't sure what to ask, but Nicola spoke quickly, "Quando posso tornare al lavoro?"

"No work for a while." Dr. Graziani looked at Alex. "He will be hard to keep in bed." Alex blushed at his words, though she knew that he was referring to the vineyard. The ulterior implication was not lost on Nicola who laughed loudly and winced as he grabbed his chest and closed his eyes in pain.

Alex managed to hide the extent of her embarrassment. "I will keep him in bed." The blush rose higher in her cheeks as she realized that she had blurted out the words without thinking. "I mean, I will make sure he doesn't get up." *This just seems to be getting worse.* She sighed. "He will follow your orders."

Dr. Graziani laughed and winked at Nicola. "Allora. I will return tomorrow. Ciao."

When the doctor was gone, Alex buried her face in her hands. "Oh my gosh, that was embarrassing."

"You are a beautiful woman. It makes it hard for a man to not think about such things."

"Well, you better be able to think about something else. I have a lot of things to learn and a short time to learn them."

"I can teach you anything and everything," Nicola teased, his meaning not lost on Alex.

"The vineyard, Nicola, the vineyard." *Yes, I'm sure you can, I am quite sure you can.*

For the next hour, Alex asked questions and made suggestions until she saw Nicola's pain level increasing. She pushed the call button, and a nurse promptly appeared. It wasn't long before the medication began to kick in, and Alex knew that it was time to leave.

"Domani?" he asked quietly as his eyes closed.

"Sì, tomorrow." Alex said as she kissed him goodbye.

When the workday was through, Alex decided that she couldn't wait until the following day to see Nicola again. She was pleasantly surprised when she walked through the door and found him propped up in bed, changing channels on the television in the room. His eyes lit up when he saw her.

"Mia bella, you are back."

"I had an idea," Alex said after kissing his cheek and taking a seat in the chair. She held up the journal and spoke before he could protest. "I know, you're not allowed to read. I've had a concussion before." She rolled her eyes. "Please don't ask me about how it happened, though."

"Now I must know." She loved the way his eyes twinkled when he teased her.

"Not gonna happen. Now, when I was home, I learned about this cool app." She fished through her purse for her phone. "It translates using the camera on the phone. It's not perfect, but I bet it's close enough that I can figure it out. There," she said when she found the phone and activated it. "Let me just open it. I downloaded it at the villa before I came over. Okay, it's ready. Let's see how well it works." She opened the journal to the bookmarked page where they left off weeks prior and held the phone over the page. "It's focusing…now translating…hold on. Okay, here it is." She looked up triumphantly and found Nicola staring at her.

"You always amaze me."

"Sometimes I amaze myself." She smiled and looked at the small screen. "I think I should bring my iPad next time, or I'll be the one suffering with headaches."

June 4, 1943

It is a miracle. Roberto's infections are getting better, and his wounds are healing. Dr. Romano says he could relapse, but for now, he is alive. I went back today, though I did not want to. I did not want to see him like that again, with death beckoning for him. I am so glad I went. His color was better, and death did not seem to be lurking. But he was still in great pain, and I fear that his wounds may be too deep to fully heal—the wounds of both his body and mind. His mother says he cries in his sleep and that nightmares plague him day and night. She said that he called my name last night, and she couldn't tell if he was asking for me or just dreaming. Papà is letting me visit after school instead of going home to help Mamma. I am grateful.

"Wow," Alex exhaled. "Talk about history repeating itself."

"Sì, but I am not battling death or wounds that will not heal."

"Thank God for that."

"Did you, were you, when you heard…"

"I was scared to death." She reached for his hand. "Don't ever do anything like this to me again."

"Sì, promesso."

June 6, 1943

I do not do anything to help Roberto. I just sit and hold his hand. I talk to him and read to him, but I do not know if he even knows that I am there. Sometimes, I think he squeezes my hand, but maybe I imagine it. Dr. Romano says I am doing all that I can, and that it is helping. I pray he is right. He is going to lessen the pain medication soon. I pray that Roberto does not suffer

*greatly. His lesions are much better, and the swelling is gone from
his face, but the skin that is gone will take much time to grow
back. The bandages will stay for some time. He looks almost like
my Roberto, but in his mind, I do not know. We will know when
the medicine is gone.*

June 8, 1943

*Roberto is awake! He is still in pain, but he is healing, and
his mind is good. When the pain is too much, he is able to take a
little medicine, but Dr. Romano wants him to not use it so much.
He believes that too much medicine will be harmful. I know that
he is right, but I do not like seeing Roberto in pain. I would bear
it for him if I could. Today, I was there when Dr. Romano
unwrapped what is left of his hands and feet. I had to run to the
toilet where I left behind all that I ate today. I was embarrassed.
Roberto is the one who suffers, and I cannot even look upon his
missing fingers and toes without being sick. When I returned, he
was crying. When he looked at me, I saw that it was not only pain
but longing that made him weep. Longing for what we might have
had. Will we ever be able to have a normal life together? I fear the
answer.*

"Will you get sick when they remove the casts from
my arm and leg?"

"I don't know. Do you have all your fingers and
toes?"

Nicola wiggled the fingers that were suspended
above him. "I think I feel all five. How about my toes?"

"You're terrible, you know. I'm pretty sure even if you had lost them, you'd still feel them. I think that takes a while to go away."

"Sì, I have heard that, so perhaps I am wrong. Do you want to check to see if I am all here?" The look he gave her let her know that he was talking about more than the appendages on his arm and leg.

"I should stop reading right now and go home. I don't know if you deserve the company. What do they have you on anyway? You have never acted like this before."

"When a beautiful woman flies around the world to see if you are still alive, it makes you want to do things with that woman." He smiled. "Things that would make you blush."

Alex was already blushing, in more than one place she believed. "Nicola, if you don't behave, I will have to leave. I may even get a judge to declare you incompetent so that I can take over the vineyard."

"Aha! I knew that was your plan all along."

"Maybe so. I am certainly the one with the upper hand right now."

"A judge would not agree. He would look at you and know that I am under a spell. He would side with me."

"Nicola, are you going to behave or not?"

"For now, bella, for now. How about one more reading before visiting hours end?"

June 12, 1943

Today, we learned that the island of Pantelleria fell to the American soldiers. They are in Italy. I am afraid. We could not trust the Germans, our allies, and we could not trust the Russians. I will never forgive them for what they did to Roberto. Though Papà says we can trust the Americans, how can I know that he is right? Will they, too, try to take our lands and beat our soldiers? Will we all be prisoners of war?

"That was short, but you look tired," Alex observed. "Shall we stop for tonight?"

"I am afraid so."

Alex closed the journal and put away her phone.

"I'll be back tomorrow, but probably not until the afternoon. We only have two weeks left until harvest."

"Maybe," Nicola reminded her. "Check the grapes every day. Do not let them get too ripe."

"Sì, I know. Don't worry. We all know what to do." She kissed his cheek and started to leave, but his hand wrapped around her and pulled her back down close to his face.

"I will not be in this bed forever." His breath on her cheek was warm and moist, and his eyes were filled with passion. Alex could not speak. She swallowed and nodded slowly. Nicola smiled and closed his eyes. "Buona notte, mia bella."

She gazed at him, and a smile played at her lips. That was some medicine they had him on. "Buona notte," she whispered.

"Be careful, take it slow." Alex tried not to hold too tightly to his torso as she helped Nicola out of the car. Luigi held the wheelchair while Giovanni and Alex eased Nicola down into the seat. It was not easy to maneuver a grown man with casts on one arm and one leg and several healing rib fractures out of a car and into a chair. All four of them were panting and sweating by the time Nicola was settled. He looked at the ramp that his cousins had built so that he could get to the villa.

"This is how you spent your time when there is work to be done for the harvest." Nicola looked away in disgust. Luigi and Giovanni shrugged it off, knowing that his annoyance was aimed at himself and not at them.

"Let's get him inside," Alex told them. She led them into the house, holding open the door and making sure there was nothing in the way.

Nicola assessed his temporary living arrangements. The sofa had been moved into the barn, and a twin bed sat in its place. The room was rearranged so that the television was visible from the bed, and some of Nicola's personal items had been moved into the room. There was one chair next to the bed, presumably for Alex or any visitors who stopped by to see him. Alex watched Nicola ball his hand into a fist up a couple of times as he tried to maintain his calm.

"Your computer is on the kitchen table. We can move it into the parlor any time you want to do work, so you can sit and watch calcio to your heart's content."

Nicola did not smile back at Alex, and his eyes clouded over. She watched him swallow hard and noticed a vein throbbing in his temple. He fisted his hand again.

"Andiamo, here we go," Luigi said, and Nicola braced himself as Luigi and Giovanni lifted him onto the bed. Alex had tried to replicate the height of the pillows that were on the hospital bed so that Nicola could sit at the angle that seemed most comfortable.

"Can I get you anything?" she offered. Nicola shook his head and looked away.

Luigi and Giovanni made a hasty exit, and Alex took a seat in the chair.

"Look, I realize this is not ideal and that you're concerned about the harvest and wine making, but everything is under control. Aren't you the one who trained your cousins? Don't you trust that you taught them well?"

Nicola looked at Alex for a moment and then sighed. "I am useless. I should be helping."

"You are not useless. Believe me, I am going to put you to work any way I can find. They might all know what they're doing, but I'm flying blind here. I've worked my butt off over the past week trying to get up to speed on what needs to be done, and I can tell you that we can handle this, but I'm going to need you to remind me of that every day. Tell me what I'm doing wrong or forgetting, keep me in line. I won't be able to make this happen without you. So don't get any ideas about wallowing in self-pity and checking out on us. You're going to work just as hard from this bed as you would in those fields. Do you understand me?"

Nicola turned back toward the window and gazed at the fields without answering.

"And another thing, Nicola Giordano." Alex took a breath and released it, pausing until he turned back to look at her. "I am not going to be your maid. I will cook, but you will feed yourself. You will let me know if you need to get up, use the toilet, whatever, but I will not be at your beck and call every time you want to turn on the TV. You will learn to take care of yourself as best you can in order to keep up your strength." Alex tried to sound tough and commanding as she repeated the instructions that Dr. Graziani gave to her even though all she wanted to do was take care of Nicola's every need.

Slowly, a sly smile crept across Nicola's face. "Will you bathe and dress me, though?"

Alex smiled. "You're incorrigible. I should call your mother and have her come stay here to bathe and dress you." She folded her arms across her chest and attempted a steely glare. Finally, Nicola laughed.

"This might be fun," he said. "We will see how tough you act when I begin to smell. You will drag me to the bath."

Alex rolled her eyes and marched from the room, concealing her smile as the color rose on her cheeks.

"The vats are clean and ready. We have them covered so that nothing gets into them." Alex sat the plate on the sick tray she had ordered online and then went back to the kitchen to get her own meal.

"This is not as good without wine," Nicola said as he tasted the pasta.

"Hey, we haven't said grace yet, and you can complain all you want, but until you're off of the pain meds, you get no wine."

After asking for God's blessing and mercy, they ate and talked about what else needed to be done within the next couple of weeks.

When they were through, Alex cleared the dishes and washed them quickly before resettling in the chair.

"I think I am feeling less pain tonight," Nicola said as she opened the journal.

"That's great," Alex said. "Dr. Graziani will be pleased."

"I think you can sit with me." He smiled and raised his brow while patting the bed with his good hand.

"Nicola, you have only been home for three days. Dr. Graziani said it will take six weeks for your ribs to heal."

"I do not want you to sit on me, but beside me." The look he gave her was akin to the way a puppy looks at his master at dinner time.

"Fine, but if you so much as wince, I'm moving." Alex moved to the bed and stretched out beside Nicola. She had to admit that this was much better than sitting on the chair.

"You've been on medicine for over a week now. Some nights, you've been asleep before I've finished reading. Would you like me to recap?"

"Recap?"

"Refresh your memory. How did you live in America and never hear the word recap?" Alex opened the journal and skimmed the pages. "It is now July of 1943. Roberto is healing. Isa graduated and spends her days tending to Roberto so that his mother can take care of his younger brothers and sisters and do her housework. The Allies have bombed and begun invading Italy, and Isa worries that they will kill Roberto for being a soldier. Paolo is still missing and presumed dead, though we know that if he were dead, you wouldn't be here."

"This is true," Nicola said, trying to concentrate with the smell of Alex's freshly washed hair so close to his face.

"Isa continues to relay messages to and from her father and battles her own frustration over taking care of Roberto and becoming more involved in the Resistance. Mussolini is growing weaker, but only those in the Italian government and the Resistance know how vulnerable he has become. That brings us to the next entry."

July 20, 1943

We hear the planes as they fly over us. The sound is not as ominous during the day, but at night, we fear that if we fall asleep, we will never awaken. Rome was bombed last night. I have always wanted to visit there but fear that there will be nothing left by the time this war ends.

Roberto is sitting up now, and his wounds have almost healed. His face is still bandaged, but every day, he looks more like himself. His skin is soft and pale, like a baby's, and we know that it is a miracle that it has grown back at all. Though he is weak, Doctor Romano has ordered that we take walks in the morning and evening when it is not too hot. The physical exercise is good for Roberto's feet and toes. I am no longer allowed to feed him because he needs to use his hands and fingers, but it is hard to watch him struggle with such a small task. Today, he threw his bowl of soup across the kitchen. His mother and I cleaned it up and gave him more without a word, but I think that if he does it again, I am going to tell him what I think. He is alive. He must stop feeling sorry for himself and work to get better. I will have to push him because I must be the strong one now.

July 23, 1943

Palermo has been captured by the Americans and the British. All of Sicily is now in their control. The Germans are afraid and are committing unspeakable acts throughout Europe. Our leader has not been heard from in days, and speculation is wild. Papà says it is only a matter of time before his rule ends.

Roberto walked on his own today. He went all the way to the end of the drive without leaning on me. I cried with tears of joy, and he smiled for the first time in weeks. He grows stronger every day, as does our love. We do not speak of the future because the present may be all we have, and we will spend the few days we might have left together.

July 25, 1943

Papà received word today that General Badoglio has been given rule over Italy. Il Duce has been arrested. I have not seen Papà so happy in a long time, but we must be careful. We do not know what will happen next. Papà says that General Badoglio has been one of us since the beginning, since he stepped down as King Emmanuel's Chief of Staff three years ago after Il Duce formed his alliance with the Führer. The command of troops has been returned to King Emmanuel, and all over Italy, people rejoice. We feasted tonight on meat from Signor Lombardi, and Papà raised his glass in a toast to Badoglio. Now we wait to see what happens next.

July 26, 1943

Today, on the feast of our patron, St. Valens, Doctor Romano told us that Roberto will never be able to have children. The damage from the beatings is too bad, and he will have medical problems for the rest of his life. Roberto pushed me away when I tried to comfort him. Why does he not understand that I need his comfort as much as I know he needs mine? I am afraid that he will refuse to see me, that he will feel like he is robbing me of something. Why does he not know that all I need is him? I ache for the loss of bearing his children, but I refuse to stop loving him. I tell myself that all this means is that we will only have more love to share with each other.

There is no festival today, only prayers to be held at sundown. Alas, I cannot even find the will to pray.

Chapter Fifteen

"The roof is finished," Alex told Nicola when she went to make his lunch.

"At last. I fell weeks ago."

"Nicola, you know we had a lot of catching up to do," she said from the kitchen. "We're doing the best we can, but the roof could wait."

Nicola scowled at her as she handed him the gnocchi soup made with sausage and spinach. "Soup is winter food. I am tired of soup."

"But Adrianna made it, and it's easy to heat up when I need to get back to work." Alex sat in the chair and blew on her soup before sipping it from her spoon. "Tomorrow, we'll begin picking grapes for the pied de cuvée. The yeast tank is ready, and Luigi and Giovanni have already chosen the area where we will start picking. I'm actually excited. I've used yeast but I never knew how it was actually cultivated and can't wait to be a part of the process. I'm amazed every day by the new things I am learning." Alex held her hand out in front of her and turned it from front to back. "Alas, it won't be much longer that my hands will be this color. Soon, they will be tinged with purple." She smiled at Nicola who was intently watching her, his scowl replaced by...something unreadable. "What?"

"I do not think you have ever looked so beautiful."
The teasing and playfulness that he had displayed over
the past few weeks was gone, replaced by an
affectionately serious tone and expression.

"Are you crazy?" Her hair was tied back in a
ponytail, and grape juice stained her clothes. There was
dirt on her cheek and forehead, and she could feel the
sweat pooling in places she didn't know she could sweat.

"I know that you are part owner of Belle Uve, but
you are doing more than you thought you would be
doing for your first harvest. You have learned so much
so quickly. You are not the girl who arrived here in
June."

Alex smiled and looked down at her soup. "What am
I supposed to do? I can't let the vineyard fail. It's our
future." She looked back up at Nicola, and their eyes
met. Alex felt a stir below her groin, and she marveled at
how just a simple look from him could send heat
through her body.

Nicola put his spoon down on the tray without
taking his eyes off of her. He licked his lips, and Alex felt
her body growing weaker. "Alex, I…" He faltered.
"Thank you. For taking care of me, of the vineyard, the
villa. I do not know what I would do without you."

"It's nothing." Alex dismissed his thanks and hastily
spooned soup into her mouth. There was not time to be
sentimental, and she needed to concentrate on work.
"I'm full. Are you finished with your soup?" She looked
back at Nicola. His bowl was still full.

Nicola looked down at his lunch. "No, I am not finished."

"Allora. I'll be back later."

She stood quickly and raced from the room. Dropping her dish into the sink, she fled through the back door unwilling to explore the feelings that stirred in her or the heaviness of Nicola's gaze. With the playfulness gone, and his senses fully restored, Alex wasn't sure how he felt about her, how he truly felt about them, but she hoped and prayed that what she thought was happening between them was real. Spending the rest of the afternoon away from him would give her time to gather the confidence to find out.

It was late by the time Alex returned, almost dark. Nicola's bowl sat on the tray that he had pushed to the side of the bed. He had been dozing when Alex closed the back door and began rummaging through the refrigerator for dinner.

Nicola sat quietly and watched Alex heat up leftovers from the previous night. He could tell that she was exhausted. Several times she stopped and rubbed the back of her neck or her lower back. He knew all too well what a long day in the field under the hot sun could do, and she hadn't even begun picking grapes yet. The days would only get longer and harder. Her beautiful, soft hands will become red from the sun and, when the red grape harvest begins, spotted purple with grape juice. They will bleed and cramp. Her neck, back, and shoulders will ache from standing all day and from reaching into the vines. She will be more tired than ever before in her life. Nicola wished he could spare her the exhaustion and the pain. He had envisioned easing her into this part of the business—picking grapes some of the day but mostly being a part of the actual winemaking process. He never intended for her to do the daily labor of the harvest.

Sure, it amused him at first. He thought of all kinds of backbreaking tasks she could be assigned. After a while, his thoughts turned to whatever tasks would force her to be next to him. He wanted to share the intimacy of tasting the first grapes, seeing the sun on her hair as they greeted the morning and went to their task, side by side, and collapsing into each other's arms after dusk when the dirt and the sweat didn't matter because they were sharing the same prize. But now, she would be doing the work, and he would be lying in bed watching from the window. Would she resent him in time? Would she quit and go home with the realization that this was not the romantic wine-country life she imagined?

He continued to watch as she straightened up, took down her long hair and retied it behind her head, and splashed cold water on her face. No, she would not leave. Somehow he knew that this was the life she was meant to live, and she knew it, too. It made her stronger, more confident, happier and healthier. She was not the same girl who ran from the States looking for a new life. She had become his, and that had changed them both.

"What are you thinking?" Alex asked when she turned and saw Nicola staring at her. She smiled and curtsied. "How stunning I am in the fashion of the season, dirt and sweat?"

"Something like that," he answered and returned her smile.

"I'll make dinner as soon as I've taken a quick shower. I hope you don't mind leftovers." She busied herself, and he could tell she was nervous. She poured herself a glass of wine and, for him, a glass of iced tea. Though not something he was accustomed to drinking, he was growing used to it, so Alex made sure there was always a fresh pitcher on hand.

"That is fine. Are you too tired to read tonight?" He knew it was unfair, that she was indeed too tired, but the thought of saying goodnight and watching her go upstairs was depressing.

"Sure. I think I can manage a second wind after I shower and eat."

"Sì. Do whatever you need to do. I have not called Mamma today. I will do that while you shower."

"Good idea. She's probably trying to let you rest, but I'm sure she's dying to call every time she turns around."

"You know her well." Nicola smiled. "I will put her mind at ease."

"I'm going to take a shower. I'll be right back."

"Allora. I am not going anywhere." But he didn't want her to take her time. As soon as she left, he wanted her back.

Fifteen minutes crawled by. Nicola chatted with his mother and then watched some of the soccer game, but it did not entertain him. When Alex returned, she wore a pink nightshirt and shorts. Her hair was wet, and he knew it would smell of strawberries and vanilla. Her cheeks were rosy from the sun, but her eyes revealed her fatigue. Even so, she began making dinner without complaint.

When Alex served their food, Nicola ate his pasta while stealing looks at her. The longer he was in this bed, the more he thought about her. It wasn't that he didn't think about her before, but now, she consumed his mind. Each time she left the room, it was as if she took all of the air with her, and he struggled to breathe. The only way not to suffocate was to think about her. It was as if she gave him life with her very presence.

They ate in silence, Alex claiming she was too tired for conversation and saving her energy for reading, while Nicola was lost in his thoughts. When he was on pain medication, he could speak his mind, tease her, try to embarrass her for his own amusement; but now he was only taking Ibuprofen as needed. He couldn't say such things without wanting more, without wanting to take his teasing and turn it into passion.

After cleaning up from dinner, Alex settled beside Nicola on the bed. She reached for her iPad so that she could use her translation app and opened the journal. He closed his eyes and rested his head on the pillow as the sound of her voice filled the room.

July 29, 1943

We have been listening to the wireless. General Eisenhower of the United States has said that the Americans come in peace and that Italy is to cease all aid to Germany. In return, the Americans will "deliver you from the horrors of war." But we cannot be delivered from the horrors of our dreams. The sound of the planes overhead, the bombings, the return of our solders, barely alive, and the loss of those buried in some unknown city in unmarked graves are all things that will live on in our hearts and minds. How are we to forget? How are we to trust a new army, a new wave of invaders? I fear that the war is not ending for Italy but that it has just begun. Roberto agreed to see me today. I have cried for two days over the possible loss of his love and the loss of our future children, but he finally agreed to see me. We cried together.

August 7, 1943

The Germans are here. While the Allies continue to fight for the South, the Germans invade the North. Papà says that our town is too small with too few treasures to interest the Germans, but is that true? Will they not seek refuge wherever they can and plunder whatever they deem as riches? Will they claim our women as their own and subject us to a fate worse than death? I have saved myself for all of these years and am still waiting for Roberto and me to be married. Am I waiting in vain for some German soldier to do to me what it is reported that they have done to women throughout Europe? Will the Americans or the British do the same? These are the thoughts that come to me when I lie in bed at night and hear the planes fly overhead. Even on nights when there is silence, I wait for the peace to be broken by screams.

August 10, 1943

Roberto and I went on a picnic this afternoon. It sounds silly, I know, to go on a picnic when we are in the midst of war, but we needed the time to be together, to rebuild what we have. For two hours, we left the war and the world behind. Mamma let us take a bottle of wine, the first we've had since the war began. Papà said it was a gift, but he would not say from whom. We drank it slowly, but I still felt the effects. Roberto learned to drink quite a lot during his time in the army, but I am still young in comparison and am not usually allowed to have so much at one time. It tasted much better than the Communion wine with which I am familiar. I was surprised, at first, that Mamma would allow us to have it, but she said that we are no longer children. She is right. We have aged many years in such a short time.

After we ate, Roberto became quiet for a time and then told me that he had something to share with me. He took a book from his satchel. It was worn, and the cover was torn. I could tell that he was nervous and maybe a little embarrassed. He read to me words he wrote with his own hand while at war:

I am alone in the night, but I see your eyes in the stars.

My heart yearns for you, but I hear your voice in my dreams.

I weep, and the rain comes down from the sky.

I know that you weep for me, too.

Look to the moon and know that I will follow its light until it shines

upon your face.

Cry no more. I am coming home to you.

I did not know that my cheeks were wet with tears until Roberto leaned over and kissed them away. "Do you not like it?" he asked me. I told him I loved it, but my words were barely a whisper. "I do not wish to make you cry," he said. "Then make me stop," I said back, and he kissed me again, not on the cheek, but on my lips, the way he did in the loft those many months ago.

I found myself moving, lying back on the blanket with him over me. He kissed me, and I kissed him back in a way I never thought I could. He kissed my lips, my cheeks, my ear, my neck. He whispered words of love, and I longed for more. I felt a deep need to show him that he is no less a man, that he will always be whole and perfect to me.

"I am ready," I told him, but he stopped. "You are not," he said to me. I begged him, but he would not listen. "Soon," he promised, and he sat up, pulling me with him. I was ashamed, and he knew it. "I love you," he told me. "Soon." I love him, too, and I will wait.

Nicola watched Alex close the book. His heart beat rapidly in his chest as he watched her she swallow and hold his gaze. She was looking at him in the same way he imagined Isa looked at Roberto.

"Alessandra," he whispered as he moved his face toward hers. He saw her close her eyes and lean toward him, and the room became dark as he, too, closed his eyes and tasted her sweet lips. She turned toward him and curled an arm around his neck as their kisses grew in urgency. Using his one good arm, he pulled her close to him. In that instant, his body betrayed him as pain shot through his chest. He gasped for breath.

"Nicola, are you okay?" Alex jumped up from the bed, her eyes wide with fright, her lips swollen and red, her cheeks brushed by the stubble of his beard.

"Sì," he said and closed his eyes. He opened them and looked at her as a smile formed on his face. "Like Isa, I am not ready."

He watched Alex smooth her hair and pull her nightshirt farther down over her shorts. She looked down, and her cheeks reddened from more than his beard. "Truthfully, neither am I," she whispered before bending to kiss him on the cheek. "Soon," she promised before hurrying upstairs.

"Mmmm," Nicola nodded as he chewed the green grape. "Perfecto. It is time."

"We all thought so, too. Maria is already on the phone calling everyone in. It looks like we'll be able to harvest the white grapes and begin fermenting them just in time to begin drying the red grapes. The vats are clean and ready, and it's going to be a perfect day. How about joining us?"

Nicola looked up at Alex. "Joining you?"

"Sì. Your ribs should be well enough for you to get into your chair and go outside for a while. You're getting around a little more."

"I do not think that dragging my leg to the toilet is getting around more."

"But you're doing it without pain. So, do you want to come outside or not?"

His face lit up. "Sì! Andiamo." Nicola reached for her hand so she could help him get to the side of the bed.

"Allora, let's go." Alex helped him move into the wheelchair. "Oh, wait." She flew to the closet and searched for a baseball cap. "You wouldn't be in your proper work uniform without your hat to protect your face."

Nicola put on the cap, and Alex pushed the chair toward the door. She maneuvered the chair out onto the porch and down the ramp that Luigi had secured in place weeks prior, when Nicola had first come home.

They went around the house to the chosen field, and everyone stopped to watch them approach. All at once, the cousins and all of the hired harvesters began clapping. Nicola bent over in the chair in a mock bow and thanked them for their applause. Luigi and Giovanni took turns pushing the chair through the field so that Nicola could be near them as they picked the grapes. They maneuvered the chair as close to the vines as they could so that Nicola could reach the outer branches. Now and then, he pointed out an inner bunch of grapes that had been missed, and Alex popped more than one into her mouth as they went along.

By lunchtime, they were all tired and hungry but pleased with the progress they had made. The tractor was full and ready to be emptied onto the crush pad where a second check of the quality of the grapes was to be done after a quick lunch. They ate quickly and went back to work. Luigi returned to the field with the workers to gather a second load while Alex, Maria, and Giovanni remained in the winery to tend to the harvested grapes. Nicola insisted on remaining with them and was able to sit comfortably by the pad. Sorting was tedious with only one arm, but Nicola tried hard to keep up with the others.

As Maria, Alex, and Nicola inspected the grapes, Giovanni prepared the fermentation tank. The grapes were crushed, separated from the bits of leaves and vines, and warmed before being put into the tank where they were mixed with bubbling CO_2 to remove the oxygen. The process was repeated with the second batch, and everything was left to sit in the warming tank for fermentation to begin. Next, the group used power washers to strip clean every basket and the crush pad. Nicola was of no use in the cleanup with an arm and a leg in a cast, so he returned to the house.

It was almost dark when Alex came inside and was met with a pleasant surprise.

"What is that smell?"

"I could ask you the same," Nicola teased.

"Very funny." Alex lifted the lid off of the pan and savored the heavenly scent. "You cooked. How?"

"It was slow, but I was able to make a simple dinner. I hope you don't mind spaghetti and Bolognese sauce. It is not fancy, but hopefully it will taste good."

"Anything will taste good right now. Do I have time to shower?"

"I am not eating with you unless you do." Nicola laughed.

"You just wait. Next year I'll be saying the same thing to you." Alex headed up the stairs and Nicola thought about her words. Next year, he would indeed be just as sweaty and dirty as she is now, and he was going to enjoy every minute of it, including the showers they could take together.

August 15, 1943

It is the Feast of the Assumption of the Virgin Mary, but we did not go to Mass, and the traditional street celebration has been cancelled. For many weeks now, Papà and I have been working at night to dig a shelter to protect us from bombs. Tonight, we huddle there with only a small candle lighting the pitch blackness of our hiding place. It smells of dirt and sweat with all of us down here—Mamma, Papà, Nonno, Nonna, and me. My sweet Nonno worries about his vineyard.

For the past several nights, Milan has been under air attack. There are fears that Leonardo's Last Supper will not survive these continuous attacks. We hear the planes as they fly overhead, and sometimes, we can hear nearby explosions. Thus far, our grapes have been spared, but Papà says that everything is a target. We believed that the Allies would liberate us from the Germans, but they bomb our cities instead.

Mamma says it is time to extinguish the candle. I know I will not sleep tonight in this dark cellar filled with the smell of sweat and fear. I pray for my family and for Roberto's family. May there be peace in Italy soon.

"But there wasn't, not for a long time." Alex looked up at Nicola.

"No, bella, not for a very long time. That was just the beginning of the bombing here in the North Country. And then raids began, and the killing of our people by the Germans."

"What do you mean by raids? Houses?"

"Everything. Mostly the museums and churches. The Germans began taking everything out of Italy, all of the world's treasures that had been here for hundreds, even thousands of years."

"But didn't the Allies get most of them back?"

"Sì, but the Italians did not trust them either. They believed that the Allies wanted the treasures for themselves. And it took some time before the Allies understood the consequences of the bombings."

"*The Last Supper*, it was unharmed, right?"

"Sì, but for a small corner. It is still considered a great miracle that it survives at all, the bombing, the weather, the years. It cannot be explained."

Nicola stared ahead, a puzzled expression on his face.

"What is it?" Alex asked.

"The underground shelter. I do not know of one. It is very strange."

"Maybe they filled it in after the war."

"Non so. Maybe."

"Shall I go on?"

"Sì, continua."

Alex scanned the next entry with her app and continued reading.

August 25, 1943

The Germans have taken all of Central and Northern Italy. The Americans and British are in the South, and Papà says that some of their soldiers are in the occupied areas trying to secure the treasures of our country, of the world. But they continue to bomb our cities. Even Rome is not immune to their weapons. I have lived in Italy all my life and have never been there. By the time the war is over, there might not be anything left to see.

Padre Lorenzo came to see Papà today. They would not allow me to be a part of their meeting, and it offends me. I risked my life to deliver messages for them, but I am not permitted to hear what they are planning next. Papà says that I am to concentrate on helping Roberto because he will be needed. Am I no longer needed? Do I no longer count now that the young men are coming back?

September 3, 1943

The war is over in Italy, but nobody seems to know it. Papà learned that today the Armistice was signed between Italy and the

Allies, but the Germans are still here, and the raids and bombings continue. Roberto is now well enough to attend our secret meetings, and I have been allowed back in. We meet underground now. It is no longer safe to meet in the open. German soldiers are going to every city in the north where they are raping the women and stealing everything they believe to be valuable. Our Jewish friends are no longer safe in Italy. They are being killed or sent to Austria. If our part in the war is over, why will the Nazis not go home? Why do they not leave us alone?

The second day of the harvest was even busier than the first. Everyone worked in the fields except for Nicola and Alex. They stayed with the tanks to ensure that the wine was fermenting properly. Nicola explained to Alex that the fermenting liquid, called the must, had to be monitored closely the first few days.

"Nicola, this one is climbing above twenty-four degrees," Alex frantically called to him.

Quite adept now at maneuvering himself with one hand, Nicola rolled over to the tank.

"We need to reset the automatic temperature control," Nicola said calmly as he made the necessary changes.

"What will we do at night? How will we know that the must isn't overheating?"

"We will all take turns keeping an eye on the thermostat. It will be fine."

Nicola was calmer and more assured than he had been in weeks. He could sense Alex's relief to have him there to walk her through the processes and routines. They were both grateful that he was not still in bed. They were especially happy that his casts would be removed later that day. The ribs would take a few more weeks to heal completely, but he was no longer taking any medication, and he was able to move more quickly and easily each day.

They turned toward the sound of the tractor approaching the vineyard and watched the rest of the crew unload a new batch of grapes onto the crush pad.

Alex kept track of the temperatures and charted the readings on the gauges while Nicola helped sort through the grapes on the crush pad. When it came time for them to break for lunch, Alex and Nicola grabbed their food and headed to the doctor's office.

On the way home, Alex cautioned Nicola not to rush his recovery. "You heard what he said. Do not overdo things."

"Sì, sì, I will be fine."

"Nicola, I practically had to wrestle my keys away from you. If I can't trust you to let me drive, how can I trust you in the fields?"

"I am anxious, sì? I need to be working and not sitting."

"You were working while you were sitting, and everything is going just fine."

Alex pulled over to the side of the road.

"What are you doing?" Nicola asked.

"Look at me, Nicola. I mean it, really look at me and listen to me."

He gave her his full attention. "Continua," he said, not hiding his impatience, and motioned for her to go on.

"You scared the hell out of me. Do you get that?" Nicola nodded. "Do not ever do anything like that again, put yourself in danger. I know that roofs need to be fixed, things happen, but you must be more careful. And that means not pushing yourself. You need to heal completely. Do you understand me?"

Nicola couldn't help himself. He reached over and tucked a stray hair behind her ear and let his finger trail down her cheek. She was so beautiful with her hair pulled back, tendrils falling loose around her dirt-smudged face. He smiled.

"Alessandra, do you love me?"

"I, uh, what kind of question is that?"

Nicola grinned at her confusion. It was certainly not the question she had been expecting from him.

"Do you love me?"

"Nicola, what does that have to do with—"

He reached behind her head and gently pulled her toward him, claiming her with his mouth. Rejoicing in the ability to touch her with both hands, he ran his fingers through her hair as he kissed her hungrily, and she responded by cupping his face with her hands and kissing him back. Forcing himself to tear away from her, he pulled back and looked at Alex.

"Do you love me?" he whispered as he looked deeply into her eyes.

"Sì," she said breathlessly.

"Then I will do whatever I need to do so that I can fully recover. Because I want more of this, more of you." He pulled her to him again and kissed her even more deeply and more powerfully than the first time before releasing her.

"Now, let us go home and finish work so that we can be alone."

Alex regained her composure, "Nicola we can't—"

"Sì, lo so, but I still want you all to myself."

Alex smiled. "I can't argue with that."

Alex made dinner that evening while the crew was planning who would take which shift during the night. This would be the only night that they would need to closely monitor the tanks. Once they were sure that the controls were working and the must was formatting properly, they would be able to let the machines do the work. That would be when the extracting and tasting would begin, and Alex was looking forward to that. They would need to start the monitoring all over again once they began drying and harvesting the red grapes, but they would have about a week in between to get several nights of sleep.

When Nicola came in, he looked robust and energized, not at all what Alex expected.

"You don't even look tired," she said as she hugged him. Before she could let go and turn back to the stove, Nicola tightened his hold on her and kissed her.

"This is what I want to come inside to every evening. It is what I have dreamed of for many nights."

"A woman putting a hot meal on the table?" Alex teased and pushed him away. Nicola just laughed and hung his cap on the hook by the door.

"I am going to wash. I trust we are reading tonight?"

"If that's okay?"

"For now," he said, and his meaning was not lost on Alex.

September 8, 1943

The Armistice was announced on the wireless today, but the Nazis continue as if nothing has changed. Papà tells us that Germans are going house to house and taking all weapons from our people. There are rumors that American and European art experts are here in Italy to save the ancient ruins, the churches, the art, sculptures, and whatever else the Nazis are taking. But the Germans are delivering notices that these are not experts but thieves and that all valuables must be turned over to the German soldiers for safekeeping. Papà has hidden, in our underground shelter, what little jewelry we have along with the candlesticks he and Mamma received on their wedding day.

I realized today that we have stopped talking about Paolo and wondering when he will come home. It has been many months since we heard from him, and there is no word on his whereabouts. We haven't even properly mourned him, yet we all assume that he is dead.

September 11, 1943

Yesterday, Rome fell to the Germans. The Vatican remains untouched, though without Mussolini, there is no longer a pact between the Axis powers and the Pope, and the safety of Pius XII is in question. I was permitted to meet with Papà and the others in the cellar this evening. Many of our neighbors are talking about fleeing, but right now, there is nowhere to go. The Germans still control the trains and the borders, and getting travel papers is almost impossible.

Roberto held my hand during the meeting and squeezed it when there was talk about fleeing. I know that he does not want to have to fight again. He would leave our home and begin again if that's what it came to. I do not want to leave, but I would go. My future is with Roberto, wherever that is.

September 13, 1943

Il Duce came out of hiding yesterday, and it was announced by the Führer that Il Duce is now the head of the Italian Socialist Republic, but Papà assures us that there is no such thing and that he has no power. Fighting continues in the south, but the Allies are making progress. Here in the North, we are still under German rule. No more for tonight. We spent all day in the fields. The harvest has begun. I can barely hold the pen in my cut and swollen fingers.

September 22, 1943

Word has come that almost 5,000 of our soldiers, the men of the 33rd "Aqui" Division in Greek Cephalonia have been executed by the German soldiers and that another 3,000 are lost at sea. We do not know if Paolo might be alive and among them. It was not his regiment, and the last we heard, he was in Tunisia, but there is such chaos with the Italian Army now that we just do not know. When I asked Papà if he might have been with them, it was the first time his name has been spoken aloud in my recent memory. Mamma began crying so hard that I dare not speak it again.

September 29, 1943

The people of Napoli have risen up against the German soldiers. All Italians are being called to protect our homeland and to help the Allies remove the Nazis from our country. I fear for Roberto who does not want to go back to war. Surely he cannot be made to fight. He cannot fire a gun, cannot walk long distances. He talks more and more about leaving, but that, too, seems impossible. Some might call him a coward, but I know the truth. He is braver than most men will ever need to be. He faced death and lived.

Chapter Sixteen

"Do you see? It is very sweet."

Two weeks after the harvest began, the crew started picking and drying the red grapes. The must had been started, and Nicola was teaching Alex the fine art of producing Amarone.

Alex made a face. "Much too sweet. And light, not heavy and robust."

Nicola smiled broadly and clapped his hands. "Sì, sì! You have a mouth made for tasting wine." He took the tasting glass from her and leaned closer. "And for this," he whispered as he lowered his lips to hers.

Cat calls and whistles came from the nearest field, and Alex blushed as she pulled away.

"Do not mind them. This is Italy, where lovers can do as they please when they please."

"Is that so? I think you're getting a little ahead of yourself."

"You are just a tease." He pretended to sulk which just made Alex laugh.

"And you have a one-track mind."

"If that were true, your virtue would not be safe with me, bella, but I am putting my own desires aside for you."

A shiver ran down her spine and settled right where he intended it to. Nicola held her in his stare, and Alex found herself melting into those chocolate eyes once again.

"The testing," she said quietly. "So far, it's good?"

"Sì, sì, it is good, but it is early. It will be many more weeks before the must is ready for the Amarone. Alex…" He grabbed her arm so that she couldn't turn away. "I will take care of you, always. You are always safe with me."

"Sì, Nicola, Allora. Perhaps it is not *your* desires that I fear."

Alex showered after dinner that evening but did not see Nicola on the couch when she went downstairs. He had asked some of the men to help him move the furniture back before they left, and Alex was part happy and part anxious to have him back in the room across the hall from her. The picking and drying of the red grapes was the most work they had done outside of the wine making since the harvest began. Even the reading of the journal had been put aside for now. Evenings were spent watching the tanks, and they all dropped into bed early, exhausted from the work of the day.

"Nicola," she called when she found the kitchen empty as well.

Thinking that he may have gone to check on the must, she went back through the parlor and out onto the porch to look for lights in the winery.

"I am here." His voice was low, but it penetrated the night and sent an arrow right into her heart.

Alex turned around and saw him on the settee. She walked to one of the columns and looked up at the night sky.

"It's a beautiful night," she said as she felt his stare. There was a pulse in the air, like a heartbeat, their heartbeats. It wrapped itself around them like a Hispanic wedding lazo that was looped around the couple and bound them together. She was bound to him, and the rope tightened each day, pulling her closer to him, binding them together for eternity.

"I have not been fair to you," Nicola said, and Alex could hear the weight of his words but didn't understand their meaning.

"What do you mean?" She went to the settee and sat next to him.

"I have not treated you like a lady, like someone I respect and..." His words trailed off, and he looked away.

"I don't understand." Alex tried desperately to figure out what he meant.

Nicola shook his head and then bent over, placing his face in his hands. After a moment, he sat up and looked at Alex. He covered her hands with his.

"Alessandra, this living together, it is not right. It is not what you deserve."

Was he kicking her out? Did he want her to leave? Her heart pounded and her eyes filled with tears. "You want me to leave?" she choked out.

"No, no, mi bella." He let go of her hands and put his hands on each side of her face. "I want you to stay, but not like this. Do you not see?" Alex shook her head and held back the tears that welled in her eyes. "Mia bella, amore mio," he cried as he pulled her to him. He pulled back and again grasped her face forcing her to meet his eyes. "Ti amo. I love you. I want you here forever."

"Then what is wrong? I don't understand," she said again.

"Amore mio, things have changed so much. You are no longer a guest in my villa, an unwanted business partner, or even someone I just want as a lover. I do not want you as a guest, a partner, a lover. I want you, all of you, for all time. I do not have a ring, I have nothing to offer you but a mediocre vineyard. But I offer you me, my love, for the rest of your life, if you will take me."

"Nicola, are you asking me…"

"Sì, sì." He looked deeply into her eyes. "Mi vuoi sposare?"

Alex couldn't stop the tears that began to stream down her face. She reached for Nicola, pulled him to her, and kissed him. It was a sweet kiss, soft and tender, and he returned it in kind. When he pulled away to look at her, she smiled.

"Sì, Nicola, lo sposerò te."

"As if we didn't have enough to do already." Maria playfully scolded Alex. "Now you want to have a wedding?"

"I suppose you're too busy to help plan and be a part of it," Alex said as they checked the final batch of grapes on the crush pad.

"Sì, I am too busy. Ho troppo lavoro da fare."

"Too much to do to be my maid of honor?"

Maria stopped inspecting the grapes and looked at Alex. Her face lit up with joy, and she ran around the pad to hug her soon to be cousin. "Sì, troppo lavoro, but I will find time."

"Look what you've done now." Luigi punched Nicola in the arm as they watched Maria and Alex from the field.

"Sì, we are in trouble."

"Not me, mio cugino, not me." Luigi laughed as he left his cousin to ponder his own fate.

"We should finish the journal soon, don't you think?" Alex placed two plates on the table as Nicola poured two glasses of wine. "Now that we will have more time in the evenings."

"If we are able to start reading at night and don't have any problems," Nicola replied. "Our days will not be so tiring now that all of the grapes have been harvested, and the must is past the dangerous time. Busy, still, but not exhausting."

"I called Father Rulli today," Alex said casually.

Nicola laughed. "That did not take long."

"Well, there is a process, you know. I figured the sooner we get that started and the sooner we get married, the happier you'll be."

"Oh, *I'll* be happier?" He walked around the table and lifted Alex into the air. "It was I who said I could wait. Do you want me to change my mind?"

Alex giggled and then gasped. "Your ribs, Nicola!"

"My ribs have been healed for some time." Nicola put her down and then turned her to face him. "We will both be happy. Forever." He leaned down and kissed her so passionately that Alex almost forgot about the virtue that Nicola had vowed to protect.

October 6, 1943

The Allies have crossed the Voltumo, the line set up by the Germans to establish their occupation of Italy. The war draws closer to us each day. The Germans are taking art and sculptures and transferring them 'for safe keeping' to other countries, but Papá has learned that the Fuhrer is building a museum in Germany to hold all of the greatest treasures of the world. They have air dropped letters to the Italian people asking us to help them save the art and keep it from the thieving Americans and Brits. I threw them into the fires that are used to heat the must tanks. The wine is fermenting, and some is bottled. We try to live each day as if nothing has changed, but every strange car brings fear of a raid, and every plane overhead sends us running to the cellar. I am so tired of war.

October 13, 1943

We are back in the war, though in truth, we were never really out of it. Italy has joined the Allies and declared war on Germany. Our men are called to fight. Dr. Romano gave papers to Roberto exempting him from fighting, which is what I thought Roberto wanted, but now he is angry. He says it is different now. Now we fight to save our own land, our own families. He feels useless, but Papá has a plan.

October 14, 1943

We met underground tonight, Papá, Roberto, Padre Lorenzo, and I. We are not a wealthy town, and our public buildings do not hold works by Michelangelo or Botticelli, but we do have something precious and rare—a rather large Robbiano that hangs over the doors in the back of the church. Padre Lorenzo worries that it will be desired for the Fuhrer's museum. There are many Robbianos throughout Italy, but none is like ours. It is just over two meters in diameter, round, and beautiful. The Virgin Mother holds the Babe, resplendent in blue and white, and lambs sit on each side of her. Roses of every color encircle them with leaves of the brightest

*green, and ivy trails around the edge of sculpture. I will admit that
I have never thought of it as anything special. It was always just
there, part of Our Lady of the Roses. I cannot say that I have ever
even looked at it for more than a second. But to hear Padre
Lorenzo say that it may be taken from us, sends a spear to my
heart. Even removing it could cause irreparable damage. A slight
bump could chip or even crack the entire work of art. I fear that
the Germans may break it if they try to steal it, but more than
that, I fear that we will break it when we steal it ourselves.*

"A Robbiano?" Alex tried to think back to her days
as an art student, but she couldn't place the name.

"Sì, Della Robbia was a sculptor and painter, a very
skilled artisan who helped sculpt the doors of the
Baptistry in Firenze. Do you remember them?" Alex
nodded, and Nicola continued. "He created a special
paint, a, what would you call it? A shiny overpaint?"

"A glaze?"

"Sì, sì, a glaze. He created a glaze for terra cotta. Do
you know what this is?"

"Sì, we use it for outdoor plants in the States. It's a
type of clay."

"Sì." Nicola' face lit up as the full impact of Isa's
story hit him. "It is a clay that, as you must know, is
orange and plain, rough and not pretty." Alex nodded.
"Allora. Della Robbia made this glaze for terra cotta.
Only he knew the secret of the glaze. He sculpted
pictures into the terra cotta. For the most part, they were
religious like most Renaissance art. He sculpted angels,
religious symbols, and many, many depictions of the

Madonna and Child. The most famous are in Il Duomo in Firenze. He painted with bright colors—yellows, blues, greens, and a lot of white, more white than color sometimes. The terra cotta was completely unseen, and the pieces were much in demand because of their rarity and secret formula as well as their beauty. On his deathbed, he told his nephew the secret to making the glaze. You see pieces now in tourist shops in Firenze and cities in the north, but even these are not made with the exact formula as it was kept secret. Most tourists do not even know of their..." Nicola looked at Alex for help.

"Significance?" Alex filled in quickly, reading his mind. Nicola' excitement was contagious, and she felt that they were on the verge of discovering something important, perhaps the very thing that Signora wanted them to find in the reading of the journal, other than each other.

"Sì, sì, significance. They do not know why these are sold in souvenir shops except that they are beautiful. By today's standards, they do not seem to be representatives of priceless art."

"Nicola, perhaps I am just as unobservant as Isa, but I don't remember seeing anything like she described in the back of the church. Am I blind?"

"No." Nicola put down the journal and jumped from the settee. "It is not there," he said with excitement. "I did not know there ever was one. There has never been anything over the doors, which, now that I know, I see is very strange. Most other churches in Italy have something over the doors. I do not know why I never questioned it before."

"Why would you? You grew up in that church. Nothing about it would seem strange or different to you."

The clock chimed midnight, and Nicola suddenly realized how late it was. "Alessandra, it is molto late. We must be up early in the morning. What do you want to do?" He held up the journal.

"Prudence would say that we should sleep..."

"Prudence?"

Alex laughed. "Wisdom. We should get some rest. Will you be able to go to sleep, or are you too excited?"

Nicola looked at Alex with hunger in his eyes. "I face that difficulty every night and have since you arrived. I will manage."

The following day seemed to drag on for Alex. Though it was Saturday, they were hard at work in the winery. She tried to focus on her tasks, but her mind was a jumble of thoughts—her growing love and passion for Nicola, plans for the wedding, the war in Italy, and the missing Robbiano. Alex was anxious for Sunday to arrive so that she could see the space where Isa said that the artwork once hung. Had it been stolen? Damaged? Lost forever in a salt mine somewhere in Europe or reduced to a pile of crushed clay?

"How's it going in there?" Alex teased as she looked over the top of the tank and into its depths where Nicola filled the bucket with the second, heavier layer of solids left in the bottom of the tank by the fermented grapes.

"You can climb down and see for yourself."

Alex laughed and hauled up the bucket.

She was learning that emptying the liquid and then clearing the tank of the solids is a process that takes several days. The liquid was transferred into smaller tanks to complete the fermentation process, and the solids were saved to be added back in later to enhance the flavor of the wine. What was not used would be sold to make other grape or wine flavored products.

At the end of the day, everything was thoroughly cleaned and readied for the next day. Nicola showered under an outdoor faucet before going inside for a real shower. He and Alex ate a light supper before hurrying onto the front porch to read.

October 20, 1943

We have devised our plan, and there is not time to waste. More and more works of art are disappearing from Italy. Papà says that many of them have been hidden in villas in the countryside to keep them away from the Germans, but some of the most priceless works are unaccounted for. Papà has forbidden me from writing down our plans and has ordered that my journal be destroyed, and I understand why, but I feel that our actions must be documented somewhere. If something were to happen to any of us, the world must know what we have done and why. Otherwise our endeavor, even if successful, will be considered a failure. From now on, my journal will be hidden so that even Papà will believe that it no longer exists.

"That explains why it was hidden in the loft and how it remained there for so long," Alex surmised.

"Sì, the loft is not often used, though I did play there as a boy. I still do not know how it was not found in all of these years."

"Perhaps it was not yet time."

Nicola leaned down and kissed the top of Alex's head.

"Sì, perhaps it was not."

October 29, 1943

It is difficult for me to write now. With the journal hidden high in the eaves of the loft, I cannot so easily find the time and the opportunity to write all that happens. There has been much rain this week, and I feared that my words would be lost forever to the dampness, or worse, to a leak in the roof of the barn. It seems that it is safe, though, so I will keep it in its hiding place and write when I can.

The rain has hampered our plans, but it has also slowed down the progress of both the Allies and the Germans. This has given us more time to make the plans firm and for Roberto to be strong enough for his part. Papà is strong and healthy, but he is not a young man any longer, and the war and Paolo's death have taken their toll on him. Padre Lorenzo is old and can do no more than direct us. The labor will be mine and Roberto's. I pray that I am strong enough in mind and body to do what needs to be done.

"Well, there it is," Alex said. "The journal was in the eaves above the loft. At some point in recent years, something must have dislodged it, and it fell onto the floor."

"Sì, birds nest in the eaves of the barn. Perhaps one of them hit it and knocked it down."

"Or Signora was finally ready for it to be found."

"I am not a believer in ghost stories, but I think that you may be right." Nicola smiled and nudged Alex's head with his chin so that she turned and looked up at him. He kissed her tenderly, and all thoughts of Isa, the War, and the journal were lost. Alex reached up and caressed his face as Nicola pulled her to him. His lips left her mouth and trailed across her cheek to her neck.

"Ti amo, Alessandra," he whispered into her ear. "I love you."

"Ti amo, Nicola," Alex breathed as she relished the feel of his lips on her skin and the sound of his words against her ear.

After a few moments, Nicola pulled back and gazed lovingly into her eyes. "I will see you in the morning, mia bella."

"Sì. Buona notte," Alex answered breathlessly. As she stood and walked to the door, she turned to look up at the starry sky. She smiled and silently thanked Signora for her gift. Not the journal or even the vineyard, but for the chance to love and be loved unconditionally.

Chapter Seventeen

Sunday morning found Alex much too excited to stay in bed. She was up earlier than necessary and ready for Mass with time to spare. Though she tried to concentrate on the homily—she was getting much better at keeping up with Padre Rulli's Italian—she found herself turning around several times to look at the empty space above the back doors of the church.

When the Mass was over, she and Nicola waited for all of the other parishioners to leave before they spoke of the missing Robbiano.

"Is it my imagination, or is the outline still there?" Alex asked as they gazed up at the brick wall.

"Sì, I see it, too. It is very faint, but it is there." Nicola seemed amazed at the discovery. "All these years, and I never saw it until now."

"Were we to meet?" Their concentration was broken by Padre Rulli's voice.

"Oh, no, Padre," Alex said as she walked to him and kissed his cheeks. "We were just..." she looked at Nicola.

"We were wondering why there is nothing above the doors. I never thought about it before, but it does seem like something is missing."

"Allora." The priest nodded. "There is a record of a priceless Robbiano that was a gift to the church in the early 1500s from Andrea della Robbia, nephew of the great sculptor. According to church records and town legend, it was stolen by the Germans during the second world war. It has never been found and is believed to have been destroyed or damaged beyond repair." Padre Rulli shook his head. "It was very tragic. The parish priest at the time lost his life trying to protect it."

Alex gasped and squeezed Nicola's hand.

"Mi dispiace, Signorina," the kind priest said. "I know it is troubling."

Alex swallowed and tried to mask her true concern. "Sì, Padre, it is most troubling."

"Grazie, Padre," Nicola said as he shook the priest's hand. "Bunona Serata."

"Anche ha a te." Padre Rulli smiled and turned to go.

"Padre." Nicola stopped him. "If the Robbiano was not destroyed, could it have survived all of these years without being ruined?"

Padre Rulli shrugged. "Non so. Perhaps if it was kept somewhere safe where the weather could not affect it. If it is in a salt mine somewhere in the North, then, sadly, I do not think so."

It was their first family dinner since Nicola's fall, and the villa was abuzz with excitement. The conversation focused on the vineyard and this year's vintage as well as the spring wedding, but all of that was outshone by Giovanni's announcement that little Marco was to be a big brother. Nicola insisted on opening a bottle of Amarone, and everyone shared in a toast to the newest addition to the family, including Adrianna who followed the Italian custom that one glass of wine per day would produce a beautiful baby. While the women washed the dishes and talked about the baby, the wedding, and how they would handle Adrianna's bridesmaid dress, the men watched la partita. Though every time Alex stole a glance into the parlor, she met Nicola's stare, and she felt the thrill of knowing that he couldn't keep his eyes off of her.

After saying arrivederci, Nicola and Alex collapsed on the sofa, his arms around her, and her head on his chest. Alex closed her eyes and found herself wanting to stay there forever. Nicola had other ideas, though, and took her chin in his fingers, tilting her head up until their eyes locked and their lips found each other. Curling into him, Alex gave herself to his kiss, and he eased her onto her back as his kisses became more intense. She knew that his ribs were healed, and that this situation was only going to become more and more difficult over the next several months, but she couldn't help herself. All of her senses were lost to his touch, his taste, his warm breath on her skin.

When she felt his need, she gently pushed him away. "I think we should—"

"Go upstairs?" he asked huskily, his eyes on fire with passion.

"Read," she managed to say between heavy breaths. "The journal. I think that's for the best."

"Allora, it is for the best," Nicola said as he reluctantly pulled back and ran his hand through his dark, wavy hair. He took a deep breath and exhaled it through his puffed-out cheeks. "But a spring wedding is too far away. We will speak with Padre Rulli about doing it sooner."

Alex began to protest. "But there is so much to do and plan."

"What is there to do? We just need the church and a tent on the vineyard grounds. You have your attendants, and I have Luigi and Giovanni. The rest is easy."

Alex smiled. "I guess having it earlier would make things easier on Adrianna."

"Sì, and on me." Nicola sighed.

November 3, 1943

Throughout Italy, works of art are being secretly crated and moved to undisclosed locations for their safekeeping. The Germans talk of Kunstschutz, their word for preserving cultural and artistic treasures, but what they really want is to take all of the world's art for their own. That will not happen here, not in our town. We go tonight to take matters into our own hands.

"Look how her handwriting changes between these paragraphs," Alex pointed out.

"Sì. Something has happened," Nicola agreed, and he read on.

I should not be here, writing this down, taking time that we cannot afford to waste, but I shall quickly note, with trembling hand, what is likely to be my last entry before Roberto and I return to our work in the moonlight. Last night, under the cover of darkness, we went to the church where Padre Lorenzo was waiting for us. He let us in, and we worked as quickly and quietly as we could. Using a rope system that Papà and Roberto designed, we lowered the Robbiano to the floor without a scratch. With Mamma's blankets, we wrapped the large piece of art as best we could and rolled it out into the night where Papà had the trailer waiting, the one that we use to carry the baskets from the fields to the winery. We loaded the Robbiano onto the trailer and thought all was well. Then we heard the command to halt. A German officer appeared in the night. He must have been watching us. He held us at gunpoint and motioned for us to move away from the trailer.

What I write next will be the most difficult thing I have ever had to write, but it needs to be done. Papà tried to talk to the soldier. He told him that we would not obey, and my own papà took a gun from his coat and aimed it at the soldier. Roberto grabbed me and pushed me behind him. I admit that I clung to him in fear. I watched my papà walk toward the soldier telling him to back down, to drop his gun, but the young man stood firm, his hand shaking. Even in the pale moonlight, I could see the sweat glistening on his skin and realized he was not much older than myself. "Halt!" he called, but Papà did not stop. He called to Roberto to get me into the truck. I protested, but Roberto told me that I would make things worse if I fought, so I went with him to the truck. The soldier yelled at us in his own language, and though I did not know the words, I understood that he was ordering us to stop. Roberto turned on the truck, and I watched as the German looked frantically from us to Papà. Suddenly, he swung back toward Papà and fired the gun. Padre Lorenzo leapt in front of Papà. I believe he yelled something, but all I heard was the shot and the sound of my own screams. As we pulled away, I watched in horror as Padre Lorenzo fell to the ground and Papà fired his own gun at the soldier. The blast was louder than the first one had been, but before I had time to wonder why, I watched as both the German and Papà fell. I screamed for Roberto to stop and opened the door and jumped out before he even braked.

Papà died in my arms.

Alex held her breath, tears streaming down her face, as she listened to Nicola read the tear-stained last words on the page.

November 4, 1943

It is done, and I am more afraid than ever. Roberto and I will take tonight's train from my beloved home. It is safest that way. Nobody else knows what happened last night nor where the Robbiano is hidden. We will take the secret to our graves. Whether that be sooner or later is in God's hands.

May He bless this land and my mother. May she forgive me for running and never discover what we have done. And may God forgive us for the sin we have committed.

Alex awoke that Monday morning with an aching heart. Throughout the night, she had been plagued with dreams, some of which were vivid memories. Her mind conjured up the scene outside the church over and over, but each time, it was Alex's father dying in her own arms, sometimes in the cold, dark churchyard and other times, on the side of the road on a hot summer day. Alex stared groggily at the ceiling and fought back tears. There were so many parallels between Signora's life and her own, though her life seemed idyllic compared to Isa's.

Though they had come to the end of the journal, the question still hung in the air. Why had Signora led them here? To this place and time, to the journal? Was it just to lead them to each other?

Alex closed her eyes and shook her head. No, that couldn't be all. She was certain that Signora wanted something more from them. Was it to find the missing Robianno? But how? It had been lost for so many years. How long? Alex began calculating the years and stopped.

She suddenly realized what day it was. Reaching for the iPad next to her bed, she pushed away thoughts of Isa and the Robbiano. She opened the tablet, and the date on the calendar app jumped out at her. The harvest made every day seem like one long one, and dates meant nothing to them as they worked. Alex shook her head and laughed at herself when she thought of how completely preoccupied she had been. She tapped on the Facebook app and scrolled through the greetings. She needed cheering up, even if it came from people she didn't even see or talk to anymore. There was just a handful of messages; after all, it was still the middle of the night in the States. When she opened her mail, she saw that she had two messages from back home, one from her mother and one from her friend, Cindy.

Tears again came to Alex's eyes as she read her mother's email. It was so full of love and promise, and Alex was immensely grateful to Signora for helping her take the first step toward reconciliation. She typed a quick response and filled her mother in on the wedding plans, though she hadn't gotten very far, and it seemed that they were moving things up quite quickly if Padre Rulli agreed. After signing off, Alex got up and dressed before heading to the kitchen for a quick breakfast. Nicola was nowhere to be found, and she assumed he had gotten an early start to the day. She was disappointed. After the rough night, she needed to see his face and feel his reassuring touch.

"Buongiorno, Alex," Maria said with a smile when Alex walked into the winery. "The oxygen levels look good," Maria continued. Alex walked over to look at the charts and inhaled the sweet smell of fermentation. "Luigi is going to go into tank numero tre to shovel it out and could use your help."

Alex looked around, peering between the tanks, and then walked to the window to look into the fields. "Where is Nicola?"

"Non lo so. Was he not with you at the villa?"

"No." Alex tried to hide her sadness. "I guess he had some early business in town."

"Sì, he is probably meeting with a new buyer," Maria agreed.

This early? That's odd…

Alex found Luigi and told him she was ready to help, and they proceeded to tank number three. They chatted, and Alex tried to keep up her spirits as Luigi cleaned the tank and hoisted the bucket up to her. After about an hour, Alex felt a familiar pair of arms slide around her as she reached the bottom of the ladder, and she let herself melt into Nicola, laying her head back and nestling it where it fit so perfectly in the crook of his neck. She closed her eyes and inhaled the very essence of him.

"Buongiorno," he whispered into her ear, his warm breath tickling the side of her face and sending ripples of longing through her. He was her rock, and she felt strengthened by his very presence.

Nicola slowly turned so that he was in front of her, his arms still locked around her waist, the bucket awkwardly clutched in her hands between them. They gazed at each other, and Nicola leaned in for a kiss just as Luigi called out from inside the tank. "Alex, dove sei? I need the bucket."

"Oops." Alex smiled and handed the bucket to Nicola before quickly grabbing another and heading back up the ladder. "Mi dispiace, Luigi. I'm coming."

When she looked back down from the top of the ladder, Nicola and the bucket of solid must were both gone. To Alex, it was as if the light and warmth were gone from the room.

When lunchtime arrived, Nicola had once again disappeared. Luigi went into the villa to clean up after rinsing under the outdoor shower. Alex didn't see Giovanni or Maria. There were no more hired hands as the harvest itself was done, and the vineyard was eerily quiet except for the humming of the fermentation tanks. Alex wondered if this was how it felt to Isa the morning she left, quiet and lonely. Alex walked to the villa to search for her family.

"Hello? Where is everyone?" Alex called when she walked through the back door of the kitchen. The house was silent and dark, which was odd for the middle of the day. She went into the parlor and squealed when a strong pair of arms grabbed her and spun her around. Nicola's lips came down hard on hers as Maria, Giovanni, and Luigi burst into the room from the front porch.

"Buon compleanno!" the three yelled as Nicola pulled back and smiled.

"Sorpresa," Nicola whispered as he beamed at her.

"How? I didn't—"

"Mia bella, did you not think that I would know it is your birthday?"

"Seriously, how did you know?"

Nicola laughed. "Tua madre. She called me."

"Oh," Alex said in surprise.

"I made Polenta Pasticciata for lunch," Maria announced.

"My favorite." Alex smiled and hugged her friend.

"Allora, let us eat while it is hot."

When they were done with their baked polenta and Fontina cheese, Maria surprised Alex yet again with a torta alla panna, a whipped cream birthday cake. With tears in her eyes, Alex thanked everyone.

"You have no idea what this means to me," she said. "This is truly the happiest birthday I've had in many years."

"Allora, there is more," Nicola said as he stood. Pushing his chair out of the way, he took a box from his pocket and dropped to one knee. Alex gasped as he opened the box and revealed a gold ring with a heart-shaped diamond.

"The engagement ring is an Italian tradition dating back to the earliest Roman times. Traditionally, a set of hands, or hands holding a heart, are the symbols of eternal love." Nicola looked into Alex's eyes. "You are my eternal love, Alessandra. So I ask again, mi vuoi sposare?"

With unstoppable tears and a lump in her throat, Alex nodded and took hold of Nicola's arms, pulling him up toward her. She wrapped her arms around his neck and hugged him fiercely. Maria, Luigi, and Giovanni clapped and whistled. Nicola leaned back and looked at Alex for a moment before kissing her, tenderly at first, and then urgently and with a fiery passion that sent Luigi and Giovanni into howls.

When they parted, Alex's face was flush, but she smiled, and her eyes twinkled with happiness. Nicola removed the ring from the box and placed it on her finger.

"The Italians chose this finger because the 'nerve of love' runs from here to the heart." He slowly ran his finger from the ring, across her hand, up her arm, and down to her heart, which was rapidly beating with excitement, love, and desire.

They held each other's gaze until Giovanni spoke. "Allora, there is work to be done."

"Sì," Nicola said quietly, taking his gaze from hers and raising her hand to his lips.

Finally able to find her voice, Alex urged the men to go back to work. "Maria and I will clean up," she told them.

After they were gone, Alex looked at Maria with a pained expression. "I need help."

Maria raised her brow in question.

"Can I please move in with you, just until the wedding? We're moving it up, but I'm afraid it won't be soon enough."

"You are afraid, Alex?"

Alex nodded and blushed.

"Sì, and this is something I've always wanted, to wait until my wedding night, and now that it's so close, I'm having a hard time remembering why I wanted to wait to begin with."

Maria laughed. "It is a curse. Lo spirito è pronto, ma il carne corpo è debole."

"Sì, the spirit is willing, but the flesh is very, very weak."

Nicola did not take the news well, but he didn't protest too much. He knew that it was for the best for both of them. But that evening, as he sat alone in the villa, he saw and felt Alex everywhere. He knew that once they were married, he would never again let her out of his sight.

Torta alla Panna

Isa, who will bake your birthday cake? Can you give this recipe to friend and have her bake? Maybe you find nice, Italian lady who will know how to bake it, but it will not be as good as mine if she does it her own way.

1 cup flour	*3 eggs*
1 cup sugar	*1 teaspoon baking powder*
1 cup cream	*Icing sugar*

Beat eggs with sugar until light and fluffy. Whip cream, and add to eggs gently. Slowly add the flour and baking powder.

Grease and flour 10" baking sheet. Pour mixture into pan, and bake at 180 degrees for 35 minutes. When cool, remove cake from pan and sprinkle the surface with icing sugar.

Chapter Eighteen

With the end of the harvest, all of the grapes crushed, fermented or fermenting, and the bottles prepared for the vintage, the winery was no longer a hive of activity. Alex used the respite to search the Internet for information about the events of November third and fourth, 1943. The first several results that her search yielded were about the 'Erntefest,' ironically translated to 'Harvest Festival.' It was the German operation that saw the annihilation of all remaining Jews in an occupied territory of Poland. Alex shivered and moved on with her search. Some of the newspaper archives required Alex to pay for a subscription, and while she hoped to avoid that, she made note of the sites.

Alex narrowed her search to include the name and location of the church, and there she found a small digitized newspaper article. She hit the translate link even though she hardly needed to anymore, but she wanted to make sure she was accurately reading and understanding the information. She read the paper's account of the shooting of Padre Lorenzo.

November 5, 1943
The body of a local priest was found outside of his church, Our Lady of the Roses on the morning of November 4. The church

doors were open, and, according to a local couple, a rare Robbiano that adorned the rear church wall was missing. The area outside of the church where the priest was shot appeared to have been tampered with, said local police. It is believed that the missing sculpture was stolen during the night by the Kunstschutz and that the priest was shot while trying to stop the theft. Authorities are working with the American Monuments, Fine Arts, and Archives program to discover the whereabouts of the piece of art.

Alex then searched for the name Doctor Stefano Abelli and the Italian word for obituary. She was surprised by her finding.

November 7, 1943

Doctor Stefano Abelli was laid to rest following a private ceremony at Our Lady of the Roses on November 6, 1943 following a sudden heart attack. Beloved by all of his patients, he is preceded in death by his son, Paolo, who is presumed to have died while fighting with the Italian Army in Tunisia. Doctor Abelli leaves behind his wife, Marta Caterina, and their daughter, Isabella Luisa Abelli.

Alex stared out the window across the fields and thought about the events of that fateful night. Isa and Roberto must have retrieved her father's body and taken it home to be buried. She wondered if her mother knew the truth and guessed that she must have known some of it but not all of it. Alex imagined that the widow would have insisted on one last look at her husband, and a gunshot wound would be hard to hide, so she certainly knew of the gun fight. Judging by the last journal entry, though, Isa's mother did not know what they were doing that night or where the Robbiano was hidden. They had to hide it quickly, and probably somewhere nearby. It had to be some place large enough to hold it but not used regularly, and in a place where the Germans, if they searched, would not be able to see or find it.

Alex's eyes stopped on the barn, and her heart stopped along with them.

"Why didn't we think about this before?" Nicola said as he opened the barn door.

"Because we didn't have all the pieces, but now it does seem so obvious."

Nicola stopped and looked at her. "Too obvious? Would not Isa's nonno or madre have found it at some point?"

"I don't know. Perhaps there are some questions that will never be answered."

They went inside and looked around for some sign that there was a hidden cellar.

"It cannot be," Nicola said as he studied the floor. "The tractor is too heavy to sit over a hollow space, and the stalls would have prevented it from being placed over there." He pointed to the horse stalls that were now used for storage.

"How big would the space have to be?" Alex asked. "We know that it could fit five people, and how big did she say the Robbiano was?"

"I think, two meters?"

They looked around the barn.

"Here." Alex yelled as she ran to the side of the barn where old barrels, bottles, and other large pieces of no longer used accessories were stored on top of large pallets. "You're right that there couldn't be a cellar under the tractor to the stalls, but what about under here? These things probably weren't here back then, and the space is the right size."

Nicola didn't answer but went right to work rolling the barrels out of the way, and Alex jumped in to help clear the spot. When the space was clear, they moved the pallets and stood, looking down at the floor. Wooden planks were hidden under the dirt, but there didn't seem to be any way to get beneath them.

"Oh my gosh, it must be here," Alex exclaimed, her heart racing. "Do you see any way to open it?"

Nicola shook his head.

Alex got down on the planks and began crawling along the perimeter of the space, feeling for any type of latch or opening with her hands. Nicola followed her lead and began doing the same in the opposite direction.

"Oh!" she cried. "Here, Nicola. I've found something."

Hidden in the shadows, on the side of a wall, was a door handle in the floor, or what was left of it. It had been damaged, purposely from the looks of how it was smashed and broken.

"How do we open it?" she asked.

Nicola jumped up and went quickly to the other side of the barn where all manner of tools hung on the wall. He located a crowbar and hurried back to the space. Not worrying about the door handle, he went to work on the planks and began working to pry up the boards. After making enough progress, he threw aside the crowbar. Splinters of wood flew as he worked to pull away the wood with his hands until finally, he located another trap door. He and Alex looked at each other with anticipation and then each reached for one side of the door and lifted it up.

Dirt and dust filled the air, and Alex coughed and waved her arms to clear it away. Just as Isa described, the space was small and dark, but it was not empty. Nicola reached in and gently tugged at the dusty blanket, but it did not move.

"Look away," he commanded, and Alex turned her head.

Holding his breath and squeezing his eyes shut, he yanked the blanket as hard as he could, and it flew at him, causing him to fall backwards. He pushed the blanket off, coughing and blinking his eyes, and sat up. Alex turned; her eyes, wide with disbelief, met his. Nicola looked into the hole and gasped.

Even in the dim light, the colors of the sculpture shone bright, the innocent eyes of the Babe in his mother's arms looking up at them, offering them peace and comfort.

"Oh my God," Alex breathed. "Oh my God, Nicola, what do we do now?"

It was a Christmas vigil like no other. There was standing room only at Our Lady of the Roses Church. People from miles and miles around came to celebrate the first Mass in over seventy years to be held in the presence of Robbiano's Madonna and Child. The sculpture had returned from extensive testing and examination in Florence just in time for the holidays. Reporters from newspapers around the world attended the Mass and snapped pictures of Padre Rulli throwing holy water on the sculpture and asking the Lord's blessing on the remarkable piece of art. He thanked God for its safe return and for the anonymous family who found it. For weeks, reporters had been calling the rectory and interviewing townspeople, hoping to discover who found the priceless work of art and how. The few who knew promised not to tell.

There was a reason Signora spent all of those years keeping quiet. Whatever it was, Alex and Nicola made a vow to honor her wishes. Perhaps it was some deep-rooted fear that the Germans would be able to trace the events back to the disappearance or death of their soldier, and they would be charged with murder or war crimes of theft and espionage. Perhaps it had become too painful a reminder of the death of her father and all that they lost in the war. For reasons they would probably never know, the story was one she did not want told, so only their family was privy to the details of the journal.

Alex and Nicola held hands as they looked up at the sculpture. Surrounded by their loved ones, Marta, Annie, Maria, Pietro, Giovanni, Adrianna, Marco, and Luigi, they celebrated Christmas as well as the return of the Robbiano. There was much to be done over the course of the next week, and they looked forward to beginning the New Year by reciting their vows on the altar in front of the loving gaze of Mary and her Son.

Epilogue - March
Little Italy, Baltimore, Maryland

A veil of snow draped across the sky and drifted down onto the already blanketed streets and yards across the city, but inside the little house, a blazing fire kept the couple warm and cozy. Signor and Signora Giordano sat on the floor in front of the hearth and read the letters and memorabilia they found in a bottom drawer in the master bedroom while they were cleaning out the house, which they would rent out until they decided what to do with it.

December 30, 1943

Dear Signora Fonticelli,

Your letter has found me well, and I am delighted that you made it to your new home. I am honored to have known you for even a short time and to have been able to marry you. I am pleased to send the enclosed photograph of you and Roberto on the altar and hope it will bring you some joy. May the Lord look down upon you and Roberto and keep you in His ever-loving care.

Yours in Christ,
Padre Anelli
St. Michael Archangel
Parma, Italy

"Ah." Nicola clapped his hands together. "So that is how."

Alex sat up and looked at her husband. "Care to enlighten me?"

"Padre Anelli is very well known to Italians. He was one of the founders of the resistance against the Germans in the later years of the War. He had many connections and would have been able to help Isa and Roberto escape from Italy."

Alex dug through the box of mementos.

"Look, here are more," she exclaimed.

February 12, 1944

Dear Signora Fonticelli,

I have located the information that you requested, and it is with great pleasure that I tell you that Paolo is alive and well. He has been in hospital in Africa and unconscious for a very long time, but he will be heading home soon. When the time comes, I will let him know of your whereabouts.

Yours in Christ,
Padre Anelli
St. Michael Archangel
Parma, Italy

March 28, 1944

Dearest Isa,

I am sorry to tell you that Nonno and Nonna have gone to be with Papà and our Savior. After fifty-three years by each other's side, they left this world only minutes apart. Mamma sends her love. She is well, though she is not the same as I last saw her before the War. She cries at night and often screams for you and for Papà in her sleep. Her heartache is great, and I fear that she, too, will join the rest of our family soon. Nonna and Nonno missed you terribly. Please find the enclosed book from Nonna. She started working on it as soon as you left. She and Nonno loved you very much. I know that you will miss them as much as I do.

With love, your brother,

Paolo

"The cookbook," Alex said through tears. "Now I understand even more why it meant so much to her." Alex pictured Signora, so young and yet so worldly, standing in the little kitchen here in Baltimore, recreating her grandmother's favorite dishes. "Do you think any of them knew about the Robbiano?" Alex asked as she leaned against Nicola.

"Non lo so," Nicola answered as he folded the letter and placed it back in the box. "There were many secrets kept for many years. Perhaps there are even more that we do not know."

Alex thought about it for a moment and decided the time was right.

"Nicola, I have a secret, too." She sat up and looked into his eyes.

"Che cos'è, mia bella?"

Alex reached for his hand and gently placed it on her stomach. She smiled and said, "What do you think of the names Isa or Roberto?"

Finè

If you enjoyed *Whispering Vines*, please leave a review on Amazon and on Goodreads. Thank you, and arrivederci!
     Amy

You may follow Amy at
http://amyschislerauthor.com/
http://facebook.com/amyschislerauthor
https://twitter.com/AmySchislerAuth
https://www.goodreads.com/amyschisler
https://amyschisler.wordpress.com

Resources

Boiardi, Anna, Stephanie Lyness, and Ellen Silverman. *Delicious Memories: Recipes and Stories from the Chef Boyardee Family.* New York: Stewart, Tabori & Chang, 2011.

Chanter, Alan, C. Peter Chen, Thomas Houlihan, and David Stubblebine. "World War II Database." *World War II Database.* Lava Development, LLC, 2004. Web. 04 Oct. 2015.

Edsel, Robert M. *Saving Italy: The Race to Rescue a Nation's Treasures from the Nazis.* New York: W. W. Norton, 2013.

Graziani, Vince and Fantoni, Antonella of Plan-It Italy Tours. http://planititaly.com

Hazan, Marcella Hazan. *The Classic Italian Cookbook: The Art of Italian Cooking and the Art of Italian Eating.* New York: Harper's Magazine Press, 1962.

La Dama Vineyards, Verona, Italy. http://www.ladamavini.it/eng/wines.html

Nicholas, John, Jack McKillop, Mikko Härmeinen, and Alex Gordon. *World War Two Chronology.* The Military Library Research Service, n.d. Web. 10 Nov. 2015.

Riebling, Mark. *Church of Spies: The Pope's Secret War against Hitler.* New York: Basic, 2015. Print.

About the Author

Amy began writing as a child and never stopped. She wrote articles for magazines and newspapers before writing children's books and adult fiction. A graduate of the University of Maryland with a Master of Library and Information Science, Amy worked as a librarian for fifteen years and, in 2010, began writing full time.

Amy Schisler writes inspirational women's fiction for people of all ages. She has published two children's books and numerous novels, including the award-winning Picture Me, Whispering Vines, and the Chincoteague Island Trilogy. A former librarian, Amy enjoys a busy life on the Eastern Shore of Maryland.

The recipient of numerous national literary awards, including the Illumination Award, LYRA award, Independent Publisher Book Award, International Digital Award, and the Golden Quill Award as well as honors from the Catholic Press Association and the Eric Hoffer Book Award, Amy's writing has been hailed "a verbal masterpiece of art" (author Alexa Jacobs) and "Everything you want in a book" (Amazon reviewer). Amy's books are available internationally, wherever books are sold, in print and eBook formats.

Follow Amy at:
http://amyschislerauthor.com
http://facebook.com/amyschislerauthor
https://twitter.com/AmySchislerAuth
https://www.goodreads.com/amyschisler

Book Club Discussion Questions

1. Put yourself in Alex's shoes. Would you have left everything behind and traveled to a foreign country to start a new life and why? Why do you think Alex did?

2. Alex suffered greatly from the loss of her brother and father. How do you think their deaths played a part in her choice to move to Italy?

3. Alex did not make a very good impression on Nicola by lying to him, especially when he was already resentful of her. Why do you think she lied? How would you have handled the situation?

4. Isa risked her life to pass secret messages back and forth between the Italian Resistance and the Allies. Why do you think she did that? Would you have taken that risk?

5. In what ways did Isa and Alex's lives parallel each other? How were the two young women alike and different?

6. Alex learned many things from the Isa she knew personally, yet she learned even more from the younger Isa in the journal. In what ways did Isa impact Alex's life?

7. Isa seems much more mature at 17 than Alex sometimes does at 22. Why do think that is? Do you believe that young people are less mature overall today than they were at that time (World War II)? If so, do you believe that the circumstances of war made young people grow up faster? Is that a good thing or a bad thing?

8. Alex had a strained relationship with her mother but was determined to make things right. How would you have gone about bringing your mother back into your life? Would you have bothered? Why or why not? Would it be harder for a child to reach out to a parent than the other

way around? How do you think Alex found the ability to forgive her mother and attempt to mend their relationship?

9. How would you have handled the discovery of a precious work of art on your property?

10. Do you believe that Isa was communicating with Alex from the grave, or was that wishful thinking of Alex's part?